50

The
Elephant Valley

Other Books by Finis Farr

Frank Lloyd Wright: A Biography

Black Champion: The Life and Times of Jack Johnson

Margaret Mitchell of Atlanta

The
Elephant Valley

by

FINIS FARR

●

ARLINGTON HOUSE
New Rochelle, New York

I

EVERY DAY that the airport was open, the noise of an incoming jet waked David Bell at eight in the morning. If he managed to get back to sleep, the roar of early buses on M Street would soon have him up and staggering toward the kitchen of his small apartment on the second floor of a garage behind a large old mansion. David was a hard waker; for two or three minutes, he looked like a man who had been stunned by a blow on the head. Then things came into focus, and he would be ready for the day. It made no difference how long he had slept, two hours or eight—as soon as he could get moving, David was all right. But he said the first five minutes were like pushing through warm gelatin with anvils tied to his arms and legs. And on the morning of his fortieth birthday, as he heard the Seven-Oh-Seven lining up over Georgetown, David felt no different from the way he had felt the day before, or even the decade before. He was alone. Somehow he got his feet to the floor, and into slippers. In the kitchen, he turned on gas beneath a saucepan, swallowed tomato juice, made toast, and poured boiling water over instant coffee. He sat by the window and looked out into mild October sunshine as his blood began to circulate again. He knew that at this time in the morning a thing he wanted to forget leaped out at him. He knew it was coming, and steered his mind away from it in slow efforts like a man leaning on a tiller to bring a heavy boat up into the wind. The bad thing had happened in the past year. Now David was forty, and that was middle age. He held to that idea—the prow was slowly coming round. Forty was middle age, David thought, and yet the newsweeklies spoke of men that old as young. Young, able—as the years went by, the magazine definition of young seemed to follow the increasing age of the publisher. They gave up when he passed sixty and entered the ranks of public oracles and elder statesmen. Still, in some ways forty might be young, if you felt that way, and David was yet to become critical of the doctrine that youth in itself had supreme value and importance. He went into the bathroom and prepared for the day, emerging to take clothes from a narrow closet and a rickety chest of drawers.

The suit that David put on had been built by Huntsman, and built is the proper word. The buttons were set in to stay forever, and the sleeves fitted narrow at the cuff. This was not the kind of suit that belonged in such an apartment. In fact, all of David's possessions that could be seen seemed out of place there. The row of treed shoes from Peal, the firm that had abandoned its bespoke business because it could not keep up the quality, the Vuitton cases, the thin-leafed wafer diary on the night table—none of these harmonized with the gloomy cramped apartment. The rooms were what they looked like—chauffeur's quarters. David was not a chauffeur.

He walked down the wooden exterior stairway, unlocked the door to the garage under his bedroom, got into his tan Volkswagen, and rolled down the gravel driveway beside the mansard-roofed house. He waited to let a bus lurch past, discharging noise and poisonous vapor into the atmosphere, drove three blocks in its stinking wake, then turned down for the Key Bridge. As he crossed the bridge David became conscious of the mellow autumn morning, and the haze that sometimes comes over the Potomac from Virginia to soften the classic edges of Major L'Enfant's town. In spite of the thing that he was keeping at bay in his mind, David felt a moment of serene happiness. It lay in his heart, an instant of warmth, and then was over as he turned west along the shore road toward the headquarters of the Company.

Soon the Company's huge building loomed among its woods and parking lots. David drove on through swarms of men and women who struggled from the insides of Detroit-made automobiles through doors that must have been designed to show off the talents of Houdinis rather than for easy exit for someone who had only wanted a ride. But among the escape artists, here and there a young man, capped and tan-raincoated, stepped from a sports car, or fellow VW owners got their feet on the ground with comparative ease. David thought that if he were ordered to pass on the fitness of applicants to the Company, he would find out what sort of car the candidate drove. For the rest, David always said a career Third Avenue bartender behind one-way glass to inspect the job seekers would be all he needed. And the only question he would ask the bartender would be, "Would you cash this guy's check?" It could be said that the science of personnel relations was one of many things that David did not hold with. But Personnel in its wisdom had evidently placed David high, for the space where he parked his VW was close to an entrance, and this was a sure sign of big rank, the brass or near it.

At the door David showed his badge, a laminated card with nothing on it but his photograph and a number. The guard was a uniformed Negro policeman with a revolver at his belt. He looked at the badge, then glanced at David's face. A friend of David's who was concerned with the Company's housekeeping had recently tested the guards by presenting a badge with Mao Tse-tung's face on it, and every guard had spotted it. This showed that Chairman Mao would not get in here, at least not without someone to vouch for him.

Like the parking space, David's office showed rank. It was spacious and looked out on woods. It was carpeted and contained a substantial walnut desk and library table, leather chairs, and the symbol of bureaucratic rank that David and his friends had often smiled at: a vacuum water bottle with glasses on a tray. The bottle was empty, for Molly Harper, David's secretary, was not the type to insist on filling water bottles or carrying coffee, though she would have done either if David had said he wanted it done. He didn't like to be fussed over, and deprecated the prevalent office coffee-brewing in the Company with the remark, "I eat and drink at tables and not at desks." Molly was a professional civil servant, a middle-aged woman married to a veteran employee at the Department of Commerce. In a way such people were the government. They stayed on while officials, Cabinet members, and Presidents came and went. David had not yet in thirteen years been able to decide whether or not he was a lifetime government career employee. He had traveled far, always coming back to Washington; and yet he had never felt rooted there. Now he wanted nothing so much as to leave the place forever.

David sat down to a clean desk. One didn't leave papers out overnight at the Company. And the drawers were as empty as if the desk were standing on a furniture dealer's floor. There were no buttons or switches under the desk, and no electronic devices in the room. David carried all he needed to know in his head, and he knew where to go for further information if necessary. He smiled briefly, thinking of some old country editor's rolltop stuffed with papers and proofsheets, or the desks of great men in the Cabinet and White House, loaded with souvenirs, memorial inkstands, pens with which some vastly important legislation had been signed, and framed photographs of their—here David closed a door in his mind, and looked up as Molly entered the room.

In government or out, your secretary told your real rank for anyone who knew what to look for, David thought. The solid brass had secretaries who were polite on the telephone *before* they found out who was calling. None of your little girls from Central Steno who might turn into jailbait, and none of your Pembroke intellectuals who couldn't type. The top men had secretaries like Molly Harper, a woman so competent and thoughtful that she seldom appeared to have allowed anything to disturb her. But now David saw that Molly was giving him a tightlipped look, perhaps the look of a person who has decided to make a complaint. This was a matter of note, although it was true that the Company had all the small problems that beset any collection of office workers—chairs too close to air-conditioning outlets, typewriters that broke down, people who smoked too many cigarettes under the noses of those who smoked none, telephones and pencil sharpeners inconveniently placed, and so on. But in the face of all this, one of Molly's greatest virtues had been to deal with such things so smoothly that David seldom heard of them, and from her expression he assumed she was now compelled to report a crisis. He was surprised that all she said was, "Mr. Sedgwick called ten minutes ago. He said he would like to see you this morning."

David's chief Henry Sedgwick always telephoned directly when he wanted to talk, without having his secretary say, "Please hold on, Mr. Sedgwick will be right with you." It was a frightening courtesy, which bothered people more than it reassured them, and David had an idea this was the result that Sedgwick wanted. Now his telephone signal lit, and it was Sedgwick calling again.

"Could you talk this morning? When would it suit you?"

"How about right now?" David asked.

"Fine, come right in."

David replaced the telephone and looked up at Molly. "That was Mr. Sedgwick," he said. "They asked me to let him know the minute you came in," Molly said. "That's nice," David said. "Take care of the minutes, and nobody will take care of you." Molly gave the standard boss's-joke smile, and then picked up the documents she had put on David's desk. "There's nothing important here," she said, and walked out, showing David the back of a trim knitted jacket and skirt. His thought was that nothing important had come to his desk for quite a while. At a time when he most needed something to do, the supply of work had been cut off somewhere above him. He rose and walked to the window. It wouldn't do to pop right up in Henry Sedgwick's office the minute after a summons—and yet, why not? The man called, David thought, and I will answer. No use playing those silly organizational games, just go right in there and see what he has to say. If anything . . .

A few doors down the hall was the wide formal entrance to Henry Sedgwick's suite, giving on an outer territory filled with secretaries and earnest-looking young men. David passed through this area, turned a corner, reentered the building corridor, and tapped at a door which he knew opened directly into Sedgwick's private room. He heard a voice call, "Come in!" and entered, closing the heavy oak door behind him. Across the large room Henry Sedgwick, sandy-haired, medium-sized, stepped out of the lavatory wiping his face with a towel. His bright blue eyes looked at David over the cloth. He walked to his desk and dropped the towel in the wastebasket beside his thronelike padded swivel chair.

"That's about the only thing that comes out of here that is not classified waste," Sedgwick said. On his desk was a round plain Mexican straw basket eight inches in diameter into which he put classified waste. That term was logical when you thought it over. Nearly every piece of paper that came into Sedgwick's office was classified—that is, stamped Secret, or Top Secret, or even Eyes Only. What he did not send on to other officials or put into locked files became waste—but it was still classified. So like all other employees of the Company, great or small, Henry Sedgwick tore paper he was finished with into fragments which he dropped into his Mexican basket. Lesser people dropped classified waste into cylindrical containers which they made out of parchmentlike drafting paper and clips. But no matter how it was temporarily stored on desk tops, it all would be gathered by secretaries who sealed it in heavy manilla sacks, which they gave to messengers who took the sacks into the cellar to be burned. All such security procedures were so deeply ingrained in the people who worked here at the Company's headquarters that no one thought them strange or inconvenient. It was merely the accepted habitual way of doing things. As a result, the security of documents was as close to perfection as any human endeavor can be.

Henry Sedgwick's spacious office had an empty look, for all its display of sofas, chairs, and tables. His desk, even larger than David's, held no personal knicknacks, and today, except for a few blue-jacketed files of papers, was completely bare. Around the walls, the bookshelves held nothing but a few magazines—current numbers, like those in a good dentist's office. The American flag on its standard by the window showed that Sedgwick held extreme high rank. He was, in fact, one of three deputies who were responsible only to the Director. He had been a banker, but not the sort who gives away radios and tea sets, and advertises for special checking accounts. He was the sort of banker who sat in a room with six partners, and the room had been in Baltimore, and Henry Sedgwick had left it only six years before. He was therefore seven years junior to David in time served, for David had come to the Company as a young man in 1952. Apparently this had never embarrassed Henry Sedgwick. He had the unassuming manner of the powerful, his courtesy was unshakable, and he had never crowded anybody in his life. Nor had he needed to. Now he came away from his great desk and sat informally leaning back on a sofa near David's chair.

"Did you rent your house?" Sedgwick asked.

"I sold it," David said, "and I've been living over the Tottens' garage."

"I rather thought you'd let the house go," Sedgwick said.

"I hope you didn't have a friend who could have used it," David said. Desirable houses in Washington Postal District Seven—the Georgetown area—were usually sold or rented privately by way of friends.

"No, it wasn't that. I was thinking you might like to get out of Washington for a while." David made no reply, and Henry Sedgwick continued, "Something has come up that would take you to New York for a time; that is, of course, if you liked it. The Institute for Strategic Research. George Rollins' shop."

"George Rollins? He's back in business?"

"Very much so. Everything checked out and working like a beaver. Same old George."

"That's interesting," David said. A few years before, George Rollins had been a deputy director, as high and powerful as Henry Sedgwick today. David made no further comment.

"What we'd like is for you to move in and give him some help up there," Sedgwick said. "You understand, David, this is an expression of confidence. By the Director's own wish."

"That's good to hear."

"You have a great track record," Sedgwick said. His eyes

flicked down and sideways toward the blue-jacketed files, then instantly away, and David now knew that Henry Sedgwick had sent for the records of his career, and had been reading them. He kept his own eyes down.

"Two commendations from the Director himself," Sedgwick went on. "I think you understand why we want you up there with Rollins."

"I've been an overt employee of the Company for thirteen years," David said. "After that, I don't see how I can act as a cutout."

"Oh, we have cutouts," Sedgwick said. "This thing is all laid on. We want you up there to give George the kind of help only a man like you can give him. George was always so optimistic, you remember?"

"I remember."

"You'll find he hasn't changed. So in addition to other things, we'll want you to serve as an evaluator."

"Of what, Henry? What's the objective?"

"At present it's mainly a sounding-board operation," Sedgwick said. "Now, you know Ben Thornton of course?"

"Very well."

"He's a little closer to it than I am, David. And he'll be happy to give you the drill. Could you have dinner at his house tonight?"

"If invited."

"Seven o'clock. He expects you, and he'll draw maps and paint pictures." Henry Sedgwick stood and extended his hand. "Best of luck, David, you're a good man. By the way —talk to Jim Ewing some time tomorrow, could you?"

David knew that in large organizations nothing ever came to a head with one person. Tom sent you to Dick, who handed you on to Harry—just to get Harry's thinking, of course, nothing substantive involved. It was true everywhere. David returned Sedgwick's firm handshake and walked to the side door. As he left the room, Sedgwick called after him:

"Come see us before you go—Dee Dee's been asking for you."

He was referring to his wife, and David said, "Thanks, I'll drop around."

Back in his office, David asked Molly to come in. He said, "I think I'm up for a long transfer out of the building. Before I go, I want to be sure you get a proper berth. Where would you like to be?"

"I'll be in Mr. Ewing's office," Molly said. "That is . . ." She stopped and started again. "That is, I know there's a slot for me there." And David was aware this was not all Molly knew or had known. She had known, before he had, that he was leaving.

There was something uncomfortable here, David thought. He had the feeling of trying to play a scene for which the lines were not yet written. He thought it would be best to try to say something honest.

"You've been a great asset to the office," he said. "And I'm going to rate your performance super-excellent, which is no more than the truth." Molly said, "I'm very grateful, David." They were about the same age, and had come to first names long ago. So far as the tone of truth in the human voice was concerned, David had almost absolute pitch. What he heard now in Molly's voice, as plainly as if she had actually said it, was, "It doesn't matter how *you* rate my performance."

"Well, good-bye," David said, shaking her firm cool hand, "and remember me to Bob." Bob was Molly's husband over in Commerce. "I think I'll be going home to pack up," he went on. "Nothing to keep me here." Molly left the room, and David looked around to see that everything was secure. There was nothing on his desk and the safe was locked. He had not opened it that morning.

As David turned in at the driveway to his apartment, a small child came to meet him. He stopped the car and got out. Topsy Totten, the five-year-old daughter of his landlord, looked up at him.

"Hello, David."

"Hello, Topsy."

"I love you, David."

"That's nice. I love you too."

The child continued to look up at him for a moment, then skipped away behind the house. At this age, David thought, they are miniature women. Then comes the gawky age, and at last, the finished product. At this the thoughts he had been trying to keep at bay every day for ten months rushed into his mind, and he felt the familiar agony. It's got to get better than this, he thought. This won't do.

2

Davᴵᴰ ᴄʟɪᴍʙᴇᴅ ᴛʜᴇ sᴛᴀɪʀs to the little apartment, and sat in a Morris chair, as weary as if he had climbed a mountain. The events of one day ten months before were so clear that he re-lived them—each a step in a still incredible catastrophe. It had been a day in early January, coming in with one of those false-spring mornings. Sitting at his office desk, David had telephoned his wife Mary at their house on Q Street and invited himself home for lunch. He had been lucky to reach Mary, who was in the front hall at home about to go out for a walk in the unseasonable sunshine. As always when she heard his voice, she was delighted. "I'll stop at the French market and get something," she said.

When David got home at a quarter past twelve, Mary was not there. This was unusual, and within half an hour David was beginning to be anxious. He walked from the living room into the narrow front hall with its French balloon prints, then back to the living room, from which he peered into the garden, now bare and dusty looking, an area that would be called the back yard in a less fashionable neighborhood.

The telephone rang. A voice said the caller was a lieutenant in the metropolitan police. David could have spoken his next words for him: "There's been an accident."

"Yes, Lieutenant, an accident?"

"We have a young woman identified as Mrs. Bell."

"Identified?"

"I have to give very bad news, Mr. Bell. Your wife has been killed."

At the police station, David found that the lieutenant had given only the bare outline of the bad news. He was now told that Mary's death was accidental only in the sense that while walking along the bank of the canal, she had happened to encounter a man who shot her in the head while robbing her. He was a Negro, unemployed, a drifter from the South. He had been captured shortly afterward with his pistol in his pocket, along with Mary's change purse and a pin ripped from the jacket of her suit.

Three hundred days old now, the terrible hours still existed in David's mind, recurring as though he lived in two dimensions of time. In one dimension, he fought to stay alive and sane; in the other, he found that he stood aside and observed himself, and his friends, as though from a great distance, but through a telescope that could bring up the slightest detail in dreadful clarity. His friends, he discovered, had sorted themselves into certain classifications: there were those who did not speak of Mary's death, although they all had sent letters expressing shock and sorrow; and then there were those who talked to David about Mary, and discussed the case—they were of the school that believed things could be "talked out," no matter how bad; and there was a third class, of those who did not refer directly to the tragedy, but tried to show sympathy by taking action in David's behalf. Among these was Topsy Totten's mother. "David, why don't you come and live over our garage? You know Topsy adores you." He had accepted the offer.

Nonie Totten, Dee Dee Sedgwick, and other women— his friends and Mary's—had come to the house on Q Street and taken away Mary's clothes. David never went back there. The garage apartment, with nothing in it to remind him who he was, had been an emotional refuge. But now, David realized, he would have to be moving on. He could not crouch in this hole forever, like a dying animal. It occurred to David now that his friend Henry Sedgwick must have come to the same conclusion. That would explain the new assignment, away from Washington. He had never thought of Sedgwick as having that much sympathy; a man who was given power as a natural right could become insensitive without realizing it. The wealthy and the powerful had to make an extra effort to be kind, for it was something that you could not fake. David knew he would have to produce an effort of the will that he had feared to be beyond him, and wrench himself from sorrow, learn to accept kindness, and somehow continue in life. He knew also that the world was a hideous place, so horrible at times that what had happened by the canal was in some incredible way, by comparison, mild and merciful. In line of business, he had talked with refugees who had been made to watch or, if they closed their eyes, to listen while their wives were being violated, and he had talked to women who had been forced to be present while their men were beaten to death. From east to west in the world he knew there had been many situations in which a bullet through the brain would be an indulgence or even a luxury: so it was, so it would always be.

David pulled two foot lockers from under his bed, and took a small Vuitton traveling case from the closet. He brought out a carton, filled it with shoes on trees, taped it up, and labeled it with the address of his father's apartment at 15 Lexington Avenue in New York. He folded overcoats and suits, shirts and shorts and pajamas, stacking them into the lockers and forcing down the lids. Little remained to go—a few reference books, a drawer of odds and ends, and, come to think of it, the shirts and other

things now at Mrs. Mendenhall's Exclusive Hand Laundry
on Wisconsin Avenue. The Tottens would not mind sending all that after him. And Monty Totten had said he
would buy the Volkswagen any time David wished to sell.
This was traveling light, a good way to go when you
weren't quite sure where you were headed.

David dialed the Sedgwick number and Dee Dee
answered, with the cheerful rising inflection that seemed
to say she would be delighted, whoever it turned out to be.
This was a dear woman. David said, "Bless you for sounding so happy. How about a drink this afternoon?" She
answered, "Wonderful David, I'll expect you." David rang
off feeling the inevitable small comfort that comes from
making a definite arrangement for the near future. He went
into the galley, found crackers, milk, and fruit, and brought
them in on blue plastic plates to eat at a bridge table. He
washed the plates, glanced at the morning's *Washington
Post*, threw it away, sat for a moment looking at the pattern
in the carpet, thought of Henry James, and decided to take
a walk.

Downstairs, David turned west and then walked north
on Wisconsin Avenue, looking into store windows, his
mind suspended between the smart-shoppers'-column merchandise and what he did not want to think of. At the top
of the hill he turned down past some embassies and back
to Georgetown by way of the old cemetery. Mary was not
buried there. In the apartment, he picked up a paperback
Anthony Powell, read a few pages, and sent it into a ca-
pacious wastebasket after the *Post*. It was doubtless great
stuff, David thought, but his attention wandered. Suddenly he knew he must sleep, and he dropped on the living
room couch. He feared sleep, for more than once he had
dreamed Mary was alive, in sharp, clean focused dreams
in which he would ask himself if he were dreaming, and
get the answer no, it was too real. In the dreams it would

be that Mary had not been killed, but had disappeared somehow, and was back now unharmed and happy, the only question being where she had been. And she would be beginning to answer that question when he would wake, an awakening to death. But now David let sleep come to him, feeling that this time it would be deep and quiet. He was right; there were no dreams, and he waked at five o'clock to fading sunshine at the windows. David got up, took off the clothes that seemed to have grown tighter while he was sleeping, and stepped into a shower bath. He opened one of the lockers and took out fresh clothes, a soft jacket and an old pair of biscuit-colored flannel trousers. Again he set out on foot, walking seven blocks to the Sedgwicks' house on Thirty-third Street the other side of the Avenue.

The Sedgwicks' house, like many in the neighborhood, looked small and simple from the street. One entered a walled courtyard, then passed through a fanlighted door to an entrance hall of modest size. But on walking upstairs, a visitor would find that the house was built into a steep rise of ground, and opened at the back on half an acre of garden, one story above the street and completely concealed. When David arrived, he opened the unlocked front door with an old friend's privilege, mounted the stairs, and walked through the drawing room, which was large enough to serve as ballroom when the Sedgwicks gave one of their small dances.

Beyond was the library, spacious and comfortable, smelling of woodsmoke, and filled with all sorts of beautiful, interesting, or amusing things. Two of the Victorian mechanical banks from Sedgwick's collection stood on a table by one of the sofas. The banks were freshly painted and in working order; one of them had a donkey that kicked a penny into a trough. The other was an Uncle Sam who bowed and pocketed a penny when it was put in his

hand. Henry Sedgwick had remarked that this one should
be rebuilt to have Uncle Sam throwing the penny away
instead of pocketing it.

Dee Dee Sedgwick came in from the garden. "*Dear
David,*" she said, offering her cheek. "I hear you're leaving us."

"I'm going to help George."

"That'll be nice."

"It will be good to see him."

David leaned back on the broad sofa, at ease as always
in this room. Dee Dee was not a woman to flutter at the
grog tray and ask a guest to mix his own drink. Instead,
she rapidly made a pitcher of martinis, knowing David
would tell her if he wanted something different. They
drank, settling to easy, unmalicious gossip about friends.
David refused another drink, but stayed talking until a
quarter of seven. Soon Henry would be home from the
office, but David decided not to wait, and answered Dee
Dee's invitation for dinner by saying he was committed to
Ben Thornton, and it was time to go. They said good-bye
in the lower hall, and it seemed like a final good-bye—for
what reason, David could not imagine. There was an odd-
ness here, though the scene was familiar still, even to the
butler who appeared, his evening duty starting now, and
opened the door for David. The butler was a dignified
elderly Negro. He spoke politely to David, who answered
in the same manner. Though he was famous in David's
circle for looking like the butler in a high-class whiskey
advertisement, the courteous old man was a preacher in
his off hours. Some of David's friends, the members of the
bring-it-into-the-open school, had asked him how he felt
about colored people now, referring particularly to the
familiar household or freelance servants of Georgetown.

"Just the way I felt before," David would say. "And
how was that?" they would ask; they would be women, and

they would have David off in a corner. "Why, no way especially," he would answer. "You know how pleasant these maids and butlers are. But their children won't be maids and butlers—or at least don't plan to be. I don't know ... I don't connect them with the business about Mary." In subsequent discussions of David, these women would tell each other, "He talks about it as if it concerned somebody else."

Over the uneven brick sidewalks David strolled to Ben Thornton's house. With darkness the air had cooled and the light from the second floor looked warm. It was a small house, one of a row along the canal. People had wondered about David's apparent unconcern in visiting houses along this row, where several of his friends lived. The murder had taken place about a mile to the west. David could not have explained it, but to him that place had no existence. Now he rang the bell, and the door was opened by a middle-aged white woman, Thornton's housekeeper. David followed her up the doll's-house stairway and entered the living room. The miniature house was not what Thornton would have lived in were he permanently in Washington these days. He had been traveling, and his wife and children were established in Paris that year.

The temporary bachelor, a tall man in a Weatherill suit, jumped to his feet from a sagging armchair as David entered the room. He shook hands with a firm grip, pointed David at a sofa and said, "Sit down and have a scoop." He beamed at David, picking up the martini pitcher and walking up and down as he stirred, very large and solid in the little room. The room had a battered, furnished-apartment look, with certain contrasting objects that might have been predicted, given Thornton's background and place in life. One might have been sure of finding on the coffee table a heavy silver box like this one, with the emblem of a college club and the signatures of Thornton's wedding ushers engraved on its cover. Sometimes such boxes had to be retired because the marriage ended in the courts, but not with Ben and his wife Susie. Another predictable item was Susie's picture in a silver frame; and near it the Director himself smiling from a similar frame, with his pipe and moustache, like a genial professor of English who gives a popular course on Tennyson and Browning.

Thornton stirred the liquor in the pitcher, peered out at the darkness over the canal, turned and filled a glass for David. In this, as in everything he did, Thornton showed an easy, friendly manner like Henry Sedgwick's. It was one of the most reassuring of all human approaches, and it worked with women, with men, with children, and with foreigners and natives of every kind; it might even work with Russians and Red Chinese, if Ben Thornton could get at them. David liked to imagine Thornton sitting them down, and offering them a scoop, and listening while they talked, with nothing ever shadowing his frank and interested gaze. It might be, David sometimes imagined, that the Ben Thorntons had been sent to take the place of the superb English who had been destroyed nearly to the last man, in two wars—the second war finishing the work of extermination that the first had so effectively begun. With their unshakable air of good will, the Thorntons could be fine ambassadors. But you seldom found them in the Foreign Service; those ranks were mostly filled with people who tried to imitate the Thorntons and did not get it quite right.

Seven years older than David, Ben Thornton had been a young lawyer starting out with the great New York firm of Livingston, de Lancey, and Wedderburn when World War Two had come along. He had gone into the active branch of the Office of Strategic Services, that ragbag of unorthodox warriors whose final achievement David would have hesitated to assess. He knew that the OSS had in-

cluded some people who had the coldest sort of nerve and
bravery; Ben Thornton had been one of them, and he had a
properly earned Silver Star for his service in occupied
France with guerillas whom he had joined one night by
parachute. Thornton never mentioned any of it, and so far
as he was concerned his medal was classified information.
In this he differed, David thought, from the President of
the United States, who wore on his coat the miniature
insigne of a Silver Star he had accepted for one flight in a
bombing plane. It takes all kinds, David reflected, sipping
his drink. You had to like old Ben, for he intended that you
should, and he knew what he was doing and how to do it.
But he was predictable. As might have been expected, he
had returned after the war only briefly to Livingston,
de Lancey, and Wedderburn. Less than a year later he was
in the Company, which was then newly founded and in
some ways the direct heir of the OSS. His law firm had
furnished a number of recruits for the Company, but this
meant no more than that one brought in another. They
ran to type, and that was where the Company had found
George Rollins. As for David, he had been teaching French
at St. Stephen's School in Massachusetts, and his experience in war had been in Korea.

David drank his cocktail and looked at Ben Thornton.
He knew that the general liking this man inspired was
shared by the Director, who would send him throughout
the world to look at certain things, and talk to certain
people, and come back and tell what he had seen and heard
without writing anything down. Thornton and the Director
would walk on fine evenings along the canal, or sit in the
Sedgwicks' garden, Thornton talking, the Director listening, quiet and relaxed, his pipe chuckling as he puffed
bluegray smoke. Yes, indeed, David thought, Thornton
was one of those people who throughout life is always a
member of the higher internal crowd. He seemed to be on

the inside by some kind of natural right. If Thornton had remained with Livingston, de Lancey, he would by now have become a partner, handling great affairs for the firm's impressive list of clients. But he wouldn't be strolling in the evening with the Director. So as anyone could see, what Thornton was doing, the life he was living, was a thousand times more interesting and satisfying than anything else he could possibly do. And to fill this child of fortune's hamper of goodies to the brim, he was rich. And even more: Susie Thornton was a darned nice girl.

Thornton poured himself a scoop and said, "I hear you're leaving."

"Washington, yes," David said. "The Company, no. It's just that Henry wants me up in Rollins' shop."

"That's what I meant," Thornton said.

"Henry said you'd brief me on it."

"I'll try to," Thornton said. "Of course, George himself knows most about it, where bodies are buried and so on. And there are some amazing bodies involved."

"As for example?"

"As for example, do you know anything about a fella called Don Marlowe?"

"Television?"

"That's the fella. He was emcee on one of those late shows. Plays the accordion, clowns around?"

"I never saw him."

"That's right, you haven't yet succumbed to the tube."

"You mean some time I will," David said.

"It's inevitable. Meanwhile, this Marlowe has written his autobiography, which you might read. I can tell you George is really interested in the man. Maybe as a consultant, that sort of possibility."

"But what is George trying to accomplish with his Institute?"

"He's only been in business a few months," Thornton said.

"I mean is he trying to run a listening post, or is he trying to make something happen somewhere?"

"My guess would be a little of both, David. By the way, there's another fella you might have heard of. He's an old creep named Jefferson Kane, a kind of general big wheel."

"Tito's pal."

"That's the man. He's also a great buddy of Kosygin and the other little number in the Kremlin."

"Very rich, very opinionated."

"You've got him," Thornton said. "And when old Mr. Kane has an opinion, a lot of people hear about it."

"Didn't I read that he has a chain of newspapers?"

"Yes, out on the Coast, plus a clutch of radio stations. And don't count radio out, my boy."

"I don't. Think of all those people listening in cars."

"Awful, isn't it? And this Kane has his own network."

"He has his own holding companies too, I think," David said.

"That's right, Consolidated Industries is one. There was a piece about it in *Fortune*. As I recall there was shipping, farming, food processing, mining, electronics, and a nice little factoring business at the top."

"I'll tell you the truth, Ben—I never did understand what factoring meant."

"In this case it means he's a money finder. He can help people who can't get help at the bank. Not that he doesn't own three or four banks too, you understand. You name it, Jefferson Kane's got it."

"And he's going to keep it, from what I hear. But I honestly don't see where George Rollins comes in, with a man like that."

"You know this Kane is intensely political," Thornton said.

"I'm aware of it, but I never really gave him much thought."

"Have you ever looked into a thing called the Kane Foundation?"

"No," David said. "Should I have?"

"It's a kind of funnel for money—millions of dollars, and all for the extreme Left."

"That's true of a good many foundations," David said.

"I agree, but old Jeff runs it into the ground," Thornton said. "On the foundation circuit, they say all you need do to get a hundred thousand dollars in twenty-four hours from the Kane Foundation is submit a plan to make the United States look bad. Do that and Kane will fall all over himself to set you up with a project—sociology, anthropology, atomic studies, political science, take your pick. But show him something that might reflect a little credit on poor old Uncle Sugar, and you can't promote him for the price of a postage stamp."

"I never could understand why these people act that way," David said. "Maybe it appeals to their vanity. So far as Kane is concerned, I can't think of anybody in the world who'd be less use to a man like George Rollins."

"I'm not so sure about that," Ben said. "It might be that George would like to get acquainted with this Jefferson Kane and try to turn him around. Or at least get some kind of say about what went on the Kane Foundation agenda. These people talk a special language. Maybe they could be persuaded to let George write part of the dictionary."

"Ben, are you being purposely vague?"

"It's just that the whole thing is a little out of focus at this point."

"Henry said you were going to clear it up for me."

"He's got a lot on his mind," Thornton said, getting up. "Let's go in and graze."

The housekeeper served perfect roast lamb and string

beans in a dining room just large enough for a table that would seat four people. After a lemon ice they returned to the living room. The woman brought coffee and said good night. David said no to brandy and Thornton left the decanter stoppered. "Don't worry about this thing," he said. "You have my assurance it's terrific. Very, very terrific. Worthy of your attention. By the way, you're seeing Jim Ewing tomorrow? Good."

Shortly afterward, David left. Thornton walked downstairs with him, and at the door clapped a firm, brief grasp on his shoulder.

"You're on to a good thing, David," Thornton said. "I'll be seeing you."

Walking home, David took from his mind the doubts that had grown there during the day and examined them. Each one melted into nothing as he looked at it. Again the comforting thought came to him that he had friends, and they realized what he needed, which was to be out of Washington when the numbness went away. When that time came—and he felt it would be soon—he did not want to be in a foreign country. He wanted to be at home, and that was in New York City.

3

N EXT MORNING David used the telephone in the Tottens' kitchen to call Jim Ewing's office at the Company. A woman's pleasant voice said, "Oh, hello, Mr. Bell. He isn't here—but I think you can catch him over on R Street." David thanked the voice and hung up. He knew that Jim Ewing often spent time outside the office at places in the District, Maryland, and Virginia, and that one port of call was a house on R Street at the top of Georgetown. He set out now in bland morning sunshine, and after climbing the hill, approached tall iron gates standing ajar between brick walls at the driveway that led to an immense mansion. There were houses like this all over northwest Washington, mostly used now as embassies, or institutions designed to extract money in some way from the Treasury of the United States—as indeed the embassies were. But this house was different. It had an unused air, and yet there were automobiles parked on what had once been its lawn, and there was some kind of security provided, for one of those uniformed Negro policemen, like the Company's guards, came out of the porter's lodge and waved David on after he saw his badge. David walked up the driveway and entered the main hall, which was completely bare. He could see where the garden had been, through tall French doors at the end of the hall, and to the right were the open arched doors of the ballroom.

David entered this huge room. There were ten or twelve people there, but the most arresting object to be seen was a square table about thirty feet long on each side. It was marked off in lines and some sort of map was traced on it. At various points were markers of differing colors and shapes. Lying at the edge of the table were rakes like those used by Las Vegas croupiers. Along opposite walls of the ballroom were constellations of bridge tables loaded with books, maps, papers, slide rules, and table-model calculating machines. Over each set of side tables hovered a group of four or five men, consulting in low tones, turning the pages of books, and working with the rules and calculators. Midway down one side of the main table was a high referee's chair. As he looked up and saw David come in, Jim Ewing descended from the chair and came to meet him.

"Good to see you, David," Jim Ewing said. "These people are in the middle of a game matrix. We have both sets of players making strategy choices on the minimax principle. And each team carries a simulated traitor."

"They know that, of course," David said.

"Why, I suppose they do," Ewing said. "Anyhow, you know the theory behind these strategy games. The players make choices among available alternatives, the total of choices determining the outcome."

"Yes, I know," David said. "I always thought of it as Monopoly with Los Angeles as a property instead of Ventnor Avenue."

"That kind of talk could put a lot of people out of work," Ewing said, as they walked down the empty central hall toward the garden. "We had a man in the Director's office only the other day who told us he was founding an entire strategic theory on the old Italian peasant game called Morra. You know of it?"

"Guessing how many fingers the other player will show?"

"That's it. The ancient rules were very simple. Two

players simultaneously show either one or two fingers, each guessing aloud how many the other will show. A player must guess correctly to win. If they're both right, neither wins."

"You're taking me back to kindergarten."

"Well, yes, in a way. Now follow this: suppose we change the rules and say that if both players show one finger, Player A wins one counter. If A shows one and B two, B wins three counters. If A shows two and B one, B wins five counters. If both show two fingers, A wins four counters. Now, the problem—is there a best way for the first player to play?"

"You're asking me?"

"I wonder what you think of it."

"I think the whole business is a crock," David said.

"And there you are absolutely right," Ewing said.

"Then why do you bother with it?"

"This operation here on R Street is a Defense Department think-shop, and I am only auditing for the Director."

"But why waste the time, if you can see it's all foolishness?"

"You could call it a talent hunt," Ewing said. "Every once in a while one of these young men says what you've just said, that game-theory exercises are nonsense so far as realistic planning is concerned. And when he does, I offer him a job where we don't deal in theories."

"That's encouraging," David said. "But I'd like to talk about my own assignment now, if you have the time." They had come into the garden, where there were a few springy iron round-seated chairs of the sort always found on the terraces and porches of such houses. In the soft and warm Washington October, they sat near an empty pool that had once contained pedigreed fish, swimming in water that had been aerated by jets from a bronze fountain. The fountain was dry and broken now.

"Amazing, this place," Jim Ewing said as he sat down. A

small man, he seemed accurately put together, and made one think of a fine watch. His late father and living uncle had their names in the title of Ewing, Ewing, Isham, and Ryerson, a La Salle Street law firm that was the equivalent of Livingston, de Lancey, and Wedderburn. Jim's mother still lived in the old apartment at 1100 Lake Shore Drive opposite the Oak Street beach on a coast of solid Chicago gold. Jim was no lawyer, but a mathematician, specializing for his own amusement in topology, a field so difficult that it made David's head ache even to think of it. Jim and his wife had been based in Washington for years now. Sometimes they traveled, and there had been a period of much foreign duty. Now he stayed mostly in Washington, living, as he did everywhere, a quiet life. Nobody knew exactly where he belonged in the Company's table of organization, but it was observed by those in a position to do so that his office at headquarters opened right into that of the Director. Moreover, this had been true in the reign of the *previous* Director. Ewing was generally believed to be trustworthy, disinterested, and dedicated, and, in fact, he *was* trustworthy, disinterested, and dedicated, an evolved professional type. David and his wife Mary had been close friends with Ewing and his wife Bet.

"Amazing," Jim Ewing repeated. "Can you imagine anyone coming to this town just to live?"

"When they didn't have to?" David said.

"Exactly."

"Kansas City beer, Omaha beef, and Chicago merchandise."

"Yes, the Levi Leiters," Ewing said. "Of course, there was Henry Adams."

"One thing about Adams," David said. "You know the memorial to his wife, in Rock Creek Park? Going out and looking at it helped me right after Mary died."

Ewing glanced at David and looked away. "Adams' wife committed suicide," he said.

"I know. The whole thing's there in that seated figure— the drapery over the head."

"My father knew Saint-Gaudens, and Adams too," Ewing said. "He never liked Adams. I wonder what he would have thought of the Kennedys."

"Not much," said David, "and neither do I."

"There's something about society Irish that bothers me," Ewing said. "It just doesn't seem natural."

"How do you like that Bobby?" David said.

"A grim little guy."

"He looks like a Beverly Hills carhop," David said.

"Bobby Kennedy makes me think of a juvenile delinquent explaining a rumble to a parole officer," Ewing said. "But what about your new plans, David? I hear you're going to give George Rollins a hand."

"I'm going up today," David said. "Aren't you supposed to brief me?"

"So I am."

"What can you tell me?"

"Nothing too specific," Ewing said, "You'll get the particulars from George himself."

"Ben Thornton mentioned a couple of names—Jefferson Kane and Don Marlowe."

"I think George may try to activate those people."

"I'd say handle those two with extreme care," David said.

"By all means," Ewing said. "You've never worked in a front before, have you?"

"I've run them but never been in them."

"You'll get a different feel of things working completely outside the Company."

"Outside?"

"I mean physically outside. You'll put it around that

you've resigned. Tell people you've done your bit, even had enough of it if you like, and resigned."

Ewing took two pieces of folded paper from his inner coat pocket.

"Here's a note I had typed up for you," he said. "It's addressed to the Director, asking him to accept your resignation for personal reasons at close of business today. And here's a contract making you a consultant. You'll notice the money works out the same. It will come through George's payroll."

"I feel strange resigning from the only important job I ever had."

"You're not really," Ewing said. "This arrangement is just to make something for those little eyes to look at."

"What little eyes?"

"In banks, David, where government salary checks come through every fourteen days."

"All right, I have a pen."

David signed the papers and gave them to Ewing.

"Here's a copy of your contract," Ewing said, handing David a sheet of onion-skin. "Now let's see if we can get you off these top-security premises."

"You still haven't told me much about the Rollins operation," David said as they walked around the house toward the front.

"It's really all George's show," Ewing said. "Best let him brief you when you get there."

"But I report to you down here?"

"Yes. Use my sterile line, you have the number. Or if you want to write, ask George for a mail drop. But this is no cross-check, David. George is trusted here."

"I was hoping you'd say that."

"Good boy," Ewing said, as he stood up. Like Ben Thornton he clapped David on the shoulder and they went on together down the driveway. Ewing said, "I had

George on the phone this morning and he said he'd like
to see you up there at five this afternoon. Can you make
it?"

"Easily. At his office?"

"He said if you could get there, meet him at the Corinthian Club."

"Be glad to," David said. Then he showed his laminated badge to the guard, stepped out on the sidewalk,
and handed the badge back through the bars of the gate
to Jim Ewing.

"Good luck, David," Ewing said, and turned back to
the big house. David walked down the Twenty-ninth
Street hill to the Tottens' house. Topsy was at nursery
school and her parents not at home, which suited David's
mood, as he did not wish to say good-bye to anyone. His
work, his friends, his colleagues—aside from his marriage,
these had been his world, and good-bye was not the word
that he was looking for. He called for a Veterans Cab,
which soon drew up in the driveway. David got in, and
the driver, a mercifully untalkative type, drove him at
high speed to Union Station.

On many occasions David liked to use the trains between Washington and New York. It gave one three hours
and more away from the telephone; and he especially
liked the way the northward journey staged itself: Baltimore, Wilmington, Philadelphia, Trenton, New York.
Still some open countryside before and after Baltimore,
and long bridges over the Chesapeake estuaries, then the
crowding structures of the super-city that David had seen
growing for years as he went back and forth. In a way he
could not have explained, the panorama outside the train
windows was always a comforting thing. When they
opened the gates for the noon Congressional, he carried
his two bags to a day coach near the front of the train
and settled on a window seat. David had stopped at the

newsstand and bought Don Marlowe's autobiography, *I Cried All the Way to the Bank*. But on this trip he intended only to rest and think; he would not even go to the dining car, but would lunch on a sandwich bought from the train vendor. This was the way, David told himself, to make time and space work for you, instead of against you, for a change.

There were not many other people in the car, but as the train began to move, a boy and a girl came in and sat near David. They might have been twenty years old, and they carried a guitar and a duffle bag. The girl had a yard of lank hair down her back. The boy's hair was long and matted, and he had a beard—not a handsome Elizabethan beard such as might have set off the face of Walter Raleigh or Francis Drake, but an indeterminate growth that had a scruffy look. Both boy and girl wore tight trousers and shapeless coats that reached a few inches below their knees. David reflected that the resulting silhouette was one he had seen many times in illustrations drawn for the writings of Dickens by Hablot Knight Browne, who called himself Phiz, and for Surtees by John Leech. It was the old Victorian outline, coming up again from the Liverpool slums, and sometimes set off with caps like those worn by Hans Brinker in the story of the Silver Skates. The boy and girl assaulted the ear as well as the eye: they had a small radio from which issued a monotonous whining almost exactly like the music that David had heard all day and all night, during visits to New Delhi and Calcutta, on the lower-caste program of All-India Radio. Everything had been done before and somewhere else, David reflected, and everything was exactly as you expected. How else could it be? This boy and girl, with their ostentatious ugliness, were bidding for attention, trying to give themselves a sense of importance, and above all to challenge their elders, as young people had always done. Such boys and girls did not make David angry. They inspired in him a mild curiosity and something on the order of sorrow. He knew they communicated with one another in a limited vocabulary that seemed to meet their meager need of verbal expression. He knew they had a small, standardized set of ideas, from which their reactions could be calculated, like those of the sheep in *Animal Farm*. Some dreary enchantment had been thrown over these kids to rob them of life, David thought. As if by telepathy the boy caught his eye and stared back with a unfriendly expression. Probably I look disapproving, David told himself, even though I am not. From their point of view he must seem like one of The Enemy. They wouldn't care at all for his suit, or for his shoes. The boy and girl got up and went down the aisle, leaving their guitar and duffle bag on their seats, the whining radio fading out as they moved through the vestibule.

The train rolled on through Maryland, and David remembered that when he was twenty, he had been a Marine private first class. He had left college to enlist when he was eighteen, in the middle of the war. As things turned out his active duty had consisted of serving in the guard detail on a transport, and mostly after the end of the war at that. But when Korea came along, after college, when he was a lieutenant in the Marine Corps Reserve, his outfit had gone up to the Choshin reservoir.

That was unforgettable, and he thought about it now. On the Koto-ri Plateau that winter, temperatures had gone to thirty-five degrees below zero. The cold broke mechanized vehicles down; unless kept running, the motors of tanks and trucks would freeze. Field guns would work too slowly; sometimes shells would fail to fire. And all the while, the winds were whistling out of Manchuria and coiling round the desolate peaks.

He remembered December 4, 1950, and Task Force Dog. They had gone to bring out those people at Chinhung in the Hagaru hills above the reservoir. David's battalion, covering the rest, was the last element of the relieving force to come down. Colonel Murray had called the junior officers around him in the razor-cold gray afternoon and said, "We're going to take our dead, wounded, and equipment when we leave. We're coming out, I tell you, as Marines—or not at all." And that was how they had done it. No one was left behind, not even the dead. Their bodies were tied to gun barrels and running boards, and carried on the hoods of trucks. They all came out, and among the living, the cold did more harm than the enemy, freezing blood to gangrene in fingers, hands, toes, and feet.

David continued to review his life as the train kept on its way. After the war he had finished college and joined the teaching staff at St. Stephen's, and he had returned there for one term after the Korean police action. And then he had been recruited into the Company along with Ben Thornton and George Rollins; and he had been promoted in the Company, so that he became acquainted with convenient parking slots, and spacious offices, as well as with circuitous travel, and odd associates, not all acknowledged, and ingenious plans, not all successful. In 1960 he had fallen in love with Mary and they had married. This marriage had been warm and good, but he could only think of it around the edges now. And so he thought of nothing at all from Baltimore until Thirtieth Street Philadelphia, and dozed off after North Philadelphia, sleeping until the train came to the Delaware River and the long sign:

TRENTON MAKES—THE WORLD TAKES

At Elizabeth the boy and girl came back and assembled their gear, glancing at David with the placid hatred, so familiar to him, that he had seen in the eyes of similar people all over the world. He did not care. Then the Hackensack Flats, the tunnel, and the vast ruin of Pennsylvania Station, cavernous, dusty, its wooden passageways infested with snakefaced hustlers lying in wait for the ill, the elderly, and the confused. David decided that he could not face the mean taxi scramble. Carrying a bag in each hand, he walked through a long tunnel to the platform for the E train uptown. On the platform stood a filthy bum, howling obscenities. David said to himself, "Home again."

4

DAVID LEFT THE SUBWAY train under Madison Avenue, walked a block east, and entered the large stone building of the Corinthian Club. Ten minutes early for his appointment with George Rollins, he sat down in a spacious room that resembled the lobby of an old-fashioned bank. On the wall behind his chair was a spirited painting that showed the action at Becher's Brook in the running of the Grand National for 1892. He picked up the *Times* and read it until George Rollins came in, characteristically twelve minutes late. Limping slightly, carrying a heavy silver-banded malacca cane, Rollins somehow managed to convey the idea that he felt David had kept *him* waiting. He drew up a chair and said, "Hello, David. How's it going?"

"I'm fine," David said. "It's nice to see you, George. How are you?"

Paying no attention to the question, Rollins said, "We have a lot to do, David. And very little time."

As David looked at Rollins, he thought of Dame Edith Sitwell's remark that faces are no longer being worn. But Rollins was wearing a face, one that looked like something that had been taken apart and put together again. David had seen that look in faces of returned prisoners, and in those of certain refugees; and in the faces of some other people who had survived what Rollins had been

through. George Rollins had always had a preoccupied
air; now he gave David the impression that he was trying
to think of at least four important matters simultaneously.
And so it appeared that George Rollins was bearing a
greater burden than in previous days, when he had never
seemed to be struggling with more than three grave matters at a time. He now started to talk as though it had
been only a few minutes since he and David had last sat
together in discussion.

"Ben and Jim will have told you what this is all about,"
George said.

"No, they haven't," David said, but Rollins kept on,
paying no attention. The same old George, David thought,
no use trying to get through to him. He settled back.

"We'll have to go carefully, David," George said. "We
don't want to set a lot of bunnies running. Not right now,
when we're between a rock and a hard place as it is."

"George," David said, "I ask just one thing: please bear
in mind I haven't the slightest idea what you're talking
about."

"I see you haven't changed," George said. "But we've
got something here that will make your teeth rattle. And
it's right down on the substantive level all the way."

David rang a bell and ordered a cocktail, while George
talked on, shaking his head when asked if he would care
for a drink. The fog of words grew thicker. "We've constituted ourselves a task force, David," George went on,
"a work party on the shirtsleeve level. We're already
phased in and set to go. All we need to do is step out and
capture a couple of bodies."

"Don't tell me you're about to make a specific statement," David said. "I don't think I could stand it."

"Specific?" George Rollins said, "This is all highly specific, David. Just pay attention and I'll read you in."

David was tempted to roll his eyes to the ceiling. Instead, he said, "By all means, George. It's always nice to know what you're supposed to do."

"The fact is," George Rollins said, "there's this man Jefferson Kane."

"I've heard of him."

"I'd like to get in touch with Kane and try to make him into a true believer."

"Translation, please."

George Rollins said, "You know his style, David, and the kind of people he gives money to," and launched into what sounded like a catalogue of the Kane Foundation's beneficiaries. As Rollins' voice went on, David stopped listening closely, and heard the words as a not unpleasant background to his thoughts. It was something he had often done when he and George had been associates; for trying to follow George Rollins word by word could be hard on the nervous system. Now he heard George saying something about Jefferson Kane's influence on world opinion. Although Rollins had always claimed it had the mightiest importance, David was not one of those who cared about world opinion, and this was because of his small respect for those who formed it. He said to George Rollins, "I don't think Kane will ever give up the party line. They flatter him too much, and they've been at it too long."

"He's running a first-class propaganda operation," George said. "And he can order unlimited space in his newspapers."

"What of it? His papers are no good—even worse than Hearst and Scripps-Howard."

"But what Kane says is reflected in the world press too."

"Nobody believes the world press, George," David said. "And aside from the standard papers, what have you got? The *New Statesman*. The *Guardian*. Forget it."

"There's more in this than you seem to think," George Rollins said.

"I'm sorry, George. I just can't figure what you want. Suppose you let me read the project, and then we can talk. 'The same language,' isn't that the way we say it?"

"You'll be contacting a man named Don Marlowe," George said, again giving David the eerie feeling that at least half an hour's detailed conversation had somehow been omitted without George's noticing it.

"I've heard of him also," David said, "and I'd like to ask, what is the connection between a man like Kane and a television announcer?"

"One of Kane's companies is a sponsor of the Marlowe broadcast," George said. For Rollins this was a highly specific remark, and David waited now, as quietly as a hunter hoping to snare a rare bird, waited for further concrete details. But George Rollins ran to form. He drew his huntingcase watch on its heavy gold chain from his waistcoat pocket, opened it, eyed it, snapped it shut, and hauled himself to his feet. The chairs at the Corinthian were not built for sudden rising.

"Come to the shop in the morning, David, and I'll show you the set-up. Four-ten Third Avenue." And he hurried away, managing to leave the impression that David had been keeping him from important affairs.

David finished his drink, and then went downstairs to the desk and asked the attendant on duty to have the club messenger take his bags down to 15 Lexington Avenue in a taxicab. He planned to walk there—it was an apartment building near Gramercy Park where his father and stepmother lived—and he hoped that while he walked, he would be able to straighten out his impressions of the last two days. As David left the clubhouse the street lights came on, and when he turned down Lexington Avenue the office workers rushed out and trampled past him like cattle on their way to the subway entrances. Once or twice they would have run over him had he not stepped aside as he made his way against their current. The faces were horrible. Yet here and there would be a face of beauty or of strength and wisdom—black, white, or some intermediate shade. These occasional human faces added by contrast to the horror of the animal masks borne along by most of the people who filled the sidewalks. But suddenly, David laughed heartily, and with such delight that a few hurriers glanced up in suspicion. What had pleased him was a neon sign:

THE ROUGHEST TOUGHEST FIGHTINGEST
MARINES IN THIS MAN'S WAR

FRANK SINATRA—DEAN MARTIN—
SAMMY DAVIS, JR.

He walked on chuckling, and an idea that relaxed a great deal of the tension about his new assignment entered his mind. It occurred to him that he had asked Rollins to let him read the statement of the project they were engaged on. Rollins had paid no attention to such a detail, but David knew that somewhere in the vast files of bureaucracy there would be a document in a blue cover, and in it Rollins' objectives would be plainly written down, in official form, with his aims, and the methods to be used, described minutely and completely. Nothing could be done without the approved project description, and it was Holy Writ; all David needed was to read it. And David told himself he would have to get used to George's maddening habit of almost never coming to the point in conversation. After all, David knew George very well and had traveled and worked on projects with him many times before. In those days, Rollins had been seated very high—as high as Henry Sedgwick was now established. And during that period, George had drawn to his desk so many details—some people felt unnecessary details— that he had gained a nickname in the Company: Joe Bottleneck. Jim Ewing had said, "Maybe old George figures the Commies will be taking us over some day, and he can tell them he was actually on their side all the time —point to all sorts of things that would have hurt them that he kept from coming off." But this was gallows humor. In stark fact, bureaucracy was no medium for men like George Rollins. They sank into it, as if into a quicksand. The specific gravity of George's personality was too great, there was no lightness, no ease. In the Company, the work was baffling and frustrating under the best of conditions. And at headquarters, the amount of detail was so appallingly great that one had to float on top of it or be smothered. This sometimes led to an offhand personal style resembling that of the British, which caused outside critics to charge, though on the whole unjustly, that the Company's career men were amateurs playing at serious business.

God knows it is a serious business, David thought. He remembered the Company's three friends in Bucharest. David and Rollins had been in Paris, waiting for word from these good and important friends. One morning at the hotel there had been a voice on the telephone. The voice spoke English with an international accent, half Babu and half BBC, in the faintly disdainful tone of a UN translator, and it inquired if David would be interested in some photographs. "Of what?" he had asked, and the voice, before ringing off, had answered that samples would be submitted. Next day the pictures were in the mail. Large glossy prints, professional work, sharp black and white, they showed the strangling of the three friends in the courtyard of an office building. Clear morning sun-

light had brought out every detail: the chief strangler
wore a belted gabardine topcoat, a furry velour fedora,
and shiny black gloves. He had a beaky face, with rimless
glasses and a small moustache, which reminded one of
the late Alexander Woollcott. He was fussy about his
work, and had everything just so. At each of the three
stakes, when he was done, he had brought the extra
length of narrow white cord down to the left and tied it
off in an identical bow. These pictures explained why
David and George Rollins had not heard from the friends;
according to the date on the pictures, they had died five
days ago. It shook Rollins, who wondered if he had delayed too long in closing accounts with the men who were
now dead. David pointed out that once these people
were blown, or exposed, there was nothing Rollins could
have done about it. "But maybe our last signal blew
them," Rollins said. "Not all three at once, George. This
took time." The chief strangler, in the tradition of the
European hangman, would have been a torturer too.

David passed a window in which a huge mouth with
false teeth slowly opened and closed. That will soon be
in the Museum of Modern Art, he thought as he passed
on. It was hard to keep one's balance at the best of times,
and every man and woman had a limit of what could be
borne. He thought of the last time he had seen George
Rollins—in Washington, two years before. In those days,
David's office had opened off the spacious room, like that
now occupied by Henry Sedgwick, in which Rollins did
his desk work. Another October afternoon, staff members
settling to the last hours of the day; Molly Harper had
entered David's room without knocking, and he could
see she was disturbed. She took him into the adjoining
room, and there sat George Rollins, scribbling away on
pads, tossing the sheets to the floor. Hundreds of sheets
covered the rug around his chair. Rollins was scribbling

in a gigantic handwriting, so that each sheet as he ripped it from the pad and hurled it away from him held no more than four or five words. All afternoon he had been doing this, and when he sent some of the writing out to Molly to be typed, she had seen that this was no code, but incoherence. Molly had read in psychiatric books, and recognized the symptom. And now George Rollins looked up at David and began to talk. It was a torrent of words linked by sound and not by meaning. David went to the telephone.

They took George Rollins away for treatment. In a few weeks David heard that he was sufficiently recovered to understand what had happened; but apathetic, feeling the effects of profound nervous exhaustion. Jim Ewing told David that Rollins had concentrated so much responsibility on himself that he had built up a pressure that almost blew his nervous system apart. He was a casualty, but not a fatal one. Rollins was a young man still. David heard that in twelve months he had recovered his tone and spirits. And now, as David walked toward his father's apartment, he thought he saw how George Rollins' case had finally turned out. Evidently the Company in its wisdom, which could be considerable, had put George Rollins on a single project which could not become so complicated as to disable his nervous system again. That made good sense. In spite of the large number of people who thought they would like to get into what they took to be its line of work, manpower was a perennial problem at the Company. No use letting a man like Rollins go to waste. But David thought, and not happily, that in spite of Jim Ewing's assurance that he was not a watchdog, he was just that: set to work beside Rollins to keep a check on him. And, he thought further, though this is not the most attractive assignment in the world, I do know George pretty well, and I probably can help him, and the Company too. But first I must find out precisely what it is that George is supposed to accomplish. Read the project . . .

David crossed Twenty-third Street and went on a short distance to 15 Lexington Avenue, a handsome and substantial building that had been his New York home as long as he could remember. He was greeted by Niles, the whitehaired doorman. Niles was a friend and they shook hands. "It does me good to see you," Niles said. "It's better than medicine to see you. The bags have gone upstairs, Mr. David."

"I hope you didn't carry them," David said, for Niles was old and frail.

"It was nothing, and the boy helped me," Niles said. The boy was Frank, the day elevator operator, a comparative youth of sixty-three. "He's just around the corner now on an errand, and I'll run you up."

At the familiar tenth-floor entrance to the duplex, David rang the buzzer. He heard light footsteps, the door opened, and his stepmother took him in her arms. Louise Bell was a pretty woman whose seventy years had worn her thin like an old silver coin.

"David!" she said, "it's wonderful to have you back! Come in and see who's talking to me, someone you know."

With her hand light on his arm, Louise Bell drew him across the hall and into the large, pleasant living room. As he walked through its archway from the hall, his heart stopped: Mary was sitting on the couch.

But of course it was not Mary, and when David looked again, he saw that this woman didn't resemble Mary at all. The fleeting likeness had been merely in the way she held her head for a moment, and the way the light had fallen over her shoulder. He knew this girl. She was Roxanna Dean, whose mother, now dead, had been a close friend of Louise Bell's. There were still young women in the world who called on old women just to see how they were getting on, and Roxie Dean was one of those young women. David had thought her attractive, but she had always seemed to him to have a look of sadness. She reminded him of Ann Sheridan as the gentle and sorrowful sweetheart of the convict in the old Warner Brothers prison melodramas. But there was nothing sorrowful about Roxie Dean now, as David shook her hand, and found it firm, warm, and responsive to his pressure.

"David, this is a nice surprise," said Roxie.

"For me, too," David said.

"Sit down and entertain us, and have some tea or a drink," said Louise Bell. A tray with silver, china, and a spirit lamp stood before her on a stand.

"I don't believe I want anything. I had a drink at the club," David said. "It's so pleasant here, Ma," he went on. "Nothing changed at all that I can see. And I'll be here for a while. I'm out of Washington—through with that work—and back in New York."

"You've been behind your curtain so long," his stepmother said, "it's hard to think of you as out in the ordinary world again."

"Well, that's what it amounts to," David said. "But there was never any secret about where I worked."

"David was too high up to be concealed," Louise Bell said to Roxie.

"I can believe that," Roxie said.

"It wasn't rank," David said. "All governments have their bureaucracies, and there's no way to hide them. Anyhow, I said when I went down there it was only temporary, and so it was. I got the idea, a year or more ago, it would soon be time to give somebody else a chance at my job." The quiet listening of the two women, in the glow of lamplight, touched David's heart. How well women knew the way to play their role of making men feel important! As he went on talking, carrying out Jim Ewing's instructions, he almost believed what he was saying. "You tend to go stale at a desk, anyhow. And so . . ." He let it drop, then started again. "New York looks no different. And what about you, Roxie? Are you still at Time Incorporated?"

"No, David, I have another job now, really a divine job, at the Olympic Travel Agency."

Travel Agency. A small bell sounded dimly almost below the line of consciousness in David's mind. Travel agencies were great listening posts, great dispatch posts. One never knew, one never really knew. He said, "On Fifty-seventh Street?"

"That's it. Do come in some time. It's really a darling place, a beautiful office, I mean the decorating. No bull-fight posters, David. This new artist. You've *got* to see."

"I certainly will."

Roxie said, "There's a friend of yours in town, did you know? George Rollins."

The warning in David's mind rang a little more loudly now. "Yes," he said, "I heard he was in town. I'm going to look him up."

"I heard someone say they'd seen him," Roxie said, and then the standing clock in the hall buzzed and clicked for a moment and pealed a quarter-hour. Roxie stood up, in a smooth graceful motion as though rising from a curtsey, and said, "I must be getting along. Thank you so much, Mrs. Bell. David, it's been so nice to see you."

But David would not hear of Roxie's going downstairs unescorted. He took her down in the elevator and put her into a cab which he was pleased to note had an old friend in the driver's seat. A few of the oldtime owner-drivers worked this building still, and so were available at this time in the evening when the fleet men tended to be pulling in. And when the oldtime drivers died or re-

tired, no one would take their places, nor the place of
Niles, who hovered as David asked, "Where shall I tell
him to take you?" and Roxie answered, "Home—Three-
ten East Fifty-sixth." David repeated the address to Frank
McGivrey behind the wheel, and said to Roxie, "I'll look
in on you at the travel agency, Roxie. I'd love to see the
place." She answered, "I hope you do. It would be nice."
And the taxi drove away. David looked after it thought-
fully. Girls who took new jobs in travel agencies, and
mentioned George Rollins—these girls were interesting
to a man in David's trade. He walked back inside with
Niles, who said nothing but stepped ahead and held open
the brassbound door that the "boy" had polished to a soft
deep glow.

"Thank you, Niles."

"A pleasure, Mr. David."

Back in the apartment, David asked his stepmother,
"Is the glorious lieutenant at home?" He was using their
private nickname for his father, who had received a medal
from the Italian Air Force in the First World War, with a
citation to the "glorioso Tenente Roger Bell." David had
thought it odd that Mr. Bell had not joined them in the
living room, for pretty girls were as catnip to him. But
his father had stayed in his study, on the top floor of the
duplex, where David now found him. When David entered, Roger Bell got up from his desk and said, "My boy,
I'm delighted to see you." Like his wife, whom he had
come to resemble in the mysterious blending of long
happy marriage, Roger Bell was thin and silvery. He was
an architect, and his study had a skylight. Its white walls
were bare except for an area of cork where all sorts of
things might be found hung up with thumbtacks. This
evening the study lights showed that the most prominent
item on display at present was the print showing a strange
dream of Piranesi, a vast and fantastic prison, its dun-

geons mounting by incredible galleries and stairs under
a roof even taller than the one destroyed at Pennsylvania
Station. For the rest, there were typewritten building
schedules, sketches, photographs, and parts of blueprints
tacked to the wall. Roger Bell took one of the photographs
from the wall and handed it to David. It showed a seaside
cottage of gray shingles and white trim with a bow window giving on a brick terrace. "Just finished, Narragan-
sett," Mr. Bell said. "David, I have men actually cry when
they find you can still get a house made of wood or brick.
Wally Dinsmore came to me the other day mumbling as
though he wanted something indecent. Finally it came
out, could I do him a Palladian villa? 'My dear fellow,' I
said, 'you're talking about my main business in life.' Absurdly grateful. Now tell me how you've been."

"Pretty well, but I've come to the end of things down
there. It may be a surprise to you, but I've been deciding
it quite a while."

"We were thinking you might, your mother and I."
Neither David nor his father ever thought or spoke of
Louise Bell as stepmother.

"I just didn't like Washington anymore, and I've traveled enough for a while."

"Enough for the rest of your life," Roger Bell said.

"I'm thinking of settling at home now," David said. "A
man ought to live in his home town. Of course I know
New York's turned horrible."

"Not so horrible, David. We're still doing business."

"It must look dreadful to *you*," David said. "You can
remember when they had a city here."

"I've lived forty years in the same building and nobody's moved me yet," said Roger Bell. "Still, there have
been some regrettable changes. Of course it always seems
that way as you get old."

"It really is that way," David said. "All the same, they

can't put me out of my own city. You understand I don't have any specific 'they.' I'm thinking of noise, and dirt, and inhuman faces."

"I understand. By the way, there was a pretty face calling on your mother. I hope you got a chance to speak to Roxie Dean?"

"Oh yes, I saw her. What's Roxie been up to, do you know?"

"What does any nice girl do in this city? She does a man's work at half the pay, looks for a husband, and keeps us all from going to hell one way or another."

"I don't think she'd have to look very hard for a husband," David said.

"Nor do I. Now see here, David, you must take your old room for a while. Give you a chance to rest and make some plans for the future. It's all ready and we won't hear of your going anywhere else. Unless, of course, you've made arrangements?"

"I'd like to have it," David said. "And I already have something to do. I wouldn't have left Washington just blindly, you know."

"Don't see why you shouldn't have if you wanted to. You're not tied by the need of a salary, thank God." Roger Bell was referring to the income David had inherited from his real mother, who had died when he was two years old. Two years later Roger had married Louise Abercrombie, in a marriage that would have been marred by childlessness except for David. He had always called her "mother" with love and trust, but it was half his real mother's property, his at the age of twenty-one, and carefully administered for him by his father before that time, that made him independent. From this source David's unearned income, after taxes, was around eighteen thousand dollars a year. The Company paid him about twenty thousand in addition; he was still drawing that pay, and intended to earn it. David went on, "For the time being I'll be doing some work for one of the foundations. There's a salary involved, so you're doubly right about no financial needs."

"But if you wanted to start out in business, something of that sort?"

"I don't believe so."

"I was going to say I'd talk finances with you," said Roger Bell. "You have free access to anything of mine, you know. You and your mother. Perhaps we ought to talk about it."

"No banking facilities needed at the moment," David said. "And I know you're the easiest man in the world to deal with."

"Ah, that's as may be," Mr. Bell said. "The fact is . . ." he stopped and looked at David, and then went on, "but let that pass. My friend, you have a preoccupied look about you. Do you have trouble? I mean, do you have a special, additional trouble?"

"It's the same trouble," David said.

"It would be."

"Have you ever read any studies in the psychology of grief?"

"I doubt they have been written."

"So do I," David said. "But I can tell you it's morbid and poisonous, just as bad as hatred."

"You're drawing a distinction between grief and sorrow."

"Precisely."

"Ah, yes. All that I can think of in writing is a text here and there in the New Testament."

"I know the ones you mean. But there's something about Mary you don't know."

Mr. Bell said nothing.

"About her death," David went on. "There's something in addition."

"You want to tell me?"

"I'm going to tell you. She was pregnant."

Mr. Bell drew in his breath, and gave his head a slight shake.

"For three months. The doctor had told us."

Roger Bell said, "Do you want your mother to know?"

"No," David said, "just you and I, and that doctor down in Washington. But just you and I *personally*."

"Thank you, David."

"I think I'll go to my room now."

"Do that, my boy. I'll see you at dinner."

David found that Louise had put his clothes away and set the bags in his closet. He washed his hands and then answered her call to dinner. Their old cook had died several years before and there was no successor. They ate in the library from trays and the chicken, rice, and salad was of Louise's making, and very good. They talked pleasantly over the food, and David could see that the older Bells were happy to have him there, yet he sensed their long familiar habit with each other which did not include him. This was as it should be, he thought; and at least Louise allowed him to help clear away and put things to rights in the large kitchen, which had an area set apart at one end that once had been known as a servants' dining hall. Six people could be fed there with plenty of room, and David could see his father's favorite coffee cups set out on a handy shelf, an indication that for breakfast at least the Bells were accustomed to the kitchen. Thus they had returned after generations to the ways of their New England ancestors. He hung up a dish towel, kissed Louise, and said, "My thanks for the wining and dining. I think I'll go to my room and read."

"You do that, darling."

David went to his room and closed the door. The room had been his retreat in boyhood, and it recorded much of his youth. Here were school, summer, camp, and college photographs. Here was the bookshelf with *Treasure Island* and *The Black Arrow* illustrated by N. C. Wyeth, side by side with *Ivanhoe* and *Quentin Durward*, and *Men of Iron* by Howard Pyle. And here were the novels of John Buchan; David smiled when he thought of the impenetrable disguises assumed by Major (later General) Richard Hannay for the deception of Baron von Stumm, Dominick Medina, and other undesirable types. But he passed up these books of his youth, for tonight he had official reading to do. He settled in a Morris chair, turned on the parchment-shaded bridge lamp, and opened the book called *I Cried All the Way to the Bank*, in which Don Marlowe told about his life.

5

NEXT MORNING David had breakfast in the kitchen with Louise Bell. His father was not yet up. Mrs. Bell said, "He's been sleeping later these days. I'm glad of it. I thought he was looking tired."

"He looked fine last night."

"Yes, he was so excited about seeing you. I haven't seen him so happy about anything for a long time. And David, I'm very happy too. You'll stay here as long as you like, won't you please?"

"Of course," David said, and he set out for Rollins' office in a good frame of mind. Half an hour's brisk walking brought him to the building at Fifty-fourth Street and Third Avenue, a new, glassy structure with an enormous metal insect of unknown species bolted to its front wall by way of decoration. David scanned the directory and read:

INST FOR STRATEGIC RES .. 2705

He stepped into the elevator, touched the "27" button and started to rise. One man had stepped in with him and David mentally photographed him: Mr. Anonymous, one of the millions who seemed to have no occupation other than getting in and out of taxicabs and stepping into automatic elevators. The man had a Central European look, with a pale, closely shaved face and heavy glasses. He was wearing one of those suits which appear to have been cut from gun-colored metal, and a doll's hat with a brim somewhat less than an inch wide. Might be in the office of a United Nations mission, David thought; they're all through this part of town. Meanwhile, as the car rose David and the man were bathed in hideous fluorescent light, while music of the kind that used to be played behind potted palms in hotel lobbies was poured into their ears from a concealed loudspeaker. Brave new world.

The elevator stopped and the man hurried out, turned to the right, and disappeared around the corner of the hall. David found 2705 around the corner to the left. The door was unlocked, and he walked in, entering a room that had chairs for callers, occasional tables with magazines, cigarette boxes, and ashtrays, and a receptionist's desk. The room was clean, smartly decorated, and empty. He heard someone moving inside and George's voice called, "Is that David Bell? Come on in."

David walked down a short hallway and found George Rollins in a sunny corner office that looked out toward the Waldorf and the Seagram tower. George rose from behind a mountain of paper piled on a huge walnut desk and guided David to a chair. The office was impressive, but as David sat down he observed that the moraine of paper on George's desk was composed of State Department dispatches, classified Confidential. In high bureaucratic circles, documents with such a minor classification were unworthy of notice, and David made a mental wager that George was using these papers merely for effect— perhaps almost as decorations. He had always liked to have mounds of paper around him, perhaps drawing some sort of reassurance from their mass.

"What do you think of the set-up?" George asked.

"It certainly looks like a foundation office," David said. "Quarter of ten in the morning and nobody at work."

"I haven't staffed up yet," George said. "There's nobody aboard so far except my girl, and she's out on an errand."

David knew that in George's language, "girl" meant "secretary." He said, "I'm sure you know what you're doing, George. I only wish I did."

"You will," George said, getting up. "Let me show you your office." He led David into an adjoining room, also spacious and beautifully furnished. There was another splendid desk, and leather chairs and couches suitable for the president of a distillery or an advertising agency. "Hang your hat here. You can get a girl for yourself any time you like."

"Do you think I'll need one?"

"You might. It depends on your paper work."

"You seem to have that cornered," David said. "And I might add, as usual. Don't forget old Joe Bottleneck."

"There's no place for old Joe around here, I promise you that."

"That's good to hear."

"We don't have time to open up any logjams, David."

"I should hope not."

"Not when we have a chance to get a stranglehold on world opinion."

"World opinion again," David said. "Honestly, George, do you believe there is such a thing?"

"What we do here is a seed-bed operation," George said, disregarding the question. David thought, Rollins is the most maddening man I ever knew, and talking to him is like giving your name to a secretary and knowing she has no intention of passing it on to her boss. Before George could go on, David said, "You can be as vague as you please about your Institute. But I've got to insist that you give me some idea of what I'm supposed to accomplish in it. Is that fair? No, there's no use asking you a direct question. Let me make a statement—that *is* fair. Now you make a statement. My mission is . . ."

"They should have told you down there, David," George said, in a mollifying tone. "I'm sorry. There's nothing in the least vague about it. You're to penetrate the Kane Foundation."

"And how do I go about that?"

"We haven't been asleep around here," George Rollins said. "Things are already laid on."

"Such as?"

"You know about Jefferson Kane's dislike for the United States?"

"Dislike is a mild term for it," David said.

"He keeps setting these people up, financing their meetings, paying for their studies."

"What people are you talking about?"

"Intellectuals, authors, professors. In the Communist countries, and from the Left in the free countries, including our own. This is your field, David, you've been studying these people for years."

"I'll admit I've been reading their books," David said, and his heart sank as he recalled his weary perusal of the world's dullest literature, the writings of socialist and Communist political theorists. David used to say, a man should be willing to do anything for his country, even read the entire works of Karl Marx, in addition to those of Babeuf, Michelet, and Fourier. He had done this, and it had been hard going. It was a great deal to ask; he had told Jim Ewing that he feared his brain might never recover from the pressure these fundamentally unreadable books had put upon it. Ewing had suggested topology to take the kinks out, and David had replied, "You are recommending straw to a camel." Now, as he listened to George Rollins, David had the familiar feeling of unreality.

"You have these Left-wing types flocking around the Kane Foundation projects," George was saying. "No matter what Kane says, his operation has just one purpose. That is, to vilify every United States policy on any and every conceivable point, just because it's our policy. That, and to sing praises for the Red Chinese, the Castroites, and the jokers in the Kremlin."

"Quite true, George," David said. "And again, what of it. Don't you know Toots Shor?"

This question was so surprising to George Rollins that he answered it. "Yes," he said, "of course I know Toots Shor."

"Then you've heard him say, 'Lie down with dogs, you get up with fleas.'"

"But I don't see the connection."

"The connection is that it's logical for those people to condemn the United States," David said. "In fact, this is all you can expect from them."

"There I disagree. We can use old Kane's foundation to tell our side of the story."

"You can't believe that's possible."

"Certainly it's possible. Not all intellectuals are opposed to the United States. Not by any means all. Just now I'm hoping to get the Kane Foundation to recognize Professor Hans Thorpe. I'm sure you know of him—famous political scientist at Southwestern University."

"Kane's crowd would call Thorpe a fascist. It's fantastic to say they'd give him a platform. Only if they were hanging him, George, only if they were going to break his neck."

"I'm not so sure of that," Rollins said, and David saw in him now the George Rollins of old, who never was known to agree with anyone on any subject. In order to get things done, George's associates had sometimes proposed to him the exact opposite. This often worked, but just as often George would suspect that he was being handled, and all activity would cease. David felt a twinge in his stomach—an old cratered ulcer was there. This Rollins, David thought—in his way, he's a terribly dangerous man. Now how can I make him hurt the right people? George was droning on that there was a great deal Professor Thorpe might be expected to accomplish. "He can slow these people down," George said. "He can present an alternate point of view, improve the image of the U.S.A. before the intellectuals in the democracies and the uncommitted nations."

"George, I know these people, as you continually call them. Please believe me. They won't let Thorpe within two miles of anything they control."

"I'm not so sure about that."

"Then I'm sure there's nothing I can do."

"Oh, yes there is," George said. "You can talk to Jefferson Kane."

"And how do I meet him? Go to one of his banks and ask for a loan?"

"Now, now," George said. "The most important thing here is for David Bell to be happy and comfortable. We can't do without him, and he must feel right." For a moment David felt the sympathy that Rollins occasionally manifested toward his colleagues. David thought it hardly fair, but he knew that in George's case, as with all self-centered people, the courtesies and sympathies that were expected of others as a matter of course were accounted to be elements of charm when George turned them on. Somehow or other, George Rollins had fixed it so that people were grateful to him when he was polite. And when you analyzed this, David said to himself, it was really a hell of a note. But there it was.

"Very well, I meet old Kane," David said. "I assume you'll tell me how."

"We do this in two phases," said George, with relish. "Phase one, you meet Don Marlowe. This television man. Phase two, Marlowe introduces you to Kane. Neat and complete."

"All I need is an introduction to Don Marlowe."

"You have it. Didn't I tell you things were laid on? Marlowe's expecting you for lunch, today." Rollins picked up a scratch pad, wrote an address with a gold pencil, and tore off the sheet. David saw that the address was one of the last apartment houses remaining near Sixtieth Street on Park Avenue.

"That's a good building," David said. "Marlowe must have paid a fortune for his apartment."

"A fortune he's got," Rollins said. "So go up and take a look. I'll be interested to see how this fellow strikes you."

"All right, George," David said. "I'll go over to the club, have a swim, and walk to Marlowe's apartment. Can I find you here later today?"

"I'll be right here," Rollins said, walking to the door with David. Outside, the building corridor was empty, but the elevator was jammed with men and women, each of whom seemed to be attached to a smoldering cigarette made from the sweepings of tobacco warehouses. As he walked toward the street, David thought perhaps he ought to take up smoking, though he regarded the habit as one symptom of insanity; but at least other people's cigarettes would not smell so bad. In the street, a thought of Roxie Dean came to him and he turned uptown. He found her travel office two blocks over on Fifty-seventh Street: pink leather walls, free-form sculpture, circular desks, and "social" help. A young man with bangs and a church-school manner told David Miss Dean was out. Surprised at his feeling of disappointment, David said he would look in again. He walked on to Park Avenue and down to the Corinthian Club.

At the club, David swam in the pool, and then stretched out in a deck chair, wrapped in several large towels, to read the papers. Greenish reflections from the water moved on the vaulted ceiling, and the light rebounded

across the newsprint. On the front page of the *Times* was
a story about the British physicist, Sir Ronald Maxwell-
Spencer, who was coming to the United States to visit
his old friend, Jefferson Kane. It was the kind of story
that only the *Times* bothered with, for the news value
was slight. Indeed, on first reading one was hard put to
it to figure out what the news was supposed to be. Sir
Ronald did not like the United States, so much was clear.
What bothered Sir Ronald was the thought of atomic
weapons in American hands. Americans, said the sage,
were the least trustworthy of mankind. Not being in an
advanced state of political civilization, these Americans
were more likely to cause trouble than the more sophisticated—and here David gently laid the newspaper on the
tiled floor beside his chair. In David's opinion, two ordinary words had been robbed of meaning: one was "sophisticated" and the other was "dialogue." He often said, "To
me, sophisticated dialogue is what Philip Barry used to
write. I don't think it means serious discussion." Whether
or not he was right, David now went peacefully to sleep.

Half an hour later, David woke and knew at once there
had been no dreams, and the brief sleep had done him
more good than many a disturbed night in recent months.
He dressed, went downstairs, and set out for Don Marlowe's apartment a few blocks up the avenue. As he
walked along, he reviewed in his mind what Marlowe had
told about himself in *I Cried All the Way to the Bank*,
which David had read last night. With this book, Marlowe
had presented the story of his life although he was only
two years older than David. An interesting man, this Don
Marlowe: at college in the late thirties, he had become
an announcer on the student radio station, and had fallen
in love with the sound of his own voice. What he especially liked was the unprepared sort of program in which
the announcer talked on and on about anything that

occurred to him, and played a record when he ran out of breath. This cut down the time Don Marlowe might have spent in the library, but led to a job on a commercial station, and then to the position of emcee with an Army show when the war came. Marlowe's war had been trouping before audiences of GIs who roared at jokes about chow lines, officers, and WACs. When Don got out of uniform, he began working before studio audiences, without at first realizing that they were a special breed of people, who would applaud anything, even an advertisement, so long as they got in free. Television came, and Don Marlowe took on a variety program that ran three hours a night, five times a week. Even if he had been blessed with major talent this assignment would have spread that talent too thin. But the studio audiences applauded as though he embodied in one performer the charm and skill of Jack Donahue, Ray Bolger, Fred Astaire, Gene Kelly, William Gaxton, and Sir Harry Lauder. They were ecstatic, those studio audiences. And what a curious crew: they looked like the people who sit all day in parks, feeding pigeons out of ratty paper bags. Then, to get in off the streets, they came to the Don Marlowe Show. In his heart, Marlowe knew this. He knew that it really wouldn't do. There were people whose applause he would have valued more than anything in the world; but these people never were part of the studio audience, or the audience that saw Marlowe's program on their sets at home. These people, whose good opinion Marlowe longed to have, would no more think of watching his show than they would have considered sitting in a grandstand and looking at the trash on a city dump.

Though there was little to envy in Don Marlowe's public, he had made incredible sums of money. He had also become an assiduous liberal. No murderer could be sentenced to electrocution without Marlowe besieging the governor to let him off; and he looked with suspicion, which he continually voiced in broadcasts and in letters to editors, on the foreign policy of the United States, whenever it failed to please other countries, including Burundi, Tanzania, and Upper Volta—and above all, he hated and feared The Bomb. With its star taking himself more and more seriously, the five-nights-a-week program ran its course and was eventually abandoned; but this meant no decline in Marlowe's fortunes. On the contrary, he now earned more money for less work—for almost no work at all, appearing half an hour each week as master of ceremonies on a variety show. This left plenty of time to cultivate people like Jefferson Kane, and to assist in activities like the Kane Foundation. If he could not be accepted as an entertainer, he would make the grade as a liberal intellectual. This was Don Marlowe's life plan. Obviously he was working for intellectual acceptance in the way that women sought social acceptance, by serving on committees with the already arrived. It was a climbing process and it seldom failed. Some day, David thought, as he neared the door of Marlowe's apartment building, somebody might actually take this man seriously. In fact, it appeared that George Rollins already had.

Entering the building, David saw that he had been right in his memory of the address. Marlowe had not made the mistake of settling in one of those new structures with paper-thin partitions, insectoid sculpture in the lobby, and the exterior effect of having been made with Meccano. Far from that, the building was a monument to comfort and privacy with a small paneled lobby and a doorman as elderly and courteous as Niles himself. "You're expected, Mr. Bell," said the man, and sent him up in an elevator with another attendant. At the eighth floor, David stepped off into a foyer with an Adam card table against pictorial wallpaper of museum grade and a gilt Chippendale mirror.

There was only one door, which showed that Marlowe's pad occupied the entire floor. David pressed the button in the marble frame, and the door opened almost at once —Don Marlowe himself had answered the ring.

"Walk in, old buddy," Marlowe said, shaking hands and indicating that David should come with him down a long hallway, and into a book-lined study. "Rest your bones. You like what I'm drinking? Dr. Pepper and vodka."

"So you've discovered it, too," David said, as Marlowe went to a grog table in the corner, opened a bottle of Dr. Pepper and poured it into a tall glass, adding ice and alcohol.

"That I have," Marlowe said, handing the glass to David and picking up his own. "The flavor is grand but indefinable."

"Quite right," David said. "There is no name for it."

"But whoever Dr. Pepper may be, he is a benefactor of mankind," Marlowe said. He dropped heavily into a big leather chair.

"A great and good man," David said.

"He ought to have a monument," Marlowe said.

"He probably has, somewhere down South." Settling in his chair, David looked at his host. Marlowe was an indoor type, with a face that seemed to be made of biscuit mix, and he wore heavily black-rimmed glasses, the trademark of the television emcee. Dark wavy hair beginning to recede from a high forehead gave him a senatorial air.

"Well, how's George Rollins?" Marlowe asked.

"He's fine," David said.

"George is a right guy."

"I've always thought so."

"You ain't just a-foolin', old neighbor," Marlowe said, dropping into the country style he sometimes affected while broadcasting. "He'll do to ride the river with, yes sirree."

David was about to answer when they heard the front door slam, and then someone walked up the hall with scuffing feet. A boy of fourteen or fifteen came into the room. "This is my son, Jeffrey," Marlowe said. "Jeff, this is Mr. Bell. He was in the Marines." The boy was loose-jointed, untidy, sullen. He did not acknowledge the introduction, but stared at David with the expression of a great potentate waiting for an especially unimportant courtier to ask a favor. David said, "Hello, Jeffrey. How are you?" Still without speaking, the boy slouched out. In a moment, an ear-splitting noise poured from the next room. The boy had turned on a record of racing-car engines tuning up.

"I have another son," Marlowe called over the din. "He's twenty years old. Peter. That's his name, Peter. Know what he's done? Come home from Duke University with a *wife*. Dropped out of college, no degree. I said, 'How do you plan to get past the guy in Personnel with no degree?' He said, 'You did it.' I said, 'That's different. I happen to have a number of salable talents, fortunately for you.'" Don Marlowe rattled ice, and took a swig of his fortified Dr. Pepper.

"What is the older boy doing now?" David yelled through the bellowing of engines.

"Course in creative writing at Columbia," Marlowe shouted back, and then yelled, "*Jeffrey! Hold it down to a roar!*" Apparently in answer, the noise got even louder. Marlowe rushed out of the room. The record was shut off, and David could hear father and son shouting at each other. As Marlowe came back, David heard the boy run down the hall and slam the front door.

"Now he's sore," Marlowe said. "He'll go back and eat lunch at school, and tell the other kids his old man's a monster. He must be nuts. If so he didn't get it from me. My analyst is a Jungian anyhow."

David could neither follow Marlowe's last remark nor

think of anything to say. He realized Marlowe was drunk, and then was startled when Marlowe apparently picked up his thought, as if by empathy.

"I'm no alcoholic," Marlowe said. "But occasionally I go on a binge."

"Sometimes it does seem advisable," David said.

"Matter of fact, I'm just coming off a big one. Instrument landing."

David smiled in what he hoped would appear to be an understanding way, but found himself running out of things to say to Don Marlowe. At this point, a middle-aged, neatly uniformed waitress came in and announced lunch. In the dining room, she served them consommé, an egg course, and cold sliced ham with mustard and pickles left on the table. Marlowe took none of it, and continued drinking while David ate.

"You certainly have a pleasant place here," David said.

"No reason for not," Marlowe said. "I have more money than I know what to do with. Even after expenses. Even after *taxes,* for God's sake." David knew from Marlowe's book that he had been married and divorced twice. Again Marlowe caught the thought.

"I'm thinking of a third marriage," he said. "That might take care of the surplus funds. I'll grant you that, old neighbor. That I'll grant." David looked interested and friendly, and nodded. He was beginning to like Don Marlowe.

The woman brought coffee to the library. David decided against brandy, or anything from the formidable shelf of liqueur bottles that Marlowe swung out from the wall beside the fireplace.

"Old George says you'd like to meet Jefferson Kane," Don Marlowe said, as he lowered himself to a leather couch. "All right, I introduce you Jefferson Kane. Bet you thought I couldn't, hah?"

"I understood you knew him."

"You bet I know him. Come up after dinner and I take you over his place."

"That's very kind of you," David said. "I'd like that a lot. Do you mind if I bring a girl?"

"By all means, old buddy," said Don Marlowe. His eyes began to glaze and his head nodded. "But now if you don't mind, amigo, I think we'll strike the set." His head fell forward, came up, and rolled loosely. "See you nine thirty. Nice of you come up. Maid show you out . . ." As David was uttering thanks for lunch and the invitation for the evening, Marlowe fell over on his side and went to sleep. David lifted his feet to the couch, loosened the shoelaces, and left the apartment. Downstairs the elevator man and doorman saw him off like a valued friend. No taxicab, Mr. Bell? But it is, indeed, a nice day to walk . . .

At the Institute for Strategic Research, David found George Rollins out, and the place in charge of a middle-aged woman wearing a hat and sitting at the principal desk in the outer office.

"You're Mr. Bell, I think?" said the woman.

"Yes."

"I am Mrs. Martin, Mr. Rollins' secretary."

"How do you do, Mrs. Martin?"

"It's very nice to see you here, Mr. Bell. Mr. Rollins has been—well, just *excited* about your coming with us." David thought this must mean George had known about the transfer before he himself had been informed of it. He wasn't sure how he liked the idea, but what he said was, "I'm glad to be here, Mrs. Martin." She was a handsome woman in standard office costume, something black, and the wearing of the hat at her desk indicated she considered herself of high secretarial rank, an executive secretary, no less. This was the kind of woman who worked for important lawyers, or corporation presidents, and had secre-

taries of her own, and was cultivated by junior executives
who treated her like the headmistress of an exclusive
school in which they wanted to enroll their daughters.
Yet here she was in an empty office. David reserved judgment, and said, "I'll leave now, Mrs. Martin. If you see
Mr. Rollins, please tell him I am meeting Mr. Kane tonight."

"I'll be glad to, Mr. Bell. By the way, before you go,
would you like me to get you a girl?"

David laughed to himself because Mrs. Martin sounded
so like a high-class procuress, but of course she would have
picked up the Rollins vocabulary. "Let me see how the
work shapes up first," he said. "I'll let you know in a few
days."

"Please do, Mr. Bell. And anything *I* can do, of course."

"Thank you," said David, and left the office. Waiting for
the elevator was the pale, foreign-looking man who had
ridden up with him in the morning. The descending car
was vacant, and they had struck a period when the
piped-in music was off. Both Mr. Anonymous and David
stood in the fluorescent silence, avoiding each other's eyes,
the standard procedure of the metropolis. On the sidewalk, David turned south, and the foreign man went north.
David thought, he's one of the old settlers in the building,
one of the pioneers, and I am the newcomer—I wonder
how long it will take for us to reach a nodding basis, as-
suming three or four elevator meetings a week. Dismissing
the speculation from his mind, David walked on down
Third Avenue to Twenty-third Street, and turned west
toward Lexington, and as he walked he questioned
whether his habit of going everywhere on foot was a good
thing in a city whose air was so thoroughly impregnated
with carbon monoxide. He muttered to himself, "I don't
like this city at all. I only love it." Still, the air at street
level was poison. The answer might be in pedestrian pas-

sageways thirty or forty stories above the streets. He would have to ask his father about this some time.

At the apartment house Louise Bell came into the hall when she heard David open the door.

"Delighted to see you back so early, my dear boy."

"I came back to look over the things in the storeroom," David said. "Mostly books—you remember, the things I sent up after Mary died?"

"Of course," Mrs. Bell said. "The key is right here." She pulled open a drawer and handed David a key tied to a block of wood. "Will you need any help?"

"Not now, thank you," David said. "I'm just looking."

"I hope this doesn't mean you're leaving us."

"I'm thinking of a small apartment, probably in this part of town, maybe around the corner in that old building at Twentieth Street."

"It's a nice place."

"I'm not sure there's anything open there, but I'd better see what space I'll be needing. I don't want to settle down on you here."

"David dear, you mustn't hurry away. Just suit yourself."

"I will, Ma. Trust me for that."

David went to the lobby, opened a door at the back, and walked down a flight of stairs into the basement. As he was approaching the storeroom assigned to his father's apartment, he heard a sound behind him. David turned in the direction from which the sound was coming, and as he did so, two men walked quietly out of the furnace room, and stopped when they saw him. The place was lit with fluorescent tubes in the ceiling, and David saw at once that the men were thugs. They had the characteristic soiled jackets and faces, and their jeans were so dirty with worn-in filth that they looked like leather. The intruders were young, perhaps not twenty-one. One was about David's height and the other was very tall, almost a freak. The tall one was carrying a hammer.

"What do you want?" David said, excitement thinning his voice.

"One side, Dad," the smaller one said, and leaped toward David, trying to hook an elbow in his gut. At the same time, the big one raised the hammer and came dancing like a boxer. Rage burst in David's nervous system. He jumped away from the elbow, ran at the big one, pulled the hammer out of his hand, and twisted his arm behind his back, forcing it high. The thug screamed, writhed loose, and started to run for the areaway stairs, stumbling and getting up again. The second thug ran past and David followed, hitting him in the back between the shoulder blades, and he fell against the wall, scrambling up and running out of the cellar. There was a smear of blood where the tough's face had struck the concrete wall. The invaders' feet clattered on the back cellar stairs, while David leaned against the wall until his heart stopped racing. Then he went to the basement extension of the house telephone and reported what had happened to the police.

6

THAT EVENING, David sat beside Roxie Dean at a divan table in a restaurant on East Fifty-sixth Street. He had called the police about half past four. At five, he had called the travel agency and asked for Roxie. Her voice on the telephone was like a shower of silver from a jackpot machine. Could she come out for dinner tonight, and meet some people later? Of course! Roxie was pleased. And for the first time in many months, David felt the happiness of a man whose evening is arranged. As he left the apartment at seven, Louise Bell stopped him in the hall.

"I hope you have a pleasant time," she said.

"Thanks, Ma."

"One thing, David. If you talk to your father later on, see if you can get him to take a vacation."

"He can afford it, of that I'm convinced."

"Of course he can, and he needs it so."

"He looks all right to me," David said. "But you know best. I'll suggest Phoenix. He's crazy about the Camelback Inn."

"Do suggest it, David. He'll listen to you."

"All right, Ma. *Vaya con Dios.*"

David's luck for the evening seemed to be in, for he picked up one of the good old cab drivers at the door.

"About to pull in but I'm glad to do it for you, Mr. Bell," said Frank McGivrey.

"Don't want to take you uptown if you were pulling in," David said.

"No, no, glad to do it," said the elderly man. "But one thing I tell you, I swear, Mr. Bell. Off duty goes the sign the minute you're dropped. No more passengers this day. You wouldn't know the dirt trash. You wouldn't realize it, Mr. Bell."

"Oh, but I do realize it," David said.

"What I've seen in this cab," McGivrey said. "You would find it impossible to believe."

"I'm afraid I'd find it easy to believe."

"True, you're a man of the world, Mr. Bell. I tell you this. My son, he's taking his Ph.D. at Indiana University, you're aware of it?"

"Sure. Bloomington, Indiana."

"Bloomington is right. Next June I'll be seeing him take his doctorate. Then I leave the streets of this city, Mr. Bell. They can have them. Have them and welcome, Mr. Bell."

"That's fine about your son," David said. "What is his field?"

"Sociology. Now let's see here, let's see now." He slowed up for Fifty-sixth Street.

"On the corner will do."

"Very good, Mr. Bell."

David got out and as he reached for his money the driver said, "That lady I had in my cab the other day."

"Yes?"

"I started uptown, this very address you gave me or near it. When we come up to Forty-second Street she says to me turn east. She says take her to the United Nations."

"Which entrance?"

"It impressed itself on my mind, Mr. Bell. It was not the entrance for the tourists and the little children from the schools. No sir. The VIP entrance it was. That's where I put the young lady down."

"I see. Well, thank you, Mr. McGivrey," David said, making up a good tip from the change.

"I thank you," said the old driver. "Like your father before you, you're a gentleman born."

The cab drove off, and David entered Roxie's apartment house, which was two doors from the corner. The building had a marble lobby with French windows that looked out on what had been a garden but was now only a desolate area of soot-coated concrete. A middle-aged doorman in a shabby uniform confronted David.

"Miss Dean, please," David said. "My name is Bell."

"She expeckin yah?"

"Yes, *Miss Dean* is expecting me."

The doorman dialed a house telephone and announced David, then drank from a container of coffee which he had standing on a window sill.

"Thank you," David said.

The doorman nodded acknowledgment over his coffee, and David stood meditating on the mysteries of what is known as a good address. In less than two minutes, the elevator door opened and Roxie stepped out. She looked attractive and happy—Ann Sheridan before Cagney has been sent to jail.

"Roxie, I'm glad to see you," David said. "I knew that would be a lucky call."

"And a nice idea," Roxie said, taking his arm. They walked out, and David said, "Let's go to the Meadowbrook." The place was a French restaurant in the same block, and expensive. "That all right with you?"

"Anywhere you say, David."

When they entered the Meadowbrook, the proprietor allowed a smile of real geniality to come through his professional mask. He was a solid and heavy man, perhaps fifty years old, and of no identifiable race or nation.

"Good evening, Mr. Bell. It's been a long time. A great

pleasure." Like all men skilled in his craft, he included
Roxie in his smile without letting it indicate whether or
not he knew her. Then Roxie said, "Hello, Charles."

"And Miss Dean, nice to see you," Charles continued,
causing a menu card to appear in his hand with the swift-
ness of a conjurer's move as he conducted them to the
narrow aisle between the bar and the cocktail tables. A
page boy took David's hat, and Charles used the menu to
tap a signal to his dining room captain on the back of his
hand. David enjoyed it quietly—there had to be a certain
amount of drama in a place like this. Roxie was known
here; she must have a beau, or several of them, with money
to spend. Now the owner, the captain, and a waiter got
them seated in the main dining room, Charles himself took
the cocktail order, and the drinks appeared almost as if
they had shot up through the crisply laundered cloth.

"My word, they're giving you the treatment, David."

"You seem to be a valued patron, too."

Roxie made no answer to that, but smiled in a gentle
way and remarked on a celebrity who was sitting on the
other side of the room. This was an actor who had once
played King Lear on television even though he was only
twenty-four years old, and now, a few years later, was a
movie star. Seated with a beautiful girl between him and
another man, the actor was "on," gesticulating widely and
giving his face a good workout.

"What do you suppose he's talking about?" Roxie said.

"God knows," David said. "I'd suppose he was talking
about himself, if he's like the actors I know. I used to see
one pretty often in the days when I went to P. J. Clarke's.
Always in the back room, always out of work. Came the
police action and I was in Korea for two years. When I
got back, my clothes were in storage and the first night out
in New York I had to wear the uniform. During the evening we stopped in at Clarke's. Here was this same actor,

same table even. Passing his table I say hello and introduce my girl. Mind you, I'm in uniform. And the actor says, 'Hello, David. I just got a call from Jed Harris. There's a great part for me but I die in the first act. Can't decide whether to take it. What do *you* think I should do?' "

Roxie laughed heartily. "Didn't he even give you 'Hello, David—been away?' "

"Not even that," David said. He nodded to the waiter, who caused their empty glasses to disappear and reappear with the second cocktail. A moment of great happiness came to him. Experience told him that it would soon be gone, but as it existed it was perfect.

"There's one drawback to this place," David said after they had ordered their food.

"What's that?"

"United Nations trade."

"Oh, really? You mean that's not good?"

"I don't mind their eating. I suppose they have to eat. But they have such bad manners."

"Oh, not all of them, David."

"No?"

"Some of them are very nice."

"Well, if you say so. I find the male ones have a tendency to light oily cigars and scream at the help. Charles could tell you some stories."

"And the women?"

"I don't know too much about their women. I guess I just don't hold with foreigners."

"You're not serious."

"Not altogether. Maybe I'm just disappointed, disillusioned."

"I'm interested in your saying that, David. I suppose your work in Washington is over? I don't know whether I'm supposed to ask about that, but your mother seemed to think so."

"It's all over," David said. "My contribution is on file. But about the United Nations, you know people there?"

"We work for some of the missions," Roxie said. "They do a lot of traveling."

"I can imagine."

"The world is getting smaller, David."

"So they say."

After dinner, the captain and waiter served Cherries Jubilee with the serious concentration of scientists performing an important experiment; and then Roxie decided against brandy. Smart girl, David thought, doesn't drink much, and probably not at all after dinner. It's the one thing that kills their looks quicker than anything else, he reflected, and yet so many of them do it. He was pleased also to see that Roxie did not say, "But you go ahead if you like," allowing a grown man permission to do something when he was, so to speak, giving the party. One smart girl, this Roxie Dean; she's been around.

"Let me tell you about the man we're going to see," David said. "He's Don Marlowe, the television star."

"Fancy that."

"He seems to be a pretty nice sort of fellow," David went on. "And he's going to take us over to Jefferson Kane's place."

"Kane? Oh, yes. Money. Russians. Red Chinese."

"That's our man. Strange evening, maybe?"

"Why it sounds wonderful, David. Marlowe and Jefferson Kane. Those names are *very* suitable for dropping. I can dine out for quite a while on Don Marlowe alone."

"There is where the whole evening may collapse. Marlowe was pretty heavily starched when I left him earlier today."

"Might not show at the post?"

"I don't know his form so I can't say for certain. But I had lunch with him, and I know when *I* drink that much at lunch and go to sleep afterward, I wake up feeling as though a mad professor had extracted my brain and substituted an order of hot Wheatena. There's no going out, I can tell you."

"I hope Mr. Marlowe doesn't feel quite *that* bad."

"We might go up and see," David said. He made a gesture as though writing on his hand to the captain, and the bill was brought. David added the waiter's tip to the total, scrawled his initials, tipped the captain in cash, and they left the table. As they walked out, David noticed that the actor was still "on," his companions furnishing a captive audience. Three large brandy glasses stood before them on the table.

"Charles may have a disposal problem," David said.

"They seem peaceable now."

"Yes, quite. Not that Charles would have any trouble."

They climbed into a taxi. After giving Marlowe's address, David went on, "One time I saw him throw out a mean drunk. This man was cursing the waiters and threatening the patrons, and Charles came up and shook hands with him, smiling all the time as though greeting a dear old friend. You should have seen that fellow move out, with Charles still apparently chatting agreeably and shaking his hand."

"What was it? Judo?"

"No, simpler than that. He was just pushing the man's hand back in the standard cop's hold, they say it's excruciating. He wasn't an old customer or anything of that sort."

"I've often wondered what they do when a valued client misbehaves."

"I've talked to Charles about that," David said. "In the first place, a bad drunk doesn't often get to be an old customer. They have ways of discouraging them. As it works out, a real souse will always keep one place where he behaves himself, so he'll have somewhere to go. But if there was trouble with a valued client, as you put it, well, the proprietor has to choose between loyalties. On the one hand, the customers who want it quiet; on the other, the man whose money he's taken. Charles told me the first thing they do is tell the drunk he's wanted on the phone. That gets him to the outer hall and then they try to talk him the rest of the way out. It usually works. A lush really knows just how far he can go."

"I hope that applies to Mr. Marlowe," Roxie said as they left the cab.

"We'll soon see," David said.

Again Don Marlowe popped the door open as though he had been waiting there. To David's astonishment, Marlowe appeared to be in excellent shape, and he looked upon Roxie Dean with obvious approval.

"I'm delighted to see you," he said, squeezing her hand. "You raise my opinion of David several degrees. Not that it wasn't high anyway."

They went to the library, where David and Marlowe had a brandy. Marlowe said he thought he had better explain about Jefferson Kane before they went over to his apartment. "He's not at all an ordinary type," Marlowe said. "He can take a sort of lordly line, you dig? You understand?"

"All that wealth," said Roxie. "And having his own way."

"That's it," Marlowe said. "Underneath it he's really a sweet old guy. I know him well."

David said, "I was wondering, Don, what your connection was. A much older man." He knew Marlowe expected to be called by his first name after one meeting, and he was almost certain Marlowe would not mind the personal question about Jefferson Kane. David knew that in Marlowe's set, conversation was frank and free.

"Yes, Jefferson is a pretty old gent," Marlowe said. "He

must be up around Sixty-eighth Street. I mean, he's easy sixty-eight years old. But the connection. David, he's furnished a good deal of the Marlowe bread and butter recently. Even some of the jam."

David's expression showed that he failed to get the meaning.

"One of Kane's companies is National Foods, and National Foods is one of my sponsors."

"Sorry, I should have known that," David said.

"It's all right, you must be the only man in the country who didn't," Marlowe said. "I even do commercials for him. Hold up the cereal box, you know."

"I'm afraid I don't," David said.

"Then for God's sake don't tell Jefferson," Marlowe said. "He's a great lover of the buck, and it would hurt him to think of any that got away." Marlowe filled a shot glass with brandy and hurled the liquor into his mouth, throwing back his head and swallowing smoothly. David watched him with interest. A professional alcoholic was usually a sipper rather than a gulper, but this was virtuoso drinking, no matter how a doctor might have classified Don Marlowe. "Care for a shot, David?"

"No, thanks, Don."

"Then we might as well move on," Marlowe said.

Downstairs, a Bentley limousine was waiting. The Japanese chauffeur closed them in the back, and got behind his wheel without waiting for instructions.

"He knows where we're going," Marlowe said. "It's always my first stop at night unless I tell him otherwise."

"This is your car?" David asked.

"It sure is, amigo. Yes, I know there's a place where you can hire them. That's what got me started. Are you impressed?"

"*I* am," Roxie said. "My goodness, I feel like bowing to the crowds."

"Speak for yourself, Roxie," David said. "I'll admit I'm impressed also."

"And you think it's pretty rich for the big civil liberties man," Marlowe said.

"Oh, I wouldn't say that, nothing of the sort. Man ought to have the sort of car he fancies," David said, but Marlowe had caught his thought all the same. They stopped in front of an apartment hotel between Fifth and Sixth Avenues in the Fifties. Here, it seemed, was Jefferson Kane's home in New York. David had learned that for all his dislike of the United States, Kane had four homes within its borders. In addition to this New York residence, there was a mansion in Minneapolis, and a hillside house in Bel Air, all kept in readiness for any time the owner might be pleased to leave the four thousand acres of his South Carolina barony. And now on entering the hotel, David noted that it was the quiet, expensive sort of place that had almost no lobby, and what he could only define as an air of ostentatious discretion. Such establishments gave several impressions at once; while Marlowe spoke on the house telephone, David thought of the eighteen floors above them—of opera singers' wives who cooked savory messes on electric stoves at one in the morning; of many-braceleted women whose lawyers disputed the wills of elderly decedents; and of high-class suicides. This place was quiet, but not always good. David would have bet a reasonable sum that Jefferson Kane owned it.

"We're to go up," Marlowe said, and they stepped into an automatic elevator and rose seventeen floors to eleven bars of Lecuona's "Siboney" on the piped-in music. "He has the top two floors," Marlowe explained as the door slid open and they got out. They were in a small hallway. A door opened and a young man in a dark suit came in and said, "Good evening, Mr. Marlowe. He will receive you in the lounge." The young man then opened another door and ushered them into the largest room David had ever seen in a hotel suite. Two stories high, seventy feet long, with French windows down one side opening on a balcony, it contained a great number of refectory tables, standing lamps, sofas, and tall-backed, Spanish-looking chairs. On the walls appeared none of Jefferson Kane's famous collection of carefully authenticated Van Dycks, Van Eycks, Vermeers, and Bruegels. Instead, David observed a series of gloomy-looking tapestries, hanging from iron spears against the yellow plaster; and some sort of papal banner was hung below the musicians' gallery.

"Dear me," Roxie murmured to David. He smiled and nodded, meaning, "Yes, whatever you think, I think so too." The young man left, and Marlowe steered them to a constellation of sofas and armchairs that were upholstered in red and blue velvet with gold embroidery. They sat down.

Roxie said, "I suppose he calls this the *small* lounge."

"He doesn't pay much attention to his surroundings," Marlowe said. "All he asks is to have it look expensive."

"There's enough carpet in this one room to do my whole apartment," Roxie said.

"Maybe we can get Jefferson to cut some off for you," Marlowe said. Then he rose, along with David, as a tall man in a blue suit marched into the room. Jefferson Kane was old, but he stood straight and gave an impression of strength—and an unpleasant expression it was when he pressed your hand in a painful grip on being introduced. He must think he's Charles getting rid of a drunk, David thought; I go for these hard grippers, such lovely people they always prove to be. They sat down, Kane taking a chair under one of the floor lamps, whose light gave David a chance to make a mental photograph. David recognized the type: Kane was vigorous for his age and proud of it, with the mean hick face that such acquisitors always seemed to have. There was no wisdom or patience in Jefferson Kane's face, and his personality struck with a blast of cold vanity. And David saw that there was more here than the self-esteem of a wealthy rube. It was expressed by a quality that lay in Kane's eyes. Those eyes had reminded David of something the moment he first saw them, and now he pinned the memory down. On a trip to Madagascar, he had come upon an excitement among the natives at a fishing wharf. They had captured a live coelacanth, a fish that scientists said should have become extinct millions of years ago. But it hadn't, and now and then a living specimen surfaced from the depths and rolled heavily in the nets. The men showed David the creature in a coffin-shaped watertight box where they were keeping it alive for the marine biologists, who would pay a great price for it. There was just enough water in the box for the thing to breathe. It was an armored fish five feet long, exuding oil from under its scales. It had leg-like fins, and a head that was a long sight uglier than anything else in the world. But it was the eyes that had compelled David's attention: eyes that should be dead, but still held all the mindless savagery of prehistoric animal creation, steadily looking up at him through the oily water as the coelacanth breathed and slowly moved the leg-like fins. Although masked, that look was to be seen in Jefferson Kane's eyes. Or so David thought, as Kane leaned back, mouthed and lit a cigar, and said, "They'd better be up early in the morning, if they think they'll get ahead of me."

"Who are you speaking of, Jefferson?" Marlowe asked.

"Anybody," said the magnate, blowing a column of smoke toward the musician's gallery. David thought he understood what Kane was getting at. The old man loved praise and approval, and he had received a good deal of it, including such undeniable distinctions as a half-column

listing in *Who's Who*. Still, there were those who criticized him. For example, he would need rhinoceros hide
not to feel the comments that his general course of action
had drawn on the editorial page of the *New York Daily
News*. That paper had often scalded Jefferson Kane for
his love for the Iron Curtain countries and the men who
ruled them. In addition, it had pointed out that Kane's
veneration for Chairman Mao was like that of a lover of
sensational literature for Mickey Spillane. Mr. Kane also
loved the African "nations" and reverenced their leaders,
except for M. Tshombe, who had no chance whatever of
qualifying for a loan at Kane's bank in Minneapolis. But
this holder of great likings had equally strong hates, and
above all, he detested his native United States, where he
said that nothing was ever done right. And this was the
man George Rollins wanted to make use of. It must be
fifty years, David thought, since anyone has made use
of *this* baby.

"Early in the morning," Jefferson Kane went on, "or
maybe not go to bed. Don't leave a call. Get started the
day before. And I'll still be long gone, long gone." Kane
knocked cigar ash on his double-breasted jacket, hit at it
with the underside of his sleeve, rolled around in the
chair to face David, and said, "Don Marlowe says you
want something, young man. What do you want from me?"

"Nothing from you personally, Mr. Kane. I was hoping
you might be interested in the work we're doing at the
Institute for Strategic Research."

"Never heard of it."

"We don't seek publicity, Mr. Kane."

"Then you're fools. Can't do anything today without
public relations. That right, Don? What are you trying
to accomplish, anyway?"

Confound George Rollins, David thought, why didn't
he give me a few specifics? He began to improvise.

"Like many foundations, Mr. Kane, we're interested in promoting free discussion, and in encouraging involvement and concern. That is, we feel that in a democracy, in an age when the world is continually growing smaller, an informed citizenship must also be a concerned citizenship."

"That makes sense," Kane said. He had been scrutinizing Roxie from head to foot, and one might almost think there was a pleased expression in his prehistoric eyes. "Go on, young man. Tell me more about the involvement." Behind Kane's back Don Marlowe nodded in encouragement and gave David a wink.

"What we hope to do," David said, "is to encourage a sophisticated dialogue, in the international academic world and on the graduate seminar level, and beyond— a dialogue in the rhetoric of charisma, you might say, Mr. Kane. We're interested in scientific humanism, and we would ask the involvement of all sides."

"*All* sides?"

"We believe that is the way to reach international intellectual consensus," David said.

"But what are you driving at?" Kane said, and David decided to give a pull on the line and see if the hook was seated.

"Our general objectives are those of Western man— of Faustian man," David said. "That is, the protection and preservation of world peace."

"Peace!" cried Kane. "There'll be no peace until that gang in Washington is disarmed!" He puffed on the cigar until the tip glowed red.

"In Washington?" David asked.

"I mean the government of the United States. We've got to get the nuclear weapons out of those people's hands."

"We at the Institute also hope to disarm the Soviets, the British, the French, and the Red Chinese," David said.

"Nonsense," said Jefferson Kane. "You can trust those people. You can't trust the Americans."

There was a slight pause, and then David said, "Well, anyhow, Mr. Kane, you have your Foundation coming along and we're always sure to hear interesting things from the people you help. Now, we at the Institute are in touch with certain authorities in the field of political science, as of course you know."

"No, I didn't know."

"We're in touch with several of these people," David said. "They have international stature, and we think they might add something to the discussions you have sponsored so generously."

"I can afford it," Kane said, and he seemed less angry. "But you might as well get one thing straight, young man. No fascist or colonialist will ever get a hearing at *my* expense."

"We have no interest in anyone like that, I assure you," David said. "You would know that the minute you looked at our roster of associates."

"Young man, I haven't time to read a long list of names."

"No, of course not, Mr. Kane," said David. "What we have in mind is to apply to your Foundation for a small number of reasonable grants. Perhaps three or four—not more than half a dozen. And we do have a short list of distinguished men and women who—uh—who have worthy projects in hand, and need financial help."

"Then why don't *you* help them?" Kane said, and he leaned back, his lips writhing on the cigar.

"Our resources are limited, Mr. Kane. That's why I'm here."

"And you think I've got money for you."

"We know you're a friend of free inquiry everywhere,"

David said. "Suppose we suggest half a dozen people, who could use your help. I could get you the names by tomorrow morning, and if they were personally acceptable to the Kane Foundation, we could—uh—proceed to the substantive level at a future time." David felt that he had spoken like a true disciple of George Rollins, and he waited while Jefferson Kane lapped at the cigar, threw his head back, and shot a volcanic puff at the ceiling. Kane made a big production out of smoking a cigar. Somehow he seemed to be angry at the cigar, and determined to beat it into submission. David went on, "You would consider a few of our recommendations for Kane Foundation grants?"

"I'll consider any group of intellectuals," Jefferson Kane said, and David thought he would use this same tone in agreeing to look at a collection of alleged old masters in an art dealer's layout. David knew that Kane never bought a picture without advice. He was pleased now to find from Kane's next remark that where intellectuals were concerned Kane also relied on a coach or professional dealer. "Bring me your list if you want to," Kane said. "I'll have Sir Ronald Maxwell-Spencer take a look at it. Sir Ronald and Lady Maxwell-Spencer will be in town tomorrow to be my personal guests, young man. Sir Ronald is an intellectual giant. He is a great man. We don't deserve him, but we have him, and that's our good fortune, young man. Get one thing in mind. If you recommend one name on your list that has anything wrong with him, Sir Ronald will know it. He knows the world of science, the world of intellect. Don't try to fool Sir Ronald Maxwell-Spencer."

"I wouldn't think of trying it," David said.

"You must know Sir Ronald very well," Roxie said. As Kane began to tell her exactly how well he did know the Maxwell-Spencers, David thought that the Englishman and his wife were indeed, as Ben Thornton would say, very, very terrific. Sir Ronald and Lady Agatha Maxwell-Spencer, David had taken occasion to find out, were dons at Cambridge, on the science side. But they got around. They had been in North Korea, for example, when the captured American airmen signed statements that the U.S. had employed germ warfare, and the North Koreans and Chinese Reds had published these statements in an attempt to excuse the typhus epidemic caused by lack of sanitation. That was the fact—the typhus came from their own filth. But there was evidence put before the great scientists from Cambridge that proved otherwise: a tray of dead beetles, another of dead field mice, and the casing from a leaflet-shell. Shortly after he came to the Company, David had seen a moving picture at a little art cinema in Budapest that had been made in North Korea at the time of the germ warfare charges. There were the American fliers, stating that they had been ordered on a mission of biological warfare; and it still haunted David to think of what had been done to make them say it. As a tip-off, they had made their statements absurd, but nothing was too absurd for Sir Ronald Maxwell-Spencer if it discredited Americans. There they were on the film, the fliers, and there also was the "International Commission of Scientists"—Sir Ronald and his lady and similar folk from Italy and France. These visitors sat across the table from the American prisoners, and they wore the old familiar look of placid hatred. And on the sound track was the Babu-voice, with its international enunciation, not that same one that had called in Paris, but like it, very like it. One gathered from his writings that Sir Ronald Maxwell-Spencer was not, on the whole, a happy man. But the camera showed him happy and complacent in North Korea.

"It would be a great privilege to meet Sir Ronald," David said.

"Understand me, *I* make the decisions," Jefferson Kane said. "But Sir Ronald might be willing to look at a list of names. He might be interested. Not that we need recruits for our foundation. I hope you realize that."

"I realize it, Mr. Kane, and it's kind of you to see me," David said. Kane stood up, dropped the smouldering cigar in a tray, and walked out. David looked at Don Marlowe.

"That means the audience is over," Marlowe said. "I don't know what you were expecting, but that's it. Matter of fact, he talked longer than he usually does. I think Roxie had a soothing effect."

"I notice he didn't offer us any drinks," David said as they got up and left the room.

"He never does except at meals," Marlowe said. "He figures anybody who can get in up here is rich enough to provide his own."

"Next time I'll bring a flask," David said. "And no Roxie."

"I don't think that's fair,' Roxie said. "I enjoyed it. And I think Mr. Kane is sweet—in a saurian kind of way."

"How's that again, cousin?" Marlowe asked.

"I think Roxie is comparing your chief sponsor to an alligator," David said. They stepped into the elevator and went smoothly down to the strains of "Karabali."

"It seems to be Lecuona night on this car," Roxie said.

"You keep throwing them right past me," Marlowe said.

"This time she's referring to a composer," David said. "Mr. Lecuona wrote this tune."

"Roxie, you ought to come on the show, you could make a lot of money with this odd-information thing. Besides getting famous."

"That would be wonderful," Roxie said.

"Then let's step in the bar and talk it over," Don said. "The drought up in Kane's hangout has parched me dry."

The bar of the apartment hotel was only about one candle-power brighter than an unlit mineshaft. They felt their way to a corner table, and a waiter whose eyes were accustomed to the gloom took an order: one double brandy and two stingers. Roxie had decided to have a drink after all; and David was surprised to note that he felt slightly put out at her interest in appearing as a guest on Marlowe's program. He decided to lead conversation away from that topic.

"How does it happen you're alone this evening, Don?" he asked.

"My girl's an actress, playing in Chicago. Her name is Peggy Alcott. And since you cousins are so neighborly, I'll breathe a secret into your shell-likes."

"If you're sure you want to," Roxie said.

"It's just a little old country secret," Don said in his rube manner, which was, of course, partially lost on David since he had never seen Don's show. "But the fact is, old Cousin Don is sort of hitting the jug a bit while Cousin Peggy's away."

"Your good influence," Roxie said.

"Hope so," Don Marlowe said.

"You don't need a good influence, with old Kane in your corner," David said. "And speaking of Kane, tell me something, Don. If you don't mind, that is."

"Speak freely, cousin."

"I was wondering if you had any official connection with the Kane Foundation."

"If official means do I get paid, the answer is no. But a lot of folks around Mr. K. don't get paid directly. Or not in money, anyhow. I told you he made a close study of the dollar. Anyway, on a volunteer basis, I'm chairman of something we call the Panel on Communications. When you get down to it, that's something on the order of public relations man."

"I thought Kane had a publicity staff," David said.

"His corporate p.r. people are good, none better," Marlowe said, "but a thing like the Foundation is special, it needs more, ah . . ."

"Sophisticated handling?" David said.

"That's it exactly."

"Speaks very highly for you, Don," David said. "And what do you say we call a Seeing Eye Dog and get out of here?"

"Good idea," Don said. "Let me take you downtown to a party. Maybe you know the host. Dick Hudson, my television producer?"

"*Isn't* this an evening?" Roxie said. "I'd love to meet him." And on being assured that it was all right for Marlowe to bring guests, David said he also would be pleased to go. In a few minutes, they got out of the Bentley in front of a town house on East Thirty-seventh Street. Every window was lighted and a sound like that of a train coming into a subway station issued from the open door at the top of the sandstone steps.

David and Roxie had been in the place half an hour before Marlowe located Mrs. Richard Hudson, their hostess. She was brittle and blonde, and was burning a cigarette in a long holder as if the smoke was oxygen and she had just climbed Kinchinjunga with an anvil on her back. Mrs. Hudson's greeting was noticeably unenthusiastic, but David felt compelled to admit that the lady was not in need of extra guests, for at least two hundred people were jammed into the main floor of her house. Coming from somewhere was a Bruckner symphony with the volume turned high enough to be heard in Long Island City. Why the police weren't there David could not imagine. The fact was that neighbors had already called the police, who had left with a gratuity from Mr. Hudson. They had told him they would be compelled to come back in about an hour, and at that time, the music would *have* to be lowered. Meanwhile, Mrs. Hudson watched her guests, standing ten deep at the bar under the Chirico in the drawing room, and seven deep at the bar on the landing, the rest getting their highballs and champagne from the trays of waiters who patiently pushed their way back and forth through the crowd. After Mrs. Hudson was carried away in the circulating movement of closely-packed guests, Don Marlowe said, "Dick Hudson's in that little room." David looked into an Edwardian den with red leather and Phil May drawings, and saw his host. Richard Hudson was small and swarthy, with large goggles, and he seemed to be engaged in a tremendous altercation with three or four other men. The group included the actor David had last seen in the Meadowbrook. The actor was drunk, and continually picking up what seemed to be a typewritten sheet and waving it around. Then Hudson would take the sheet of paper away from him and they would all talk at once, although what they were saying melted into the general noise so that David could not make it out, even though he was standing only a few yards away.

"That's the performing arts Vietnam advertisement for the *Times* they're discussing," Marlowe said.

"Discussing seems to be a mild word for it," David said.

"Oh, they're in perfect agreement," Marlowe said.

"Then I'd hate to see them have a slight tiff," said David.

"We ought to see that too before the night's over," Marlowe said, and then the slow heaving of the mob bore him away. Roxie clung to David, and the projection of a heavy table made a small area in which the crowd did not press.

"What a crush," Roxie said.

"Free liquor will always draw a crowd."

"True, but what a crowd. Hello, Billy." Roxie reached out and touched a young man on the arm.

"No!" cried the young man. "It can't be! It's not possible! Darling!"

It turned out that this young man, who now embraced Roxie and kissed her cheek, was Billy Aubrey, the decorator who had done the travel agency. He was an engaging fellow, and his acknowledgment when Roxie introduced David was considerably more cordial than that accorded by Mrs. Hudson.

"A ghastly affair," Aubrey said. "I can't think what I'm doing here."

"Look here, Billy," Roxie said. "Be sensible for a minute. David's family tells me he's going into a new apartment. Why don't you get him for a client?"

"I could show you a sample, David," Billy Aubrey said, setting a world's record for getting on the first name basis, in David's opinion. "I'd like to show you my own place. It's a gorgeous apartment, only it's a total mess just now. But run this through the computer: orange lacquered walls, plaid furniture, and a simply gigantic purple suede sofa."

"It sounds great, Billy," David said, "but not quite my style."

"No, I suppose not," Billy said. "I guess you'd be wanting one of those butch places. But I could do it for you."

"I haven't an apartment yet," David said. "Let's see how things work out."

"Roxie has my number. Give a ring if I can help."

"I'll do that," David said, and Billy Aubrey left them.

"Thank you for being nice to him," Roxie said.

"I don't mind those people," David said.

"He brings out righteous wrath in the tough types."

"I'm not tough," David said.

Roxie looked out over the crowd. The smoke hung thickly over their heads, the din was a solid thing, and people yelled to be heard. Everyone looked angry. Beards, flannel shirts, fantastically towering hair; dinner jackets with narrow satin shawl collars; black ties tucked under lace collars; long dresses, short dresses, pajamas, nothing right, everything wrong—so it looked to David Bell and he had attended many a party in his time. Roxie said, "You're not enjoying yourself."

"Nor you."

"You're so right."

"But you haven't met Mr. Hudson."

"I really don't care," Roxie said.

"I think now would be a bad time to interrupt him," David said. "They're getting up a manifesto."

"Nobody would mind if we slipped away, then," Roxie said.

"Nobody I can see."

In the lower hall they found Don Marlowe, and managed to convince him they would prefer to get home under their own power rather than in his limousine. If it was all the same to them, Don was staying, for it was said that Truman was expected any minute, and he did not mean Harry.

"All right, children," Don Marlowe said, "go ahead by yourselves if you want to, and the birds will cover you with leaves."

"I'll call you tomorrow about that list of names, Don," David said. "And thanks for everything."

"You're welcome, amigo. It was trouble none."

Going up Third Avenue in a taxi, Roxie said, "David, you have the most amazing friends."

"Everybody I saw today," David said, "I was seeing for the first time. Except you."

"Meaning old friends are best, I hope."

"Meaning old friends are best."

As he left Roxie in the lobby of her apartment house, David said, "Does going to lunch tomorrow or the next day appeal to you?" And Roxie said, "David, I'm so sorry, but I just can't do it either day." This sort of answer put masculine ego in danger, and David made the indicated retreat to the terrain where dignity survived. "Let me telephone you." "Do that, David, I'd love it," Roxie said. She gave him a cousinly kiss on the cheek, stepped into the elevator, and the door rolled shut.

Rolling down Lexington Avenue toward his own home, David felt empty and tired. It wasn't because of Roxie. If a man was interested in a girl, he could only accomplish so much in one evening with other people around. Roxie was the first girl he had taken out since . . . he became eligible to ask girls out for the evening. He didn't expect her to make things right, he only wanted to show himself that he might not be forever maimed by the way his wife had been taken from him. It wasn't the Roxie part of the evening that had him down, he told himself now as the street lights of early morning moved past. It wasn't even the old crocodile, the old coelacanth, Jefferson Kane; nor was it that genial candidate for the alcoholic ward, Don Marlowe. David's depression of spirit came from the people at the Hudson's house. He knew nothing would come out of the Washington they criticized but the spectacle of bigmouthed politicians dancing the Watusi and the frug. The stink of Washington, the idiot clamor of New York—enough to make a dog sick, David thought. But there must be a country beyond the Meccano, beyond Park Avenue and Pennsylvania Avenue. And in that country, perhaps, a basic and essential reality could still be found. The cab drew up at 15 Lexington Avenue, and David got out. After paying the driver, he strolled for a few minutes in front of the building, admiring the traffic lights as they stretched over Murray Hill. An early mist made the asphalt reflect the lights, first a necklace of rubies, then a necklace of emeralds. As long as he could remember, David had liked to see them change, as though in a magician's trick.

"I don't see how they can ever take *that* away," David murmured to himself. He mounted the steps, rang for the night doorman, and went up to bed.

7

NEXT MORNING before he set out for the Institute David
had a caller. He was Detective Thomas Wilson,
working out of Manhattan East. David took him into the
library and said, "What can I do for you, Detective
Wilson?"

"We have those guys who tried to jump you," Wilson
said. "They're basement thieves. Prowlers, we call them."

"How did you spot them?"

"We acted on information received, Mr. Bell. The same
pair pulled a job in the cellar of a Second Avenue candy
store last week. They fractured the old storekeeper's head
with their hammer."

"Are you charging them with the Second Avenue thing,
or with attacking me?"

"Just the robbery, Mr. Bell. The storekeeper's wife identified them. You don't have to come into it. By the way, you
did a good job there. The one fellow, you tore the muscle
and broke the bone. The other one, he's got a broken nose,
where his face hit the wall, and a broken collar bone.
Where did you hit that son of a bitch, anyway?"

"On the back, high."

"A little higher you'd have killed him."

"That's what I had in mind. At the moment, I was sore."

"I don't blame you, Mr. Bell. I swear to God, this
city . . ."

"I know. Are you sure you won't need me in court?"

"That's what I came to tell you about. We don't need you, and you'd better stay out of it for your own sake. These people could charge you with assaulting them."

"But it was in my own basement, and self-defense."

"That don't mean anything in New York, Mr. Bell. Remember, this is in juvenile court. The judge will probably yell at the cop for bringing them in."

"And turn them loose?"

"Of course."

"Could you let me know what happens?"

"I'll be glad to."

As he walked to the door with the detective, David said, "I appreciate your coming up here. How long have you been in the Police Department, may I ask?"

"Next year I got my twenty years and I'm leaving the city. They can have it. I'm going to Southern California, get into plant security work. I can make easy my salary here, and I'll have the pension. The wife likes Los Angeles, we've been there already. My oldest kid can finish college out there, and there'll be better schools for the younger ones. California, here I come."

"I like Los Angeles, too, if they can lick the smog," David said.

"Oh, they'll find a way to lick that," Wilson said.

"But ride clear of San Francisco, it's a phony town in my opinion," David said.

"You called it on that town, Mr. Bell," Wilson said. "The wife and I, she has relatives. I've had a chance to study San Francisco. New York wasn't bad enough, they have to *imitate* it. No good."

Pleased as one always is upon coming to agreement on a firmly-held opinion with a stranger, David shook hands with Detective Wilson and thanked him again for his advice. Then David went back to the kitchen and was pleased to find his father sitting over coffee. Louise joined them and David told them about the party at the Richard Hudsons'.

"Theatrical parties used to be a lot of fun," Mr. Bell said. "But this one sounds like too much."

"I imagine they start to go wrong when you get television people," David said. "A straight theatrical party shouldn't be so bad. But I don't know that I added anything to the gathering, other than a very pretty girl."

"Roxie is a lovely thing," Mrs. Bell said. "She's a nice girl, too."

"You are right as always," David said. "Now I must get along to the office. Good-bye, all."

Roger Bell went to the door with David and said, "Give me a few minutes one day soon, will you, David?"

"Of course."

"I haven't brought you fully up to date."

"Let's make an engagement right now."

"That's much too formal, my boy. Just look in at the studio next chance you get."

"I will do it," David said, and his father smiled. It was a very good smile, with briskness and cheerfulness in it, a heartwarming smile, from which David had drawn strength and encouragement all his life. He walked to the office sustained by it.

On the premises of the ISR, David found Mrs. Martin typing away, but George Rollins was not to be seen.

"He said to tell you he'd be in later," Mrs. Martin said, turning in her swivel chair as David approached her desk. "He was absolutely delighted by the Kane development."

"That's good."

"Mr. Rollins told me things would begin to hum when you got here," Mrs. Martin went on.

"I don't know about that, only the second day on the job," David said. He was not happy about Mrs. Martin, and wanted to make sure she didn't know it. And so he added a banality, "We have to do things one step at a time."

"Oh, don't I know it," Mrs. Martin said. "And Mr. Bell . . ."

"Yes?"

"Someone has been trying to reach you for the last hour. A Dr. September."

"Dr. September?"

"That's what he said, and he's with Mr. Kane. He left this room number, at the Pomerania Hotel."

For a moment David had thought this might be a joke of Don Marlowe's, but he decided against that theory. No one who kept a Bentley could have anything to do with the Pomerania, so much was sure. He picked up the slip of paper Mrs. Martin held out to him.

"I'll call this Dr. September," he said.

"Let me ring the hotel for you."

"Thanks, Mrs. Martin, but I'll dial it. I don't like to ask people to wait for me." Henry Sedgwick was not the only man who called people direct, David told himself as he asked the hotel operator for Dr. Harvey September in room 2925. The operator clicked off, then came back and asked who was calling.

"David Bell, returning the doctor's call," David said.

Another silence, during which David theorized that the operator was consulting a list.

"I will ring them."

"Hello! Hello! Who's this?"

"David Bell, returning a call to Dr. September."

"This is Dr. September speaking. May I help you?" The voice was like all the daytime radio health experts in the world, plugging a patent food.

"Doctor, I think you wanted to speak to me. I have a message to call you here at my office, the Institute for—"

"Oh, David *Bell*. Sure. Of course. Mr. Bell, Mr. K. wanted me to get in touch with you."

"I see."

"Wonder if we could hold a little conference."

"I'd be glad to see you, Dr. September. Could you give me some idea of what it's about?"

"Not on the telephone. Definitely not on the telephone," said the announcer-voice, with a hint of putting David in the wrong.

"Would you like to come over here? We're on Third Avenue in the Fifties."

"Prefer you come over here, Mr. Bell."

"That suits me, Doctor. What time would be convenient?"

"I'll be free in half an hour. Can you make it?"

"Certainly. Half an hour. I'll be there."

The lobby of the vast and vile hotel on Sixth Avenue was crowded with prosperous-looking people, many of whom were queued up like refugees in front of the reservation desks. David meditated on the scene as he hunted for the house telephones. Some people said there was an unwholesome docility in the American public, and this hotel might almost seem to prove it, at least for the patrons lined up uncomplainingly in the grim, low-ceilinged lobby. The Ritz, the Marguery, the Chatham, the New Weston, the Vanderbilt, the Gladstone, the Savoy-Plaza, and dozens more, all gone. For some dubious reason, probably having to do with inflation of money, these civilized and comfortable hotels had been destroyed. Up in their places there had risen office filing cabinets of glass and steel. And their former guests who did not wish to travel in automobiles and put up in garages were handed over to the Pomerania and similar enormities. For a moment David stood and watched them as they filed past reservation clerks whose standard of civility seemed to be modeled on that of receptionists in a county jail. He shook his head, and dialed room 2925.

"Hello! Hello! What call is this? Who is this?"

"Dr. September, are you having trouble with your line?" David asked. "I'll ring off if you're trying to get outside."

"Who is this?"

"David Bell downstairs in the lobby. Will you come down?"

"No, no, come on up, you got the number?"

As the automatic elevator rose, packed like a subway car at rush hour, it occurred to David that Dr. September's telephone manners might be open to criticism. He'd better turn out to have a lot of innate charm and geniality, David thought, or *I may not like him.* He laughed, and the miserable bellmen and guests turned their blank faces toward him. The car went past his floor but he made it on the way back down. Par for the course, where the guest is king. Twenty-nine-twenty-five was a single room and its door stood open.

"Mr. Bell?"

"I am he."

The man who stood back to allow David to enter was of medium height and build. He closed the door, pointed out an armchair, drew up the chair from the writing desk, and sat down.

"I am Harvey September. Dr. September."

David nodded and smiled. The man's eyes were dark, with a sideways slant; the general flavor of having something to do with selling, which David had noted in his voice, was even stronger when one was able to get a look at this Harvey September. He had a small, black moustache, with pointed ends, and David wondered if it was possible that he waxed those ends. Great industries of the past: number one, the moustache wax industry, David thought. Again he chuckled, and Dr. September picked it up.

"Glad to see you so happy, Mr. Bell," he said.

"It's one of those days, I think," David said. "Everything seems to be working out right."

"And we want to keep it that way," the man said. David continued to draw in his general impression. It was evident that the doctor had spent a lot of money for his clothes. Also there was a considerable glinting of gold about him. Oversize links shone in his cuffs of white-on-white. A heavy gold clasp held down his necktie, and his wristwatch sat on a band of golden links. The watch was studded with extra knobs and appeared to have four or five hands and two or three systems of numbers running around the dial. David and Jim Ewing had a theory that a watch like this one was a reliable indicator that its wearer was what they referred to as a four letter man. David knew it was childish, or at least unscientific. But that was how he felt, and he believed he had often been proved right. And he was convinced now that a life-long friendship was not about to start. The telephone rang, and Dr. September seized it, snarling and barking.

"Call later!" the doctor shouted. "No further disturbance at this time, you understand me? I'm in a meeting."

One could almost think he had been conditioned to the sound of a bell like Pavlov's dogs, for he now seemed perfectly calm as he pushed the telephone back across the writing desk and handed David an embossed card:

SYSTEMS ANALYSIS, INC.

DR. HARVEY SEPTEMBER

PROGRAMMING SUPERVISOR

"I'm a Doctor of Philosophy, by the way," September said. "Took my degree in social psychology at Princeton."

David looked impressed, and said, "And I believe you said you wanted to talk to me about Mr. Kane. I expect you're a consultant of his?"

"Much more than that," said Dr. September. "We're a problem-solving team, working on confidential assignments for Mr. K. outside his regular staff lines."

"You say you solve problems. I suppose there'd be a good many?"

"More than you can imagine, Mr. Bell, where a man as big as Mr. K. is concerned. Corporate communications, community relations, program evaluations, Telex communications facilities, management psychology, human relations management, all that side of things. We write the big ticket."

"It does sound interesting," David said. "But I'm wondering just what you might want to talk to me about."

"I'll get to that," Dr. September said. "We also take an interest in personnel. Anybody coming into the Kane organization, we check them out, run the Rorschachs on them, and the Minnesota Multiphasics. You know what that is, of course."

"I don't believe I do."

"It's a multiphasic personality inventory, a scientific tool. We'll run you through it this afternoon."

"Run *me* through?"

"Like always, when anybody wants to work with Mr. K."

"But I'm not planning to work with him," David said. "There must be a mistake somewhere."

"Mr. K. never makes mistakes," September said. "He sent me your name at six o'clock this morning. Said get the usual work-up on this fellow."

"Evidently he got the idea I'm applying for a job," David said. "Nothing was further from my mind."

"You don't seem to understand, Mr. Bell. Mr. K. wants

the psychological picture on everyone he's associated with. That's one of the reasons for my group."

"Then I wish you'd tell me a little more about your group."

"We never talk about our activities, Mr. Bell. All we can say is we're in business to make things easier for Mr. K."

"He's your only client?"

"I didn't say that."

"Doctor, I hate to cut this short, but I don't see that we're accomplishing anything."

"Don't you understand what I want, Mr. Bell?"

"I'm afraid not."

"I'm suggesting that you run through a few of our tests. As a basis for my report to Mr. K."

"You mean to say that just to hand a man a piece of paper I have to be analyzed?"

"We hardly go as far as analysis, Mr. Bell. The multiphasic is merely a well-known psychological tool in personnel selection."

"I've already said I'm not asking for a job," David said. "I have a job."

"So we understand," said the doctor smoothly. "You were fortunate in making a connection so soon after leaving Washington."

"I don't think my affairs are up for discussion."

"Mr. Bell, I'm only trying to make you see that when you take it upon yourself to get in touch with Mr. K., you're not dealing with an ordinary man."

"I realize that more and more."

"What we do, Mr. Bell, one of our most important functions, is that we *protect* Mr. Kane."

"Perhaps he needs it, Dr. September."

"We're convinced that he does, Mr. Bell. We have had experience." The doctor took off his heavily framed glasses, and massaged the bridge of his nose. He pulled out a handkerchief, heavy as a napkin, and polished the lenses, lifted them, and peered to see if the glass was clear and clean. As he did so, the light fell across his eyes and David saw their essential and unguarded look. It was the coelacanth look: old, so old, and expressive of deadly strength and purpose, but without mind. For an instant David imagined he felt a blasting cold in the room, the freeze of mindless pre-history when something was preserved that should have died. Then the glasses went back on and the doctor was what he had seemed to be when the interview began, an aggressive salesman-type with overtones of quack psychology.

David stood up and said, "Well, it's nice to have seen you, Doctor. I'll go along now."

"I believe you're living down on Lexington Avenue," September said as he walked to the door. "Lovely neighborhood. But they say there's trouble with hoodlums coming in."

"Is that what you hear?"

"Why, yes, that's what I hear," said Dr. September, opening the door. "I understand it's a serious problem. By the way, your parents are living down there too, I think. Makes a problem. I mean, older people, things can get very dangerous for them. I hope you're careful."

David had heard this sort of talk before. Once in Vienna a man had talked in just this tone, and a few days later, David had opened a chocolate box, addressed to Mary, that contained a live snake. The man who made the threat had disappeared, a wise move on his part. And David had heard other threats, and recognized them, and known that they were meant to be recognized. He could not be mistaken now. It came clearly into his mind that if anyone harmed Louise or Roger Bell, he would kill that person. David looked now at Harvey September. He said nothing. But the doctor got the message. He stepped back into the room. When he suspected danger, the coelacanth would go behind rocks at the bottom of the sea. The only way to kill it would be to drag it to the surface and batter its head in. David continued to look at the doctor. Then he said, "It's kind of you to take an interest in my parents. If I were you, I wouldn't doubt that they are very careful. Very careful indeed. Good-bye, Dr. September. I'll tell Mr. Kane I saw you."

David walked to the elevators, while Dr. September stood motionless beside his open door. On Sixth Avenue, a cold wind was blowing spirals of trash past the Columbia Broadcasting Building. Fine particles stung David's eyes, and he took a taxicab back to the Institute.

"Mr. Rollins is here," said Mrs. Martin brightly.

"Thank you," David said, and walked into George's office. Rollins was barely visible behind the mountain of paper, but when he got up and went over to a sofa, with David taking a chair nearby, he looked fit and well—the old George Rollins. As a friend, David was glad to see this; as a colleague, he feared the worst. Rollins at the top of his form could stop a dozen projects in their tracks with endless tinkering. Now he said, "It's great that you're here, David. With your help we'll be phasing right along. I understand you saw Kane, and I'll bet you have everything on wheels and ready to roll."

"I've met him."

"How did you like him?"

"Have *you* ever met him, George?"

"Briefly, one time at the Gridiron Club dinner."

"Then you ought to know that 'like' isn't an operative word with Kane. If you mean could I stand him, the answer is yes. Just barely."

"You make a good impression on Marlowe?"

"George, I don't know. I doubt if he paid much attention. But he seems a genial sort."

"Oh, very."

"I must say he's a two-fisted drinker. And George,

there's something miraculous about it. I left him after lunch yesterday, sleeping it off. Went back at dinner time, and he looked as healthy as a Maine guide. I don't know how he did it."

"That's simple enough," George Rollins said. "He takes drugs."

"What do you mean?"

"I mean dexedrine, benzedrine, paracodeine, demerol, paraldehyde, anything like that. They're all hangover killers. Don doesn't believe in hangovers. He knows what to take."

"And you supply him," David said.

"I don't say that, but I wouldn't like to see him suffer," George said.

"George, there may be things in this that I don't need to know. If so, don't tell me. So far as I'm concerned, Marlowe can pop it in the main line if he wants to. Right now I want to tell you about Jefferson Kane."

"Go ahead, David. You're always worth listening to."

"Not having any idea what you wanted me to say to Mr. Kane, I improvised. I told him we needed some grants to help associates of this Institute do their work."

"That's a good approach," George said.

"Good approach to what?"

"I want to get close to this man, make use of him. He has power."

"So I've been hearing," David said. "Anyhow, he'll consider a list of our candidates for Foundation money. I told him I thought he'd want to present all sides. I had a pretty girl with me and maybe that smoothed things over."

"You had Roxie Dean."

"How did you know?"

"She told me."

"You seem to be sitting in the center of your web, like Professor Moriarty."

"Nonsense, David. I've known her all my life and she books our travel at her agency. Talked to her this morning about a trip I'm taking."

"You use her agency?"

"Always like to help a friend. Go on about Kane."

"He said he'd be willing to consider people we recommend. But only to consider, George. I don't know that anything will come of it."

"But he did listen to you."

"Yes, Marlowe had no trouble getting us in there and he said the old creep talked longer to me than to most."

"And now the troops are blooded," Rollins said. David recognized it as one of his favorite phrases, which he often used when something had been given a start.

"There's more to it, George," David said. "This morning I heard from a Dr. Harvey September, who says Kane told him to call me. I went to see him and he said he runs some kind of psychological service for the old man. He talked a lot of nonsense about wanting to give me some tests—said he had to do it for anyone who was associated with Kane. But that wasn't really the point. What he wanted to give me was a threat."

"You sure of that?"

"I've heard enough of them to know."

"But why threaten?"

"George, they must know all about us. Your background and mine. I don't see why we try to kid them."

"I haven't suggested that we try to kid anybody," Rollins said.

"This man was talking about protecting Mr. Kane. You wouldn't say you meant Jefferson Kane any good, would you?"

"I wouldn't spit down his throat if his guts were on fire."

"Then George—surely Kane must know that? And

believe me, this September was giving me the message loud and clear: lay off!"

"You make it sound as if Kane had a private Gestapo."

"Haven't you heard of stranger things being true?"

"Maybe."

"As I see it," David said, "the only way for me to make sure that Kane lets anyone like your Professor Thorpe within a mile of his operation would be for me to denounce the professor as anti-American. I'm almost serious about that. I might even try it."

"David, we're not going to try to force Thorpe into this Foundation. Thorpe will be one name among several on a list that you'll submit."

"We can try," David said. "I'll see that Kane gets the names of your people. That I can do. But Kane said he'd turn the list over to Sir Ronald Maxwell-Spencer, and that's all we'll ever hear of it. By the way, are the names ready?"

"I'll put together a list for you, David," Rollins said. "We mustn't go too fast at this point."

"But you gave me the idea we were in a hurry and didn't have much time."

"That's true in relation to the big picture, David. In specifics, we want to be sure of each step." This was the old Rollins talking, and David gave a shrug of resignation.

"Let me know when you're ready," he said. "Meanwhile, I'll do what I can to keep the Marlowe contact alive." On this familiar inconclusive note, David ended his conversation with Rollins. He had debated with himself the question of asking George for a copy of their charter, the written project. Then he decided that this might irritate his friend, who had always been sensitive to any implied disagreement. David would get a copy of the project from another source. It would be easy enough to do. He went into his own office and closed the door. At his desk, he dialed Jim Ewing's sterile line in Washington, and the answer came almost instantly after one ring.

"Hello," said Jim's voice in a calm, offhand tone.

"It's David."

"How are you, my boy?"

"Very well, and calling from George's establishment."

"How's George?"

"As usual."

"He is, eh? Look, David, I'm about to fly up there. Care to have dinner?"

"Like to."

"How about the club around six, six-thirty?"

"I'll be there. And Jim . . ."

"Yes, old man?"

"Could you set up a secure channel for me to get a copy of our project?"

"Your project? Ah, yes, of course. Will do. See you then."

David's next call was to Don Marlowe's apartment, with the intention of leaving a message, for he could not believe Marlowe would be up at half an hour before noon. But it was Marlowe's voice on the wire, not sounding in the least like a man in pain. David said, "I wanted to thank you again for taking us to the party."

"You left too soon," Marlowe said. "Truman didn't come but the police did, and then later two actors had a fight. And you'll see the Vietnam ad in tomorrow's *Times*. From the performing arts."

"How is it?"

"Old Uncle Sam gets a lacing, cousin. It goes pretty far. I don't think it will appeal to you."

"Why not to me?"

"Well, I have an idea you're the Straight Arrow type, old neighbor. Am I wrong?"

"I don't know, Don. Tell me something. Do you know a man called September?"

"Of course. He writes the big ticket. He'll tell you himself."

"Is he close to Mr. Kane?"

"According to September, yes."

"And he is around the place, so to speak?"

"Very much so. I expect you've met him?"

"Why?"

"Oh, Harvey always takes a look at new playmates."

"I see. Now Don, I'd be most grateful if you would tell Mr. Kane something for me."

"Come on up to lunch and fill me in. Dr. Pepper is flowing freely."

"I'll bet. Sorry I can't have lunch today. Anyhow, it's my turn. But will you tell Mr. Kane that our director is delighted to hear of his interest and that we're canvassing our membership to make up a good list of prospects for the Foundation? Would you mind?"

"Sure I'll tell him. And listen here, neighbor, don't you be a stranger, you hear?"

"I hear you. Let me call when we're ready, huh? That suit you?"

"Very good, cousin. Take it easy now."

David hung up the telephone and proceeded to plan the rest of his day. When he had decided what to do, he left the office, with a nod and a smile to Mrs. Martin on the way out. Today she was typing away furiously, but on what, David could not imagine, and he was too steeped in the etiquette of his profession to inquire. David operated on the principle of need to know. Know only what you need to know, and forget that as soon as possible: such were his principles in the matter of curiosity about other people's information. He went downtown on the subway, ate lunch alone in the apartment, and then took the subway back up to Seventy-ninth Street and the New York Society Library. David's great-great-grandfather had been among the founders of this library, and his father still held the family membership. In practice he had no more privileges than any annual subscriber, but that he would certainly have been, for he loved the place. He spoke to the ladies on duty in the main hall, then went to the reading room on the second floor.

There was a fire in the fireplace, and the room with its portraits, armchairs, and tall windows looked like the Subscription Room at Boodle's. In one of the armchairs sat a youth in skin-tight trousers and corduroy jacket, frowningly reading an article on Italian directors in *Film Quarterly*. A girl with long pigtails, apparently dressed to go down the experts' trail at Stowe, was making notes from a pile of French magazines. Was she from Barnard, Hunter, or Finch? One couldn't tell, but it was obvious that things were all right here. David went into the stacks, where he spent the afternoon until closing time at five o'clock studying the career and achievements of Jefferson Kane. Many a directorship, many a partnership did Mr. Kane hold. It also appeared that he had a taste for setting up foundations. One almost had the feeling that he collected them, in the way that lesser men accumulated golf clubs and old tweed coats. At any rate, the great Kane Foundation was only one among many. There was, for example, the Industrial Research Foundation of New York, with an address on Tenth Avenue. David thought that over: industrial research; it could mean anything. All this and more was to be found in *Who's Who*, the *Directory of Directors*, and other works. It seemed that Jefferson Kane was no man to hide his light; and yet nowhere was there a reference to anything called Systems Analysis, nor to a man called Harvey September. There was a biography, *Jefferson Kane, His Life and Purposes*, written by a man who specialized in portraits of living or recently dead public figures. The writer had studied his subject with care, and the book gave a multitude of facts. Among other things, David learned that Kane was an educated man. He was a graduate of historic Plato College in Ohio, an institution which still had a slightly daring air because of its traditional connection with the Underground Railroad. Many noted Americans had been educated there, and Kane was a trustee of this bastion of respectability. Moreover, he had made large gifts to the college. David thought he must have learned *something* from his professors. Had young Kane studied history? Politics? Knowing about this might give a clue to the Jefferson Kane of today. But for once the biographer had passed up a chance to cite small specific items, and mentioned only "the general literary course leading to the Bachelor of Arts degree." For the class of 1918, what would that imply? During those years, as David now discovered, Plato College had not deposited its catalogue in the New York Society Library.

Outside on Seventy-ninth Street at five o'clock, David was pleased to see that the wind had died down and the particles of crystallized soot had settled. All at once it was New York in the fall as it could be at its best, invigorating and crisp. He walked up Madison Avenue to Ninety-sixth Street, then over to Fifth Avenue, down to the Fifties, and back to Park Avenue, timing himself to reach the Corinthian Club at six-fifteen.

He found Jim Ewing in the library, reading a British magazine called *The Field*. When he saw David, Jim jumped up and they went into a room where talking was permissible.

"Ernesto!" cried Jim as they shook hands. "Did you kill well?"

"I went in over the horns," David said. "But it was not good."

"It became bad?"

"It became bad afterwards," David said. This was a routine they often went through, and it delighted them every time. Jim rang a bell and they ordered drinks.

"I see you were reading a righteous magazine," David said.

"Oh, yes," Jim Ewing said. "It's in my bloodstream. Always the same picture of some nice old boy with a name like Commander H.C.B. Hay-Pauncefoote, together with a forty-pound grilse, taken in the lower reaches of the Wye. There'll always be an England."

"I don't know about that. It's mostly down the drain."

"Don't pay any attention to these musical acts. They're just fads."

"I don't object to their entertainers," David said. "I'm thinking of people like Sir Ronald Maxwell-Spencer."

"Please. We'll be eating in a few minutes."

"And I may soon be talking to him."

"Good Lord," Jim Ewing said. "As bad as that?"

"It seems that he's old Kane's chief political adviser."

"That figures."

"Aren't you up on Kane?" David asked.

"Not especially."

"I think you said he and a man named Marlowe are—people of interest."

"In what way, David?"

"Something in the nature of a target in George's show."

"Oh, yes. George is pretty thoroughly autonomous. I thought you knew that."

"I don't know anything. It's about time I took a look at the project, don't you agree? I like to see things written down in black and white before I make any serious moves."

"On this thing, we've been happy with George's planning."

"George's *what*?"

"He seems to know what he's doing."

"But Jim, you know George when it comes to making a plan. Delay as long as possible and then start out full speed in the wrong direction. Great muzzle velocity but no aim. I've heard you say that."

"This proposition is a little different, David. Let's put the details off until after dinner, shall we?"

When they had eaten dinner, David and Jim Ewing settled in a large deserted room under John J. Audubon's tremendous painting called "Dog and Pheasants." They decided a glass or two of Carlos Primera would do no harm, ordered, and sat quietly for a few minutes collecting their thoughts over the Spanish brandy. Then David said, "This is all very puzzling."

"I don't see why it should be, David."

"I feel a lack of direction."

"George ought to supply that. He knows the drill."

"Jim, I can't just work from day to day, meet this guy, go to see that guy. And you'll never make me believe anybody seriously thinks a gang like the one around Jefferson Kane would change its spots because somebody likes George Rollins. And I can't believe anybody takes Don Marlowe seriously. A television announcer and a toady of the Left! Haven't we better things to do than bother with a fellow of that sort? I think so, and I've put in a few years at this work. Jim, as a friend, please tell me, what's going on?"

"That's hard to say in specifics. Hard to be specific on these things."

"Now you're talking like a bureaucratic bag of wind."

"Thank you very much."

"I thought better of you. I thought a lot better of you than that."

"I don't know whether I ever deserved your good opinion or not."

"I'm sorry I took that tone with you," David said. "Please overlook it."

"Perhaps you weren't wrong. Your standards are pretty high."

"Don't get sore, Jim. Think of what's happening to me."

"I'm not sore, and I am thinking of what's happening."

"There's no reason in the world we should get into an argument," David said. "The whole thing is easily solved."

"I wish I could hope so."

"But Jim, it's so simple. All I have to do is read the plan, and then I'll know where the Rollins operation is supposed to go, and I'll be perfectly happy. All I need to do is read the project."

"Ah, yes. The project."

"I'd have asked George for it, but I decided not to. No use stirring him up. You know how he is."

"I know."

"So I've asked you to set up a channel so I can have a look at it. I ought to have done that before I left Washington."

"That wouldn't have been any good," Ewing said.

"I don't follow you."

"To tell you the truth, David, there is no project."

"But that's not possible! How can we be in business without one?"

Jim Ewing drank the last of his Carlos Primera and put the glass down softly. Then he said, "You're not in business."

"You mean I'm called off, already? Taken off the project?"

"There is no project, not the sort you've been accustomed to at the Company."

"But this is appalling. What are you trying to tell me?"

"David, we're friends," Jim Ewing said. "I've been trying

to decide what to do about this and I've concluded the only decent thing is to tell you the truth. And the truth is, you're in the elephant valley."

"What does that mean?"

"It's the place where the elephants go to die."

"Would you mind speaking plainly?"

"I shall do so. You know the Company, David, the pressures that build up. People break down and can't go on. Or, sometimes, they just don't work out. So if things get to be too much for them, or they simply don't measure up, they become a disposal problem. With the opposition it's very simple. A bullet in the head. But we don't do that. We have to have a place where they can go. A valley for the dying elephants where they can end their days harmlessly while the Company goes on. But you asked me to speak plainly. Of course there isn't one *place*—it can be in Washington, or in New York, or in other cities all over the world. Offices like the one George has, where people like George can go through the motions, and be reasonably happy, and stay out of mischief. After all, we owe these people something."

"But Jim, why *me?* What makes *me* a dying elephant?"

"It's going to be hard to tell you."

"You're talking about places where broken-down people can take refuge. Very nice idea, though I don't know that I'd care to use it. But the point is, I haven't broken down."

"The Company says you have."

"That's impossible."

"I'm afraid not."

"But how could anyone say such a thing, even a bureaucrat?"

"I'll try to explain, David. It has to do with Mary's death."

"Have you *any* idea what you're saying?"

"I know very well what I'm saying. Remember, I'm talking as a friend."

"You mentioned Mary."

"I did, and here is exactly what happened. About a month ago, you took your annual health checkup, didn't you?"

"As usual."

"You remember talking to the psychiatrist?"

"For about two minutes. I soon had enough of him."

"Maybe you should have talked longer. His report to Henry Sedgwick was that, in his opinion, the shock of Mary's death had left you seriously disturbed."

"I should think so. I'm still disturbed."

"He meant in the technical sense."

"Some kind of nut, eh?"

"The doctor said you revealed latent transvestite tendencies."

"The man's insane."

"I couldn't agree with you more, David. Most of these people are half cracked, undoubtedly. But they have power. This one told Henry you were talking of merging your personality with some woman or other, identifying, as he put it. Recommended you be relieved of your work load, and have some treatment."

"Identifying with some woman!" David said. "Now I see what set him off. Let me tell you what happened exactly as it happened. For years I'd been taking this annual checkup with the Company's medical department, one of our few fringe benefits. Never saw the psychiatrist before. This time, there was a Dr. Greenway—psychiatrist —on my list of people to consult. First psycho man I ever saw in the Company. As you know, we came in on our security clearances and personal records without anybody asking us if we got excited looking at bird cages, or nonsense of that sort. I spotted this guy right off, this

Dr. Greenway, as somebody I wouldn't consult as a chiropodist, let alone psychiatrist. Jim, he had rimless glasses and instead of regular socks, he was wearing socklets that barely covered his ankles, and one of those metallic suits, and a huge metal clasp on his tie."

"It's true," Jim Ewing said, "you can tell a lot about a man from his clothes. Strange that more people don't realize that."

"And even if this guy had *looked* right, he was finished with me the minute he opened his mouth. I realized, of course, that they'd rung him in on me to see if I had blown my stack because of Mary. Friends who saw me every day had done this to me. They didn't have enough confidence in their own judgment of me—working with me, and talking to me every day. Had to ask the witch doctor, a fine way of doing business. Well, I won't reproach *you*, Jim. I'll just tell you what happened. This Greenway asks me how I felt about Mary's death—can you imagine the impertinence of the fellow?—and I said I didn't care to discuss it. 'Oh, but we must discuss it,' he says. I said, 'Must we indeed? I'll be the judge of that.' He says, 'I'm not used to having patients talk to me like that.' 'That's too bad,' I said. 'And what gives you the idea I'm a patient?' 'That was an unfortunate expression, Mr. Bell,' he says, and goes on, 'Now let's try to be friends. If I can, I want to help you.' The obvious reply to *that* was that I hadn't asked for help, but I said nothing. So now he asks me how I feel about colored people, and especially the Negroes. 'Feel about them?' I asked him, 'How am I supposed to feel about them? I'd say offhand it depends on which ones you mean.' 'Well,' he says, leaning back in his chair and puffing on the old pipe, 'what I'm interested in is your feeling toward Negroes as a whole. Is it one of hostility?' I answered, 'Taking them as a whole, which is a tremendous generality, if you ask me if they make me feel like Harriet Beecher Stowe, the answer is, they do not.' 'Make you feel like who?' he says, picking up a pencil. 'Like Mrs. Calvin Stowe, Doctor,' I said. 'Mrs. Henry Ward Beecher's sister-in-law. And now, if you don't mind, I have other things to do.' And I walked out."

"It's incredible," Ewing said. "Yet people like that are drawing salaries."

"And people like my friend Henry Sedgwick."

"It was Henry's doing, all right," Ewing said. "He called me and Ben into his office, and said he thought you'd better be put out to pasture. Ben asked him if he was sure it was necessary, and Henry said he based the decision on a psychiatric report. Well, that's the big juju nowadays, the big magic. All big organizations have those people, and you'd think they'd be useful with our outfit if they are anywhere. But the trouble is, the danger is, so many of them are frauds, or fools, or plain ignoramuses from diploma mills. Demand for witch doctors is running way ahead of supply."

"I can see why there's a demand. They give a man like Henry the chance to enjoy doing a cruel thing without having to take the responsibility for it."

"That's hard on Henry."

"And I'm so damned sorry about that. Let's by all means not criticize Henry. But I'm determined not to quarrel with you, Jim. Let's have a drink." He rang the bell and an attendant came to take the order. It was another shot of Carlos Primera in the large glass for David and the same for Jim Ewing.

"I won't defend Henry Sedgwick," Ewing said. "But I can explain what he did. He goes by the book. The book says if the juju man puts a curse on David Bell, then find a place for David far enough away so the curse won't spread. Perfectly logical, once you accept the juju." The attendant came back with the drinks and Ewing said, "Thank you, Bobbie." He took the chit before David could reach it and signed his name. "I ought to buy these, I think," he went on. "Not that it makes me feel any better."

"Much obliged," David said. "The thing that gets me is that apparently nobody dared to raise the question. Here they put it in my record that I was supposed to be clear off base and there's nothing to it, absolutely nothing at all."

"Nothing but some little guy's feeling of inferiority and resentment at your assured manner, plus a ludicrous lack of understanding of what you were talking about. This business of trying to educate everybody is a terrible mistake."

"Hiring that idiot at the Company surely was."

"Which idiot are you referring to? Henry or the quack?" Ewing asked.

"Either. Both."

"It beats me," Jim Ewing said. "What it finally comes down to is Henry Sedgwick taking orders from a guy who wears socklets and a metal thing on his tie. I swear it beats me. But I have to tell you, as I said, and you may as well face it: you're cut off from the Company for good."

"It was kind of you to keep me on the payroll," David said, "but I don't need the money. I have a bundle from my mother's estate. You know about that. Imagine if I didn't. First, it would dawn on me that I was wasting my time. So, what about a job in ordinary life? I'm in my forty-first year. Too old by far for the big corporations. Teaching? Not in college, no advanced degrees. Back to St. Stephen's, or the wheel of a taxicab. 'Change your act, or go back to the woods.' You remember that old routine of Victor Moore's? However, I have my own income, I can start a business, or write, or just loaf if I feel like it. But I want you to tell me, what about the men in my position who don't have money of their own?"

"David, the elephants don't know they're dying, and don't realize where they are."

"That's hard to believe."

"But it's true. I've had occasion to study a great many of these cases. Of course yours is entirely different. Now what do you plan to do?"

"What do you suggest?"

"I don't know what to suggest."

"And I don't know what to do."

They drank the last of the brandy, found no more to say to each other, and left the club.

8

THAT NIGHT David had a dream. Mary was clear and her
voice the same as always; and he kept telling himself
it *was* a dream, and yet it could not be, for there she
stood before him. She had been away, believed lost or
disappeared, and now there was something baffling about
it, that would presently be explained. He woke. It was
light outside, and he got up, took a showerbath, dressed,
and went to the kitchen to make coffee. Louise Bell came
in, wrapped in a robe. She looked at David's face, said
nothing, went to him and touched him, then sat across
the Formica as he drank the coffee, knowing that he was
all alone.

By the time David got to the office the dreary shameful
feeling of the dream had abated to emotional numbness.
George Rollins was in his room, and David compelled
himself to enter it and sit down near the huge desk.

"Have you a few minutes, George?"

"Of course. Anything on your mind?"

"Only that I have it on good authority that we are wasting our time."

George Rollins got up from his desk chair and walked
to the sofa, leaned back, and carefully balanced his fine
old shoes on the edge of a low Chinese table.

"You have it on good authority that we are wasting
our time. Who do you mean by *we?*"

"I mean you and me and I can't say how many others."

"This doesn't sound like you, David. You never used to get discouraged when we had just blooded the troops."

"George, the troops are going nowhere."

"You've been talking to Jim Ewing."

"Well . . . yes."

"He's fun to be with, but there are lots of things he just doesn't know," George Rollins said.

"Not about the Company," David said. "I'd say he knew everything about that. Don't tell me he isn't right by the horse's mouth down there in Washington."

"That's the point, David. The real business of the Company isn't in Washington at all."

"The headquarters is."

"You're wrong, David, absolutely wrong. You've only been here, what is it, two days? And you don't know anything yet. When I say 'business' I *mean* 'headquarters.' Think that over, if you please."

"Then I wish you'd talk to Jim Ewing."

"I couldn't possibly talk to him. There's too much he doesn't know. He's on the outside, not you, David. And if anybody's wasting time, it's Mr. James Ewing."

"Are you sure of all this?"

"Of course I'm sure."

"Don't you consider Ewing your superior officer?"

"Not in any way. He has nothing to do with me."

"But don't you report to *somebody?*"

"I certainly do."

"In Washington?"

"No."

"Shouldn't I be in on this?"

"You will be, David. Just go easy."

"I can't operate in a vacuum."

"You said yourself you only wanted to be read in on what you needed to know."

"I need to know what I'm doing."

"Do you mean on the policy level or the substantive level?"

David held up his hand as though stopping traffic.

"Please, George," he said. "No more federalese right now. I'd like to do some thinking. Maybe we can talk some more another time?"

"Any time," said George affably. "I have a lot of things to show you. Primary objectives. Secondary objectives. Tertiary objectives. Targets of opportunity. Don't worry about any of it, David. Just leave it to me."

"George, I honestly doubt if I can help you here. But suppose I go ahead with the Kane thing and see what comes of it. There's something odd about that guy, and I'd like to learn a little more about it. Personal curiosity, nothing better to do. All right?"

"David, you know it's all right. We can't get along without you."

"There isn't any question but some kind of personal threat came through to me. And there was some trouble down at the apartment. So I don't want to lose contact with Kane just now. Somehow I think it wouldn't be wise."

"I always trust your judgment, David."

"Then suppose I feed him our list of applicants for Foundation grants. Have you got it for me?"

"It should be in your 'in' box right now."

"All right, George. I'll see what I can do."

At his own desk, David found a typewritten list giving the names of ten professors of political science at various American and Canadian universities. He noticed that the paper was stamped SECRET, and he laid it aside. Long training, now part of his reflexes, told David a paper with that stamp could not be taken out of the office. He would simply have it typed over, or perhaps Mrs. Martin could give him an unstamped carbon copy. A small matter, really. Just now it was most important to straighten his thinking about his job, his career, and his obligation. He remembered how Weir of Hermiston had marched up the great bare staircase of his duty, uncheered and unafraid. But it was not immediately plain what David's duty was. And a thought that David began to turn over in his mind was that this Institute for Strategic Research might be made into a useful thing after all. Why not be just that, an institute for strategic research? Surely strategic research was a good thing. And there could not be, could there, too much of a good thing? As a platoon leader, David had absorbed the theory of limited objectives. Acting on that theory, he now decided that at the least he would meet Sir Ronald Maxwell-Spencer and his lady, and submit Rollins' list of names. He was fairly certain what Kane and Maxwell-Spencer would think of anyone recommended by Rollins and the Institute, but he would go this far for George's sake. And he had another reason, as he admitted to himself: he wished to find out more about Dr. Harvey September. The elephants might be dying, as Jim Ewing had said, but this was a personal thing.

His telephone rang and Mrs. Martin announced a Detective Wilson on the wire.

"Good. I'll talk to him."

"Mr. Bell?"

"Speaking, and how are you?"

"Pretty fair, considering everything. Thought you'd like to know about those bums that tried to mug you."

"Certainly would."

"Well, the judge in juvenile court turned them loose, that was to be expected. That's routine."

"So now they're running around free again."

"Oh, yes, of course. But there was an interesting thing.

The judge paroled them in the care of a citizen. He wasn't in court but he had a lawyer there."

"Anybody I know?"

"I don't think you'd know the lawyer, but everybody knows the guy who sent him. He's on the television. Don Marlowe."

"Don Marlowe you say."

"That's the man. You must have seen him."

"I know who you mean."

"The more money they make, the less sense they got."

"I'm inclined to agree with you on that," David said, and after an exchange of good wishes, the conversation ended. David thought it over for a minute or so and then called Marlowe's apartment.

"Hello, Don? Dave Bell here."

"Good morning, cousin."

"How about lunch? My turn."

"I'm afraid I can't go out for it."

"What's the trouble?"

"No trouble. It's just that I like to sleep right after lunch. You come up here, I want to see you."

"All right, Don. Twelve-thirty?"

"Do it, neighbor."

In Don Marlowe's library, David refused a Dr. Pepper with or without vodka. Marlowe said, "I'm going on a quiet two-day drunk, David. After that I'll be on the wagon for a while. Foundation business is warming up, Sir Ronald will be in town, and I'll need my wits about me. Also, Peggy's due back in New York. She gets pretty sore if I hit the sauce too much."

"I can understand that," David said. "Now listen to me, amigo. I want to ask a serious question."

"You have my ear, camarado. What can I tell you?"

"I want to know if you sent a couple of thugs to beat my head in."

"A couple of what did you say?"

"A pair of young hoodlums, with a hammer to cave in my skull."

"Why would I do that to you, old buddy?"

"I don't know."

"Then I don't know why you ask."

"It's not fantasy," David said. "Two young bums tried to mug me in the basement of my own house. They got away but the cops caught them later. This morning your lawyer came into court and made you responsible for them. Now you must admit that it does look a little strange."

"Yes, it does that," Marlowe said. He went to his grog tray and mixed a drink. "But these aren't the first kids I've helped. I've done this for a good many kids in trouble with the law. I'll admit there have been some disappointments."

"I imagine these two were disappointed when they didn't break my head."

"I know what you're thinking," Marlowe said. "You're thinking I haven't done very well with my own." He was right. That thought had entered David's mind, as he remembered the surly boy he had met in this room. Marlowe went on, "But don't you know a boy will very often refuse to hear common sense from his own father, and welcome it from somebody else? You, for instance. And that's what I wanted to see you about. Would you talk to my boy?"

"Which one?"

"The older one, the younger one's hopeless."

"You said the older boy was named Peter?"

"That's right."

"I haven't met Peter."

"I'd like to introduce you tonight, at dinner."

"I'm sorry but I can't make it for dinner." David was

planning to ask Roxie to dine with him, and in any event did not wish to become a star boarder at Marlowe's house. Enough was enough. He went on, "Of course I'd be delighted to meet Peter any time."

"Stop in after dinner if you can make it," Marlowe said.

"That ought to work out."

Luncheon was announced, and afterward David left Don Marlowe sleeping on the library couch as he had before. It was amazing what the human system could stand, David reflected as he returned to the office of the Institute. As he entered the building, he saw coming out the same little man he had noticed the first day. Pretty soon I'll be an old settler too, David thought. Or would he? Would the elephants move to another valley? He sat down at his desk, struggling not to surrender to a sudden great heaviness of spirit that seemed to be moving him to surrender, to turn his back on shadowy problems that he felt he could not grasp even if he faced up to them. With an effort of the will, he told himself a man should always complete his day by seeing a sympathetic woman. He called the travel agency. There was difficulty with the agency switchboard. Someone seemed to think he was a customer, and said, "Miss Dean is busy at the moment, could I help you?" Infuriated, and filled with adrenalin, David managed to say politely, "I'll call again." At this moment he heard Roxie's voice, and it sounded so happy and gay that his bad humor vanished.

"Roxie, it's David."

"Oh, hello, David."

He couldn't be sure, but he got an impression that Roxie was now just a little bit less gay and happy. At any rate, he asked her if she could join him that evening.

"David, I'm so sorry, but I can't."

He kept disappointment out of his voice and said, "I'm sorry, too. Have a nice time, Roxie, and I hope to see you soon."

Putting down the telephone, David was surprised at the depth of his disappointment. He said to himself, it's obvious the girl has a steady beau, but how I hate to be turned down. And yet somehow the chagrin was a good thing, putting to flight more agonizing emotions. David found that he was now able to concentrate on immediate problems. One was to find what actualities had been brought about by George Rollins and his Institute. George had said that it was all genuine, that the unrealities were in Washington. David did not believe this. And yet his friend and colleague had seemed completely sincere. He knew also that George Rollins was a poor liar; in fact, Rollins never had been known to lie. This was not so much from high ethical standards, David feared, as from impregnable self-confidence. And so, after hard thought on the entire matter, David came to the conclusion that there must be some kernel of fact in what Rollins had told him. It would be distorted, and grown beyond proportion in George's mind; but there must be an area of reality. George was out, and it occurred to David that this might be a good time to consult Mrs. Martin. He got up and walked through the office to her area. She looked up brightly from her typing.

"Mrs. Martin," he said, "I'm wondering if there is some kind of statement or outline around here, something that defines the Institute."

"Defines, Mr. Bell?"

"Something for possible members or contributors. Not classified, a public statement."

"Perhaps you mean our prospectus."

"That might be it. May I see it?"

"Of course. I thought Mr. Rollins had shown it to you."

Mrs. Martin went to an unlocked file and took out a printed pamphlet.

"I think this is up to date, Mr. Bell." She opened it and turned a few pages. "Yes, it is. The very latest."

"Thank you very much."

At his desk, David read the beautifully printed booklet of thirty pages, admiring the academic prose which was like that of a college catalogue. The meat of it was a listing of some three dozen research projects made possible by Institute grants. They were for studies in history, economics, and political science, and all were beyond criticism from any point of view—they were safe, sane, dull. David was unable to make out how the completion of any of these studies would benefit the United States. He also noted that nothing listed was far enough to the Left to earn the approval of Jefferson Kane and his Cambridge dons. But in the elephant valley, he reflected, what difference did it make? He laid the booklet down on the rich walnut of his desk, whirled the big chair, and looked out at the Waldorf and the Seagram Tower. Over New Jersey, the haze was thickening to smog.

The door opened and George Rollins came in. He drew up a chair, sat down, and looked David over in a speculative way, but also with the cheerful and friendly look that had characterized the old unconquerable George Rollins. Considering what he had endured, he nowadays appeared to be an admirably relaxed and adjusted man, though much older than when David had first met him. George now said, "You have a big day coming up. I've just heard from Don Marlowe. He says Sir Ronald Maxwell-Spencer and his wife have come in at Kennedy, and you're to lunch with them tomorrow."

"When I left Marlowe he was all set for the big sleep."

"He's awake now."

"I wonder why he didn't call me?"

"He had some other things to tell me about, David. You'll meet at Kane's place, at twelve-thirty. This thing is phasing along very nicely now."

Rollins got up and went to the window, moving with

the slight limp he had acquired. He stood there looking out as though on the bridge of an aircraft carrier, checked on Seagram's and the Waldorf, and returned to his chair. David got an impression of energy—nervous but purposeful. This, too, was the old George Rollins.

"David, I'm going to speak substantively," he said. "And mostly about Jim Ewing. I've disagreed with him many times. I'll tell you now what it always comes down to. Jim doesn't believe in working through fronts."

"I'd say he doesn't believe in fronts that don't work."

"He doesn't want them to work. He's constantly telling people they're struggling in a vacuum and nothing can be done. And he certainly got at *you* soon enough."

"But George, he must know what he's talking about. He's a deputy director in everything but authority, and maybe even in that."

"The way those people work," George said, "they try to make you think they know where every single body is buried. They could overlook a few. In fact, a whole cemetery."

"George, you don't reach me with figures of speech. But if you have anything concrete to tell me, I want to hear it."

"Now, Professor, don't get angry with me," Rollins said. "Here's something concrete for you. What have they got down there, Jim Ewing, Ben Thornton, Henry and the rest of them?"

"They have a headquarters organization. A large one, filling a building of considerable size."

"Right, a huge building with signs pointing to it, calling attention to itself twenty-four hours a day."

"They couldn't make it invisible, George."

"Nor would they wish to. That thing is *supposed* to draw attention."

"Away from something else?"

"Now you're catching on."

"Don't try to tell me an entire government bureau is a deception exercise. I just won't believe it."

"You never had a closed mind before, David."

"I hope it's always closed to fantasy."

"Fantasy is wrong, eh? Then let's phase out the fantasy. I'm not suggesting you deal in that. But think a minute. Do you remember that report you wrote, on the nature of organizations?"

That was one thing David could hardly forget. For two years he had studied the biology and morphology of human organizations—how they were born, how they grew, what structures they took, and how they died. His work was an incalculably small part of the Company's great production of paper, but it would have been worth a doctorate at any university. The finished study had been laid on only four desks. But David was used to writing for small audiences.

"I remember your conclusions so well," George said. "One was, 'The importance of the administrator will be measured by what he approves rather than by what he initiates.' By God, you're right. Has Henry Sedgwick ever initiated anything?"

"No, and forgive me, George, neither did you."

"And I almost killed myself with worry over granting approvals. 'Report on the theory of organization.' Yes, quite a piece of work you did, old boy. I wonder if you recognized your most important conclusion."

"What did you think it was?"

"You made one discovery, David. I'll quote it to you: 'When a bureaucratic organization has failed to achieve its objective, the only way to reach that objective is through a new organization.'" George Rollins folded his arms, nodded vigorously, and went on. "You never said a truer word. You came down to fundamental fact."

"Are you telling me there *is* a new organization?"

"That's what I'm telling you," Rollins said.

"Then I've come into the new organization in a peculiar way. They dropped me in Washington because of a psychiatrist's report."

"Did you have any symptoms?"

"No, it was just that some fool made a mistake and Henry Sedgwick didn't have the decency to check it."

"How did it happen?"

"I was brusque with the doctor, and he failed to catch a common literary allusion."

"And you're the guy who wants plain talk."

"Yes, if it's about something important. I didn't think the psychiatrist was important."

"Those people helped me a lot," Rollins said.

"I'm glad they did, and I'm glad you're all right now."

"Thank you, David. The fact is, Henry Sedgwick has done you a great favor."

"I wish I could think so."

"And I'm going to do you another one."

"I doubt if I can survive another favor like Henry's. Maybe you'd best let me alone."

"I'm going to help you the way I was helped."

"I'm not in the market for doctors, George."

"This has nothing to do with doctors. Forget about doctors. I'm going to introduce you to Colonel Andrews."

"And who is he?"

"You'll find out."

"After Henry Sedgwick I don't suppose a mere colonel can do me much harm. When do I see him?"

"I've made the appointment for tomorrow evening after dinner."

"Where?"

"Meet me here, David. After that leave it to me."

"All right, whatever you say."

"Stick with me, young fellow," George said. "You'll see what a black operation really looks like."

George left the room, and David sat for a moment arranging his thoughts. He saw that, following proper procedure, Mrs. Martin had locked up the list of intellectuals that Rollins had stamped SECRET. He went out to Mrs. Martin's desk and found that the four clean and beautifully legible copies had also been stamped.

"I can make you another copy, or we could cut the stamp off," said Mrs. Martin helpfully.

"No, this will be all right," David said, picking up a legal-size pad and writing down the names. "They can do the secretarial work at the other end."

Mrs. Martin acted as though David had conferred an enormous favor on her, and they parted on terms of high office courtesy. In his mind, David was facing the idea that Mrs. Martin could very easily begin to get on his nerves. He knew this was a sign of fatigue and boredom, and so put on his hat, went out, and strolled up to Fifty-seventh Street to look through a few galleries. He saw a good show of Peter Blume, and some things he would have considered buying had he been really rich. David liked all advanced art; or it might be more accurate to say he liked *looking* at all advanced art. Today he was saving the Madison Avenue galleries with their blowtorch sculpture and slapstick constructions for another time, in the way a movie fan would save a festival of the Marx brothers or Laurel and Hardy. He left Knoedler's comforted and refreshed, went down to 15 Lexington Avenue, took a nap, put on clean clothes, and had dinner with Louise and Roger Bell.

"Curious thing," Roger Bell said as they sat after dinner.

"What was that?"

"A magazine agent got in here today."

"Indeed?"

"Yes, came and rang the bell, tried to start a sales talk with Louise. Appalling people, try to sign you up for ten and fifteen years."

"What did you do?"

"I happened to be downstairs," Roger Bell said, "and I sent him about his business."

"What was he like?"

"Utterly nondescript."

"Salesmen aren't supposed to come in here," David said.

"Of course they aren't," Louise said. "I asked Niles how this one got in, and he didn't know."

"You mean he slipped past Niles in some way?" David asked.

"That's what it must have been," Louise said.

"If it happens again I hope you call the police," David said.

"Oh, I don't know that we ought to do that," Roger Bell said. "Make trouble for a poor devil. I got rid of him, never fear."

"Did the man leave anything?" David asked.

"Leave anything? What would he leave?" said Mr. Bell.

"An order blank, anything of that sort?"

"No, why should he?"

"I don't know, I was just curious. I wondered what magazines might be using such people."

"I can't say." Mr. Bell spoke in an offhand way, but he was looking at David keenly. It might well be, David thought, that his father had sensed his anxiety. They were close, and Roger Bell knew the tones of his son's voice. David got up and said, "I have to run uptown for a while. Seems I've promised to talk to the younger generation."

At Marlowe's apartment, David found his host entertaining a young woman in the drawing room.

"Peggy, this is David Bell," Marlowe said. "David, Peggy Alcott."

The girl was startlingly beautiful. Peggy Alcott had red hair, blue eyes, and golden freckles on a background of cream. She did not look as much like an actress as David had expected. Of course, there was no rule as to what actresses looked like, when you thought about it. But she did look a damned sight too good for a television announcer, that much was certain. Her handshake was firm, and David said, "I'm delighted to meet you, Miss Alcott."

"Call her Peggy," Marlowe said. "No last names around here. You're lucky to see her, as well as delighted. We thought it was going to be a long run in Chicago."

"What happened?" David asked.

"A revival of *Design for Living*," Peggy Alcott said. "With Rex McKenzie, Jeremy Wayne, and me. We died out there, in public."

"Poor girl had to hit the railroad ties back to New York," Marlowe said.

"Not that bad," Peggy Alcott said. "The airlines are still flying. But poor Mort. Morton Roth, our producer. It was a big disappointment for him."

"Hadn't you done it last summer on the Cape?"

"Yes, that's where Morton saw us."

"I may hold up the cereal box," Marlowe said, "but we lock the audience in."

David was embarrassed to hear Marlowe come so close to the truth. In his opinion, one honorable defeat on the stage was worth ten years of television, but there was no way to say this without being rude, and he said nothing. "Come on in the library, David," Marlowe said. "Peter's waiting for you."

Peter Marlowe was a thin young man who gave an opening impression of intensity and shabbiness. His wife Pamela was small and plain. At first she seemed mouse-like, and then one picked up a glance of intelligence in her eyes. She had nothing to say after the introductions but sat watching David as though she expected him at any moment to perform some extraordinary feat, something as remarkable as disappearing in the center of the room, or bursting into flame from spontaneous combustion. David found this flattering, and he formed a good opinion of the quiet little girl. As to Peter, David almost immediately got the idea that this boy would be hard to like. By the time they had exchanged only a few words, David also knew that he had embarked on one of the oddest scenes of his life. Marlowe had left the room as soon as he introduced them. Now, from Peter's attitude, David got the impression that Marlowe must have told his son "Lieutenant Bell" had all the answers, and that he was willing to argue for these answers, and impress them on the young. Unconcealed hostility was the boy's reaction, and David's thought was, I cannot say I blame him. Another thought was: how did I get into this?"

"I don't know why your father calls me lieutenant," David said. "I've been a civilian for a long time."

"Dad told me you were doing the government bit," Peter said.

"Yes, I've been in Washington off and on," David said. "But that was non-military." For a moment he felt that he was in the position of a man being interviewed for a job. This was what happened, he decided, when you agreed to cast bread upon waters. So he might as well go on. "And when it comes to what's going on in Vietnam, I really don't know what to say to a younger man. Korea was simple compared to it."

It was curious, David thought, that he had been about this young man's age when he had gone to Southeast Asia with the Marines. Not much more than twenty years separated them now. And in twenty years if they were both still living, Peter would be David's present age, and

David—for a moment he looked ahead, and hoped he saw an old sturdy man, with some kind of integrity, like a baseball umpire, calling them as he saw them.

"Maybe I just ought to enlist," Peter said, squaring off at his problem with the immense and terrifying self-centeredness that these young people seemed to have. He had not led up to this topic with any general talk about the state of the world, nor had he offered David any sort of reward for sharing his interest, such as a crumb of respect or courtesy. This was going to be like interviewing a refugee or a defector, trying to help lift the weight of insufferable misfortune. David had done it often enough, and always came out exhausted at the end.

"I thought of enlisting, all right," Peter went on. "But I guess it wouldn't work. Like I don't want one of those clods telling me what to do and what not to do."

"You might not find it so bad," David said. "You could take your wife along and live off-post for the time you were in this country. Maybe your father would help with an allowance. I don't see anything against that arrangement."

"No, man," said Peter. "None of that. Too much chance of being sent away and shot."

"You have pretty good odds against that," David said.

"What are you trying to do, recruit me into the army?"

"Nothing of the sort, Peter. You brought it up, not me."

"It's a lousy hang-up, any way you look."

"What are you doing right now?" David asked.

"Nothing," Peter said. "What's to do? There *is* my writing. There's that."

"You're clear out of college?"

"College is long gone."

"You know that leaves you open to the military? Even though you're married?"

"Man, what do you think we're talking about?"

"Uh, yes. Talking about you, I think. You might finish your undergraduate work, and do it well enough to keep free of immediate draft. Then perhaps you could go into graduate school."

"But I'm out of college, I said."

"I thought you were taking a course in creative writing."

"Not any more. Man, was that a bring-down. Those clods knew nothing. They've all sold out."

"Which clods were these, Peter?"

"The teachers and critics. *Hemingway*, for God's sake."

"I have some friends who are writers," David said. "If I asked them, they might be willing to read what you've done."

"That's no good," Peter said. "My work is free form. They wouldn't understand it."

So it went, with David marveling that a boy only twenty years old could have developed one of the most tedious and suffocating personalities he had ever met. For all of that, young Marlowe had a sensitive look about him, and his face was appealing when he smiled. He did smile occasionally, so there might be hope. Yet David was baffled and exhausted by the talk, and he thought of the dreary curse that seemed to have fallen on so many young people of this generation, leaving them unhappy and inert. In the Second World War, David's only fear had been that it would be over before he could get there. That was how it turned out, and he had ridden the transports back and forth after the U-boats had surrendered. Then later, in Korea, he had learned the score. Falstaff was right: the man with honor was he that died o' Wednesday. Perhaps it was a matter of example. David's father had gone to war at a time when young Americans had been enlisting in Canada out of impatience at their own country's slowness to "get in it." Lord, what fools these mortals be. And yet, in a way that couldn't be explained, those young men had been right. It was a personal thing. And now, David thought, there was nothing he could say to a boy like Peter Marlowe. Nothing, at least, that Peter would wish to understand. Finally he said, "I hope you didn't expect me to have answers. I only know everyone has troubles to face. You remember Hamlet: 'The readiness is all.'"

"I don't remember that," Peter said. "I don't relate to Shakespeare much."

"You might keep it in mind," David said, getting up. Pamela gave him a cool childish hand, and Peter said, "Well, thanks for talking, anyway."

That boy will never grow up to be a Lord Chesterfield, David thought as he went back to the drawing room. But then, according to some authorities, the Earl of Chesterfield was not really a nice man. David walked into the drawing room and found that four people had joined Peggy Alcott and Marlowe during his conversation with Marlowe's son. The newcomers were Rex McKenzie and his wife Lola, who was a well-known theatrical designer, and Jeremy Wayne with a pretty girl. The two actors, though handsome and fit, were well past forty, possibly past fifty. No need to worry about military service here. Nevertheless, they had worries and, like Peter Marlowe's, their worries were intense and personal. But these veteran players knew how to make it appear that disappointment had not touched them. They had shaken off the disaster in Chicago, and were now discussing prospects in New York. They acknowledged Marlowe's introduction of David cordially but briefly, and continued their conversation.

Jeremy Wayne said, "My agent is talking about daytime television. The soaps." He struck a melodramatic attitude and intoned, "It's come to this!" Then he turned to Marlowe and said, "Sorry, old boy."

"Don't knock it," Marlowe said, looking around the beautifully decorated room. Wayne's present home was a small bedroom at The Lambs.

"Dear boy, I wouldn't dream of criticizing," Wayne said. "I've seen your show. You're the greatest thing since Sir Henry Irving in *The Bells.*"

Rex McKenzie said, "I've seen a few of the soaps, and really, they're quite interesting." For years he and his wife had saved and invested, and they could afford to wait between jobs at their house in Connecticut or their service flat in an old West Fifty-eighth Street hotel.

"We know about you," Wayne said. "Why don't you produce a show yourself?"

"I might at that," McKenzie said. "But where can we find a script?"

This led to a fierce argument about the state of dramatic writing; during a pause in the discussion, David said good night and left. Going down in the elevator, he thought to himself that Peggy Alcott had sparkled in the gathering, though with remarkably little to say, considering that she was an actress. Long ago when he had been a youth first going out in New York, David had heard a man of experience say, "Actresses aren't women." The words had stuck in his mind and he had come to believe them. And yet this Peggy Alcott—she had the look of a faultless girl. David could testify that they did exist.

As David stepped from his taxicab at 15 Lexington Avenue, he looked up and down the street. It was a little after eleven o'clock, and the sidewalks were empty. But down by Gramercy Park, under the red eyes of the sign that warned motorists to turn, a man was standing. As a rule in New York, people did not stand on sidewalks, they hurried on. David thought about this as he went up to the apartment. He looked in at Louise, propped up in bed with her Tensor light adjusted for Angela Thirkell or Agatha Christie. Roger was on the next floor in his studio.

David went to the closet in the back hall off the kitchen
where there were mops, buckets, and rough tools useful in
the household. He found a heavy wrench, and wrapped
the head of it with rubberized tape. Dropping the wrench
in the pocket of his topcoat, he stepped out into the service hall, brought up the automatic freight elevator, went
down to the basement, and out onto Twenty-first Street
by the back entrance and stair. He stepped around the big
iron waste-cans and looked over toward Lexington Avenue. The man was still there, and David now saw that
he looked familiar. He walked over to him.

In the pale red light he saw that the man was his lobby
and elevator acquaintance from the Institute. The hunch
came very strongly now, and the sense of danger.

"Good evening," David said.

The man said nothing.

"Are you looking for something?" There was no answer, and David then said, "Whatever it is, you won't find
it on Gramercy Park. *So get the hell out of here.*"

The man was startled into speech.

"What did you say?"

"I said get to hell away from here."

"You cannot say this," the man said, and now David
heard the old international accent he had been expecting.
"You have no right. I am deeplohmat."

"That makes no difference to me. I've seen you before.
Get moving."

"You are fasheest?"

"Never mind what I am. Go over to Twenty-third and
Park and down the hole. The subway. And don't come
back."

The man looked around.

"Don't look," David said. "Move."

The man took a step away, then hesitated, looking back
at David.

"Good-bye for now," David said. "And remember something. If I catch you down here again, I may kill you."

The man hurried off toward Park Avenue South. David went back into the house, thinking how easily he could have made a fool of himself, except for that overpowering hunch. If the man had been legitimate, he would have yelled for the police, or shown identification, for David had made it plain he was no mugger. He had merely told the man to go away. He wanted this to be reported, and he knew it would be. Then the situation might develop, and if it did, he might have the satisfaction of showing Jim Ewing that something had happened in the elephant valley after all.

9

JEFFERSON KANE sat at the head of a table for six in the
dining room of his hotel apartment. At his right and
left were Lady Agatha Maxwell-Spencer and David Bell.
At the other end was Sir Ronald with Peggy Alcott and
Don Marlowe at his right and left. In attendance were
two waiters in livery, the dining-room captain in a dinner
jacket, and the hotel's catering manager, a bulbous person
in black jacket and striped pants. The reverent waiters
were handing round the entrée, two platters of lamb that
had been heated and sliced at a side table by the catering manager himself. Sir Ronald Maxwell-Spencer now
inspected this offering as though looking for evidence
of biological warfare, and asked, "What is that?"

"Southdown lamb, sir."

"I shan't touch it. Take it away and bring me a grilled
bone."

David thought Sir Ronald sounded like the bad-tem-
pered man in *The Pickwick Papers,* ordering accommoda-
tion at a coaching inn, and not in any way like a guest
at a remarkably attractive lunch table. On the way over,
Don Marlowe had said, "We're going to graze pretty well
today." But David had not believed it; remembering
Kane's lack of hospitality on the previous visit, he had
resigned himself to mean fare and no drink. To his pleased
surprise, they had started their drinking with Rainwater

Madeira, and a glorious claret appeared with the lamb. So it had turned out that the old scoundrel could do himself well when he wanted to, and David was grateful. Kane paid no attention to Sir Ronald's complaint, and kept on talking to Lady Maxwell-Spencer. An imposing sight, she had a large cylindrical body, the same width all the way down, wrapped in thorn-proof tweed. The lady appeared restless, as though not happily cast in the role of listener. But she was going against a stern opponent in Jefferson Kane, who evidently saw no reason why he should be silent at his own table. When they sat down, he and Lady Agatha had gone after the conversational opening like two hockey players slapping for the puck in a face-off, and Kane had won. Now his voice brayed in endless self-congratulation, while at the other end of the table Sir Ronald had taken over the talk, and was demonstrating that his conversational style, for the United States at least, had its foundation in the word "your." It was your Empire State Building, your Queensborough Bridge, your McCarthyite witchhunts, and your Washington fascism, the last being the result of crimes committed by your Ike and Foster Dulles.

Belligerence was the key to Sir Ronald's personality. David recalled that his father, a prosperous solicitor, had sent him to Winchester and New College, an enviable start in life which he now seemed to feel a disgrace. As if to conceal his social and academic origins, he had managed to get a defiant sort of scruffiness into his appearance. He probably would have been happiest, David surmised, in a uniform such as the Chicoms wore, with a coat buttoning under the chin, a sulky-driver's cap, and pinned to the chest, in Sir Ronald's case, the order of Lenin, plus whatever they gave with the Nobel Prize. As it was, David felt that Sir Ronald's wrinkled, snuff-colored suit was a contrived effect, and he would have bet money that the "American" necktie, with its floral pattern, had been included as a touch of obvious contempt for fashion. And God alone knew what reason Sir Ronald had for adding space shoes to his costume. But don't take this baby for a fool, David told himself, sipping the noble claret and admiring Peggy Alcott's performance as a sensible young woman interested in what Sir Ronald had to say. David remembered Ben Thornton's words—Maxwell-Spencer was terrific, very terrific. In Ben Thornton's lingo, terrific usually meant dangerous.

Sir Ronald's loud voice went on. ". . . Then we'll see. We'll see what your American government does *then*. We will see whether your people have learned anything at all." Peggy Alcott looked as happy as though Maxwell-Spencer had just told her Paramount was on the telephone. We Americans certainly can take it, David thought. Imagine one of us behaving this way in London. They'd never get over it. This was the man who was to advise Kane about George Rollins' roster of authors and professors, but David did not bring that subject up during lunch. He kept it out of the conversation until half an hour later, when the company had left the table and moved into the two-story main hall of the suite. Sir Ronald had taken a generous amount of wine along with his bone, salad, and lemon ice. He now accepted a Partagas cigar and a glass of brandy. If ever he were approachable, this was the time, and David said:

"Sir Ronald, I wonder if you've heard of the work my Institute is doing?" He was quickly made aware that the greatness and importance of Sir Ronald Maxwell-Spencer made it impossible for him to know what anyone in New York might be doing. With that point established, David was able to call on Don Marlowe for help. Marlowe explained that in anything concerning the Kane Foundation, one must be conscious of public relations, of community relations. To that end, Mr. Bell had some suggestions to make as to the personnel employed on foundation projects. In short, he wanted to submit a list of candidates for grants. Sir Ronald Maxwell-Spencer opened his mouth and took a deep breath. Obviously he was on the point of denouncing both David and Marlowe, when Jefferson Kane said, "I hope you'll give me your opinion of these people. I may need it. It might be useful." And there was no roar from Sir Ronald. He extended his hand and took the list that David had drawn from his pocket. Just how he was to make Dr. Thorpe's name jump off that list and into Sir Ronald's favor, David did not know. But he felt that he had accomplished a task, even though an absurd one, when he placed the paper in Sir Ronald's hand. Now I can start thinking for myself, David thought, and about time, too. Shortly afterward, the party broke up. Sir Ronald and his lady went to their own suite in the hotel, and David parted from Marlowe and Peggy Alcott in the street outside.

The Bentley glided away, and David stood alone for a moment, strongly tempted to spend the afternoon in getting drunk. But that wouldn't do. That evening he was to meet George Rollins and call on Colonel Andrews— presumably the man who really had the answers. If so, he hoped that Andrews would bring him more peace of mind than he had been able to give Don Marlowe's son. What a life, what a world! David turned into a drugstore, found an unoccupied telephone booth, and called Roxie Dean. Again the voice like a shower of silver, happy, bright. Could she join him for a late drink that evening? "Oh David, that's such a good idea. I'd love to."

As he walked the rest of the way to his office, David felt that in some ways, it was a pretty good world after all. He smiled on Mrs. Martin, and offered a mild joke, which drew decorous laughter. George was out, but in his own room David found a pile of State Department dispatches with a note from Mrs. Martin that Mr. Rollins had thought they might be of interest. David plunged into the mass of paper, hoping to find some kind of clue to a more serious purpose in George's Institute for Strategic Research than he had yet been able to make out. But it was no use. Either the dispatches were too dull, or Jefferson Kane's catering was too good. In half an hour, David was fast asleep.

Later in the afternoon he waked, and felt more kindly toward the authors of the State Department documents, for anything that gives refreshing dreamless sleep should be valued and appreciated. He bundled up the papers and carried them out to Mrs. Martin.

"I see no reason to keep these," he said. Mrs. Martin took the tall stack of mimeographed sheets with a slightly hurt expression.

"They're classified Confidential," she said. "I'll put them in a locked file."

"By all means."

David went out into the hall to see if he could find an office door that might be labeled in such a way as to indicate the presence of the man he had seen at Gramercy Park. He found that few of the doors were lettered, and the names of firms told nothing. They ran to such titles as International Securities, Ltd., or Research Associates, or Consolidated Factors Corporation. To David these had a distinct air of dubiety, and made him think of Kane's numerous foundations, and Dr. September's Systems Analysis, Inc. There were also doors bearing nothing but the office number, behind which there was evident activity. Making a full circuit, he turned the corner of the hall, and ran into George Rollins.

George said, "Are you taking a constitutional? How many times around equals a mile?"

"I might ask you the same."

"Come into my office, I have things to tell you."

In George's room, David said, "Before *you* start, let me bring you up to date. Last night I found a man hanging around 15 Lexington as if he had the place staked out. And I've seen him around here, too."

"Any idea who it was?"

"I was pretty grim when I told him to go away, and he said he had a right to be there because he was a diplomat. Might be United Nations talent."

"Are you sure about all this?"

"Either sure or seeing visions."

"And you think one of Kane's people passed you a threat."

"I'm certain of it."

"There's nothing for it now, young fellow, we'll have to read you all the way in."

"Does that mean telling me exactly what you're trying to do?"

"Just about that, David."

"You could have saved time by telling me the first day I was here."

"Well, first I had to, uh—"

"You had to look me over. We didn't know each other, was that your thought?"

"We haven't worked together for quite a while," George said.

"Don't you trust anybody?"

"No, I don't," said George Rollins. "Do you?"

"Come to think of it—no."

"This isn't a good business for trusting people."

"You put things nicely, George."

"I don't mean to get your back up. I want you to be happy."

"Was that what you had to tell me?"

"No, I want to explain about what you're going to see tonight," George said. "In a way, you're going to see your own creation."

"Something *I* created? I don't think I'll ever understand you."

"Stay with me," George said. "You still don't realize how I listened to some of the things you said when we were working together. Do you remember what you said when the Director's face appeared on the cover of *Time*, and then on the cover of *Newsweek?*"

"There was no reason he shouldn't, being one of the best known men in the country."

"That was your point, David. You said you wondered if it might not be better in the long run if the boss of the show was some little anonymous man hidden away behind a stamp and coin shop. You were joking, but it impressed me all the same."

"You're flattering, George."

"Mind you I didn't say it amused me. I said it impressed me. Many a true word is spoken in jest."

"And out of the mouths of babes."

"No, no. Nothing of the sort. What I want you to understand is that we do have something very much like that. The little shop, the anonymous man."

"Colonel Andrews?"

"That's what we call him. I wanted to be sure you wouldn't judge him by the place where we find him working."

"Surroundings don't always tell the whole story," David said, glancing around the room where they sat.

"Sometimes they're not supposed to," George Rollins said. "Meet me in front of the building here, at nine o'clock tonight."

At dinner Roger Bell said to his son, "I know you're busy these days. But I'm still hoping you can give me

a few minutes. Any time of day or night would suit." The
best of parents did not know how easily they induced
a feeling of guilt. David immediately said, "How about
tonight?" and then remembered he was seeing Roxie after
he got rid of George Rollins. He added, "It would be
pretty late."

"That won't matter," Roger Bell said. "Look in the studio
when you come in. If I'm not up, we can make it another
time."

Peering from a taxicab as it slowed in front of the office
building on Third Avenue, David saw that for once George
Rollins was on time. He came across the sidewalk with
lifted cane, calling, "Keep the cab, David. We have a few
blocks to go." He hauled himself through the door, knocking his hat over his eyes in the process, collapsed on
the seat, and said to the driver, "Sixty-second and Madison." They rolled on, and David said, "Who do you suppose designed these taxicabs, anyways?"

"The devil in hell designed them," Rollins said. "I'm
old enough to remember cars with running boards. We
had a Pierce, designed so you could actually get in and
out."

"Extraordinary idea."

"Yes, wasn't it? Here we are, driver. This will do."

They got out in front of an art store, one of those places
that always has a window full of Meissen figurines, silver
candelabra, jade napkin rings, Chinese chessmen, heavily
framed Alpine landscapes, and paintings of jolly-looking
cardinals in red robes, savoring glasses of wine. David
often wondered who painted these pictures, of which
there seemed to be an inexhaustible supply, and yet no
market whatsoever, for he could not recall ever having
seen a customer in any of these shops. Now that the building of baroque movie palaces was a thing of the past, he
was not able to think of any conceivable demand for these

works of genre painting. Yet here they were, and there were a dozen similar stores up and down Manhattan. Most curious. It was another thing, David told himself, that he would never find out; another of the minor frustrations in life. There was no use trying to discuss it now with George Rollins, who was gloriously indifferent to painting, music, and architecture. And so David followed George silently as he stepped to the heavy glass door and rang the night bell. Although the door was locked, the interior of the shop was fully lit, and in a moment David saw a young man come through the store to the front entrance. Peering through the glass, the young man raised his hand in a gesture of recognition to George Rollins, unlocked the door, and held it open for them. They entered, and without a word the young man led them down the aisles to the rear and opened a side door into the service hall, where he pressed a button; a signal buzzed, and a fire door slid back. George and David walked through, the fire door closed behind them, and David saw that they were in a windowless, plainly furnished reception room. An ordinary office door was ajar in the opposite wall and a voice called, "George? Come on in."

They crossed the reception room and entered an office furnished with well worn chairs and tables and a modest metal desk with one telephone and several folders of papers on it. Through the windows David could see locked steel shutters, and he heard the breathing of an air-conditioning machine. Except for a certain shabbiness, the place might have been a minor desk-wallah's office in the depths of the Pentagon. A man rose from behind the desk. He was tall, thin, sixtyish, and had a neatly trimmed grey moustache. On the left side of his face a white scar ran from chin to cheekbone. He walked around the desk as

George said, "Colonel Andrews, this is my colleague David Bell."

"It's good to see you, Mr. Bell. Nice of you to come around. Have a chair and we'll have a talk." They sat down away from the desk and there was a pause as David waited, feeling it was not his place to open conversation. At this point the telephone rang and Colonel Andrews reached over for it.

"Andrews," said the Colonel. At the other end a voice began talking in a high and excited gabble like Donald Duck. "Hold on and slow down," the Colonel said in a relaxed and unworried tone. "There's lots of time. Just tell me your own way." The voice continued talking, in bursts, but less rapidly. David could not quite make out what the caller was saying, but the Colonel glanced at George and David in a friendly way as if to include them in his end of the conversation as he said, "I see . . . well, we're not supposed to win the cold war *tonight,* you understand . . . no complaint, no criticism whatsoever . . . don't worry about Washington . . . I'll take care of Washington . . . keep up the good work . . . at the usual time, right. See you then." He hung up, and said, "George, you know how some of these people are. Have to be spoonfed. It's the business we're in, I suppose. Now, how is your operation going?"

"We're up to strength now that we have David on board."

"I'm glad you were able to get this fellow," Colonel Andrews said. "One of our greatest problems is manpower, as you know."

"I didn't have time to give David much of an orientation course," George Rollins said. "And I thought perhaps you could read him in, on the need-to-know basis."

"By all means," the Colonel said. He got up and went back to his desk, seated himself, and leaned back in the plain oak swivel chair. "Mr. Bell," he went on, "you're about to start on the most important piece of work that ever came your way."

"That's good news, Colonel," David said. "I've been trying to get a sense of direction and not succeeding very well."

"I can understand that. You've been used to computers, plans, charts, and projects."

"There has been a great deal of paper, yes, sir."

"We don't bother much with paper around here. What interests us is results. By that I mean deliveries on target. It was bound to develop this way, Mr. Bell. The other outfit smothered itself to death."

"The *other* outfit?"

"The Washington group. Jim Ewing. Ben Thornton, Henry Sedgwick. They're all friends of yours."

"I'm not so sure."

"For their sakes, I hope they're your friends. You may be able to do them some favors before the year's out."

"I don't suppose I have anything against them," David said. "Certainly no personal complaints. But I don't see myself able to do favors for anybody these days."

"That is what makes our work so rewarding," the Colonel said. "The way it opens up, everything coming together. One piece fitted with the next piece, then suddenly we can all see the entire design. And we make our move." He put his hands flat on the desk and looked from George to David. This Colonel Andrews, David thought, has an undeniable air of knowledge and authority. "Where you were working, Mr. Bell, that wasn't possible."

David decided he didn't wish to answer that remark, and he was fairly certain no reply was expected. He knew one thing: he wouldn't work in a place for thirteen years and speak ill of it afterward until he was absolutely sure what was at stake.

"Out here," the Colonel said, "we do more with less. Or more accurately, we do *something* with less. We work on first principles. As you know from Marine training, the principles of war are absurdly simple. The actualities are what make it complicated and difficult. As the organization is now constituted, we allow for actualities. This makes the organization what it has not previously been— a thing of logic."

"The *organization*, Colonel?"

"The organization—the one the world thinks is run from that big building in Virginia." Spoken in the steady voice of Colonel Andrews, the words carried weight and conviction. David looked into the man's scarred face and asked, "And the Director?"

"I am the Director."

The strength of the man seemed to come from his calmness, David thought, from the way he sat with his hands quiet before him—no fumbling at ears or chin, no taking off and putting on of glasses, no hair-caressing, no lapel-smoothing, no pipe-stuffing, no cigarette-lighting; here was someone without nervous mannerisms. He was persuasive because he was so reassuring. "I know how you feel," the Colonel said. "It takes a while to get used to the idea." He stood up and extended his hand. "You stick with George Rollins, Mr. Bell. He's a good man."

"Thank you, Colonel," David said. As they turned to go, Colonel Andrews added, "It's a small group actually. That means I can always be called or seen. George will give you the number, or you can come in. Any time you need me. There'll be no channels so far as the three of us are concerned. All right with you, George?"

"Of course, Colonel. That's the way I want it."

On the sidewalk outside, George said, "Satisfied now?"

"There's something about that man," David said. "I swear, I think he's made me believe him. And yet . . ."

"You heard him say it takes a while to get used to the idea. I was like you, state of shock after my first interview. But you're going to be all right."

"Well, I think I *am* all right," David said, as George raised his cane and signalled a taxicab. "No thanks, I'll walk. Good night, George. See you in the morning."

It was now ten-thirty and he was to meet Roxie in fifteen minutes in the bar of the Meadowbrook. Waiting in the bar, chatting with Bruno, the room captain, an idea came to David, and he asked, "Does a man named Jefferson Kane ever come in here?"

"I know who you mean," Bruno said, "but he is not a customer here."

"Do you know a Dr. Harvey September?"

"Not one of ours, Mr. Bell."

"Ask Charles to speak to me, will you?"

"I will tell him."

In a few minutes Charles appeared at the small table in the alcove of the bar where David was waiting for Roxie.

"Have you a minute, Charles?"

"Of course."

"Won't you sit down?"

Charles did not hold with sitting at customers' tables, but he was not busy that evening, and David was a friend. He pulled out a chair.

"And how are you, Mr. Bell?" Charles said.

"Pretty good. I'm waiting for a friend, and things don't look as awful as they have on occasion. I'd like to ask you a favor."

"Anything you say."

"Bless you for saying that before you know what it is. I was just talking to Bruno and asking him about some people I'm interested in. But they're not your customers. Still, you might have heard about this man." He took from his pocket Dr. Harvey September's card. "I've found that you often know more than you say."

"I hope that's true, Mr. Bell, but I know very little." Charles took the card and held it to read in the light from a parchment-shaded wall fixture. "Systems Analysis Incorporated. Sounds like credit card business." His face held an expression of distaste. "Would you like me to make an inquiry?"

"Could you?"

"We use the Appletons, Mr. Bell. It's my impression they know everything about everybody. I could have this checked through." Charles was referring to the Appleton International Protective Agency, the old and enormous private detective firm which he used as security against thievery in the staff and the writing of bad checks by customers. David thought an Appleton Agency report on Dr. September might be an interesting thing, and he said, "That would be fine if you could do it. If there's an extra charge, please let me pay."

"There won't be any charge," Charles said. "They owe me a lot of service anyhow. They haven't been doing much for me. The last bad check artist I took care of myself. He had the nerve to come in again and try to lay another one on me."

"And what did you do?"

"I had Bruno take him in the back and knock hell out of him. It's the only thing they understand."

"I don't envy you, Charles. You're in a hard trade."

"But where else, Mr. Bell, where else would I make what it's brought me? And I think this lady is looking for you." Charles got to his feet, greeted Roxie at the entrance, and went away, taking Dr. September's card with him.

"Hello, Roxie. You look great," said David, as he rose and pulled out a chair. She was beautiful, with her characteristic happy-sad expression that had interested David

as long as he had known her. He had an idea that seeing
this girl helped keep away the unacceptable dreams that
made him re-live the loss of Mary on waking. Unacceptable was the word: a few more of those dreams, and he
would be a different man, and by no means certainly a
sane man. What a fool the Company's doctor had been; it
was not hatred that put David in danger, it was grief.
That could be a drug, and one had to ration one's self
away from it. As he looked at Roxie now, David knew
that if the dreams could be controlled, he could state his
position in life so far as women were concerned with
some precision: Mary's death had paralyzed his emotions
with a deep, unspeakable suffering that probably would
never end; but this he could learn to live with. Other
people did, and so could he. It had been overpowering
sorrow, but the yearning memories, and bitter regret,
might sometime and somehow be an initiation into another state of mind, another condition of heart. He believed now that his friendship with Roxie had something
extra in it, and that it might soon begin going in the
direction a friendship between a man and woman ought
to go. And yet, here was a girl who knew George Rollins,
and who changed a cab driver's instructions to go to the
United Nations building. Perhaps she was a consultant to
the Company—the Company, itself perhaps only a huge,
wornout shadow. It could be, in some strange manifestation of mindless bureaucracy, that she was supposed to
keep track of David Bell. He suddenly thought of Brue-
gel's picture, "The Blind Leading the Blind," and the
trusting face of the central blind man, who is about to
fall over an obstacle in the path.

"George Rollins spoke of you the other day," David
said. "Have you known him a long time?"

"All my life," Roxie said. "He was older, of course, but
he went to my sister's dancing class when we still lived

on West Forty-ninth Street. They took our house down to build Radio City. Did you know that, David?"

"You couldn't have been living when they built Radio City."

"Oh I definitely was," Roxie said. "I guess I'm older than you think."

"I hadn't speculated about it. You're just a child."

"As a matter of fact, I *have* a child."

"I didn't know that," David said.

"I've been married and divorced. I took my own name back but I have a little boy five years old."

"I didn't know that at all," David said. "Where does the boy live?"

"Where do you suppose? At home with me," Roxie said.

"But when you work?"

"I have a wonderful Scotch nurse, and a perfectly swell Negro woman who comes for odd hours, and then Lewis has two adoring grandmothers."

"Lewis is the boy's name?"

"Yes, I married Lewis Russel. Didn't you know him? He was a member of the Corinthian Club."

"I don't think I ever met him."

"He had race horses."

"Oh, that Russel. No, I didn't know him."

"Well . . . we were divorced a year after the baby was born, and right away Lewis married Constance Trask. And two months later he was killed in a wreck coming home from a party, on Sunrise Highway. Constance wasn't with him."

"I see."

"So my son has no memories of his father."

"Roxie, in this case it may be just as well."

"I think so, David."

Roxie had ordered a stinger, while David, who did not

have a favorite drink as many men do, had settled on a
Dr. Pepper and gin, served by an imperturbable waiter.

"Drink snobbishness is a funny thing," David said. "I
have friends who wouldn't want to be seen with anyone
putting down this mixture."

"It's true," Roxie said. "A lot of people think Scotch and
soda is sophisticated, bourbon not so good."

"With bourbon and ginger ale marking the complete
outsider," David said. "People are sensitive about it. I've
been in Texas and above a certain educational line they
get nervous if you say you'd like Jack Daniel. 'Oh, we have
Scotch,' they always say. And they do, too. But tell me
something, Roxie. Why am I always discussing drinks
when I'm with you?"

"Because we're always drinking, I suppose."

"Surely not to excess. I'll show you I can change a subject in midair. What do you think of the United Nations?"

There was no question about it, Roxie was startled. She
looked up quickly and said, "Has anybody mentioned me
in connection with the United Nations?"

"Nobody you'd know," David said. "But I think you
went over there the other afternoon."

"Good gracious, David. Do you have a network of
agents in your pay?"

"It's more like Sherlock Holmes and his Baker Street
Irregulars," David said. "I have my Gramercy Park Irregulars. I just didn't want you to forget I used to be a spy."

"Sometimes I wonder if you still are."

"In New York?"

"Perhaps not staying in New York. Don't take me seriously, David. I heard you say you were through with
Washington."

"I got very uncommunicative down there," David said.
"The habits that grow on you can seem very strange. For
example, I still tear up all the mail I get, and burn it.

After reading it, of course. I even do it with circulars that come in the mail. You know, record albums of the masters, and ads from travel agencies."

This would give Roxie a chance to mention her booking of a trip for George Rollins. David would like to surprise Rollins by telling him where he was going, because he felt there had been enough mystification on George's part. But Roxie did not rise to the opportunity. That was admirable, but was it an agent protecting the privacy of a client, or was it because of another sort of professional training? Roxie picked up her gloves and said, "I do have to go home now, David. I hope you don't mind."

"I mind very much, but it can't be helped," he said. He rose and put money on the table. If Roxie wanted to go, he would not delay her by waiting for a bill to sign. As he hoped, she recognized the gesture.

"We don't have to go as though the place was on fire," she said.

"It's all right," David said. "And I'll see you to your door."

A few steps down the street to Roxie's house, a sisterly goodnight kiss, and she was gone. In spite of an impression that it had been a rather empty little date, David felt warmed and encouraged. This girl was beginning to have importance for him, and he was not afraid to accept that fact. He started to walk home, then remembered that his father might be sitting up for him, and hailed a cab.

When David entered the apartment at 15 Lexington, he found his father on the duplex's first floor, prowling the library.

"Oh, hello," Roger Bell said. "I was looking for a book. Friend of mine wrote trying to locate a quotation."

"Tell him to try the *New York Times*," David said.

"Just what I mean to do. Have you a few minutes? Let's go up to the studio."

They climbed the stairs and entered the big room under the skylight. Roger Bell turned a switch and flooded his worktable with light which reflected on his cork wall board. David walked over to see if anything new was pinned there, and saw that his father had put up an old photograph from the First World War, a snapshot taken at the Italian aviation training camp outside Foggia. His father was posed with Albert Spalding, Fiorello La Guardia, who had been camp commander, and Steve Philbin, the old Yale halfback. In flying the Caproni bombers, Roger Bell had always said, they had been in more danger from the airplane than from the enemy. That, of course, was not true, but it was the way those people talked about that war, when they talked about it at all. And at this moment, Roger Bell was in a serious mood. David could recognize it from the way he sat at his table, arms folded and leaning back in the Barcelona chair which was a touch of approved modernism in the workroom. Roger Bell sat just out of direct light and his head did not have its usual confident tilt. For David his father was a man who could be as expressive in stillness as in motion, and the signal that came to him now could be read in only one way: discouragement.

David said, "I have an impression something is wrong. It's always been the other way around so it sounds funny to say it, but can I help?"

"You help by being in existence, my friend," Roger Bell said.

"Then there is need of it?"

"In a way. And you do come into it. I'll get to that part. Let me wind up here and take a run at it. I have to put something in words, and that makes it a little frightening. David, the other day I meant to tell you something, but what you told me—about Mary—was enough sad news for one day. But I do have to tell you this. About

a month ago, I went to the doctors and they discovered
a tumor in my lung."

"Are they sure of it?"

"Quite sure."

"You had a second series of pictures?"

"And a third. It's there all right, and almost certainly
malignant. They've been treating it with rays, and reduced
the size quite a bit. And now they are going to operate."

"When?"

"Early next week. Louise knows about all this, but I
didn't mention the cancer aspect to her. And won't. You
see, if they can get the whole thing out, we still might
be all right. At least, we might be all right for quite a
while—measure it in years, three, four. That would be
pretty good considering my age and all that sort of thing.
During that time I might die of heart failure or be run
over by a *New York Post* delivery truck. You never know.
It's just this possible immediacy that shakes my nerve
a bit."

"You don't seem shaken up. I think I'm the one who's
shaken. We just can't have this, Dad. We can't have you
sick."

"As I say, David, they aren't certain it's malignant, and
if it is, they may be able to kill it all one way or another."

"Who's the doctor?"

"The surgeon is Ted Kenyon. He'll tell me the truth
after the operation, just as he has so far. He's a good man."

"Is that old Dr. Kenyon?"

"No, his son, your classmate at St. Bernard's." Roger
Bell smiled. "Something has happened to time, David.
You'll find out soon enough. A boy I took to see Thurston
the Magician at the Palace is opening my chest at New
York Hospital." David remembered the trip to the Palace
well. His birthday—he and little Ted Kenyon had been
seven years old. They sat silent for a moment, with David

trying to send waves of courage and hope into his father by *willing* the old man a share of his youth and strength.

"I said you came into this," Roger Bell said at last. "And here is how. I want to ask you a favor. Suppose they cut me, and find out they might as well have left it alone. In that case I shouldn't have much longer. What I'm thinking of is the end. They don't like you to take up room dying in hospitals these days, and I'd be down here at the apartment. Now it might get bad. Get to where it wasn't dignified, you know? In that case I'd need access to an escape hatch, an emergency exit. What it amounts to, David, is this: I may have to fall into the hands of the enemy, but I don't propose to be tortured. Now I understand that in your former line of work they have a certain pill or capsule. All you do is bite on it, so I've heard, and that solves the whole thing then and there."

"They're known as L-pills," David said.

"I was wondering, could you get me one of these?"

"Yes, I can get one for you."

"And you will?"

"Of course."

"Thank you, David. You have no idea how that lightens the anxiety."

"Dad, things are going to be all right."

"Yes, they are, my boy. By hook or by crook, things will be quite all right." He hunted on the worktable and found a small card. "This isn't the quotation my friend wanted, but I like it: 'But fie upon that knave death, that will come whether we will or not.' Do you know it?"

"John Donne?"

"John Knox."

"What was your friend looking for?"

"He wanted to know who wrote 'The boy stood on the burning deck.'"

"Felicia Hemans."

"Oh, to be sure. 'Casabianca.' I must write to Wally Dinsmore in the morning. You know how these things prey on one's mind."

"They do indeed. Will you be turning in now? It's pretty late."

"In a few minutes, David. You've done enough for the moment. You go along."

"All right, Dad. Good night."

"Good night, Son."

As David prepared for sleep he tried to keep up the willing of encouragement to his father, but bleakness was growing in his heart. He did not want his father to die, ever. But when the time came, when that knave death insisted on his entrance—then David wanted his father to die in his sleep, or at the drawing board, quickly. He remembered how little he had understood Roger Bell some years before when he had commented on the "great good luck" of a friend who had picked up a bridge hand at his club and fallen from his chair, dead before he hit the carpet. At the time David had thought, it is never lucky to die. Now he was not so sure.

10

THAT NIGHT David dreamed about his father. Again it was a clear dream, like a moving picture in sharp black and white. The plot of the dream was that his father had been away under mysterious circumstances, and after having been written off completely had suddenly returned. Now there was something wrong with Roger Bell, something discreditable, and there was a question of what to do with him—a disposal problem. David waked to bleak misery and a feeling of loss and shame. As he dragged himself from his bed, he thought this was almost as bad as dreaming about Mary. What was the edge of pressure beyond which a man could not go? David had an idea he might soon find out.

In the office, Mrs. Martin said that Mr. Marlowe had called. There seemed to be a slightly accusing note in her voice, and the mild but deadly reproof of a secretary talking to the junior executive who is ticketed to become that month's man of extinction. David wanted to say, "Look here, Mrs. Martin. You know nothing about me. If I have my way you will never know anything about me. But I'd like to tell you this: I don't need a job. So I'll come and go as I please. And I'll thank you to mind your own business and allow me to take care of mine." How shocking this would be, and impolite, and hurtful to the feelings of a relatively defenseless person. My nerves are tuned up pretty high, David told himself, that I can think of such a thing. And so instead of scolding, he said, "I'll call him at once, Mrs. Martin. No, I'll dial him, thank you."

On the telephone, Don Marlowe came quickly to the point.

"How about coming to the show tonight?"

"I'd like to, Don."

"I have something important to tell you, and no way to get loose till after the broadcast. This is the day we put it all together, you understand, old son?"

"Of course, rehearsals," David said. "I didn't think you made it up as you went along."

"That's what you're *supposed* to think," Marlowe said. "I know your kind. You've never seen us."

"Maybe not, Don."

"Then join the merry throng tonight. Nine o'clock, Studio 8-H. You'll do it?"

"I'll be there."

"Bring Miss America too, if you like."

"Good idea. See you."

Ten minutes later David was once again regretting that he had made a call to Roxie Dean. He had thought it would be pleasant to take her to Marlowe's show, and had made that suggestion by telephone. It was too bad, Roxie said, it was maddening, but she couldn't go. After David had hung up, he thought about the Roxie situation and decided it was not at all good. I don't have to have a house fall on me, he thought; this is the invitation to go and keep going. And George Rollins can take his chances with that girl. George is old enough to know what he is doing. But it was all regrettable, David admitted to himself; he realized he had been hoping that he could come to a place in his friendship with Roxie where each would assume that all evenings would be passed in the other's company. Of course there had been only the smallest encouragement. But this sort of thing shouldn't happen to a man. Nothing in his life now seemed to be clean-cut or crisply outlined. Everything doubtful, ambiguous, and hard to explain. He stood up, and tossed the *Times* unread into the wastebasket. He would go up to Charles's and have lunch.

David was the first customer to arrive at the restaurant. He caught Bruno settling into the dinner jacket that he wore by day and night, and Maurice the bartender polishing cocktail glasses.

"Good morning, Mr. Bell," said Bruno. "Mr. Charles would like to see you. Could you go in the office?"

Charles's office was not meant for display. It was no more than a broom-closet, almost filled with cases of liquor and cardboard cartons of glassware that barely left space for a small desk and two straight chairs. Rising courteously as David edged his way in, the restaurateur displayed a pair of red and gold Hawes & Curtis braces that would soon be hidden under his black waistcoat and jacket. It was part of his calling to dress like an undertaker; the suspenders showed his personal taste.

"Please sit down, Mr. Bell." Charles kept to formality of manner with David even though he had known him for almost twenty-four years, since he first had come down from Cambridge as a college boy learning how to drink and take women to dinner and the theater. "I asked you in here because I have information and you might not want me to be telling you where people could overhear."

"You work fast," David said.

"So do the Appleton people when a customer calls," Charles said. The Appleton International Protective Agency was a legitimate business—they made sure everyone understood that. Somewhere along the line, they had government connections—but not precisely that, not technically or actually that. What it came to was that men who had served their time in the great and famous Bureau then joined Appleton. They would know a thing or two, these former Bureau men, and they were discreet. And there were things that AIPA would not do. For example, they did not do any divorce work. However, if a client needed divorce work, they were happy to direct him to a subsidiary company that had no objections to such an assignment. And they did not do industrial espionage. But their Research Department was very good at *counter-*espionage, and one way or another, Appleton clients seemed to get what they wanted if it was at all possible to obtain. In the matter of Systems Analysis, Inc., there was plenty of information available. For it seemed that Systems Analysis might be a rising rival of the huge and venerable AIPA and its two or three peers in the private detective business.

"They don't like this September at all," Charles was saying. "He's been picking up accounts here and there. The biggest one is Jefferson Kane."

"But what does he do for Kane?"

"Anything he wants, as I understand it," Charles said. "My man at AIPA is sending up a written report and I'll mail that on to you. Meanwhile, I'll try to give you what he told me over the phone. To begin with, my man said to stay away from this September. He said don't touch him with a ten-foot pole. I said I didn't intend to. 'Well, be sure you don't,' my man said. 'That guy will kill you.' And Mr. Bell, it turned out he meant literally kill, murder. He says there have been cases where Systems Analysis has started investigating people, and then all of a sudden, no more people. It seems there's an area where private investigators get so close to the crooks you can't tell the difference. And the next thing you know—there *is* no difference. Where there's money, there's bound to be thieves. And where there's thieves, some of them will kill you. My man says it's known in the business, don't get this Harvey September mad."

"Then that might apply to his clients, also."

"So I was told, Mr. Bell. It's privately said if old Jefferson Kane doesn't like you, the best thing you can do is get out of town."

"Or what?"

"My man says people are out in Forest Lawn right now because they got in that old gentleman's way."

"He give you any examples?"

"Do you remember that patent case, an inventor suing one of Kane's companies?"

"Vaguely."

"This man was a suicide. Jumped off the roof. Left a note."

"A fake?"

"That's what the Appleton man said. He told me it's easy to fake a suicide."

"I don't know how easy it is, but I'm damned sure it's been done."

"You and me both, Mr. Bell. There's police that come in here, captains and inspectors, very nice, quiet. I've talked with them late a few evenings. In times like these, don't be surprised at anything."

"I'm not," David said. "What else did you get on September and his outfit?"

"My man said it was getting to be a big thing. They weren't sure how big. Systems Analysis doesn't advertise, and they're quiet in the way they go after business. Apparently it's a matter of recommendation. A man like Kane will tell a friend, another big wheel like himself, you see what I mean?"

"Good Lord," David said, "I suppose they're sitting around at Sea Island and Kane says, 'I had a smooth job of murder done the other day. Let me give you the fellow's name.' Like recommending a barber. It's too fantastic."

"A man like Kane wouldn't know the details," Charles said. "He'd just know something had been bothering him, and it wasn't bothering him anymore."

"The problem solver."

"How's that, Mr. Bell?"

"That's what I heard Dr. September call himself."

"Then you've met him."

"Oh yes. And he's a barrel of fun."

"Be careful, Mr. Bell. I don't want to lose a good customer."

"Thank you, Charles," David said, and he stood up. "Mail me your man's report when you get it, will you?"

"A pleasure."

"I do appreciate this."

"And you'll have lunch with us, I hope?"

"Seems like a good idea."

After lunch, David shook hands with Charles and started walking uptown, his objective again the stacks of the New York Society Library. This time he spent his afternoon reading and making notes on Sir Ronald Maxwell-Spencer and certain of his colleagues. Sir Ronald was a strange man, an inexplicable man; equally hard to explain were his idolators, the writers who had made him figure-head of a cult as uncritical as that which had centered around the fiddle-scraping, poodle-haired old Dr. Einstein. In these writers' eyes, the most preposterous statement Sir Ronald could make had the force of divine command, graven on tablets and brought down from Sinai. Perhaps this idolatry was one explanation of Sir Ronald's curious failure of mind when faced with any comparison between the United States and the Communist parts of the world. Perhaps the years of slavish flattery had rotted the Maxwell-Spencer mentality to a point where it failed in logical analysis. Critical of the United States to such an extent that the smallest flaw could not escape comment and condemnation, he saw perfection in all the doings of the Soviet

Union and its satellites, and his love and longing for Red China was like that of John Henry Newman in his Oxford days for the Church of Rome. David supposed that as individual choice this was all right: let every man decide what appeals to him. But not in the name of science; Newman had not claimed to be a scientist. He would have thought that beneath him either as Anglican or Roman.

But Cardinal Newman had been dead a long time and now, in his way, Sir Ronald Maxwell-Spencer was one of the most powerful men on earth. He had cast himself in the role of infallible oracle, and had been accepted as such. Very few were the people who dared to debate Sir Ronald, and most of them were not qualified to do so. For what one needed to argue with Sir Ronald was not knowledge, but fame. And the famous ones of the world, as a rule, did not like to appear under public scrutiny with another equally famed person nearby to distract attention. The world's great men were like the oldtime vaudeville stars who went on as single acts. They felt no need for partners or straight men. The huge vanity of this era's public figures, David thought as he looked through the material on Sir Ronald, was worse than that of actors, who at least tried to entertain. The bigwigs had read their own publicity so long that they now believed the mere sight of their faces was sufficient to collect and hold an audience. He thought of fireside chats, and leaders of cities and nations in the hands of make-up men, while hacks, ghosts, and toadies fed the teleprompter with lines up to the moment the red light came on and the director behind his glass said "Take it." This was a hell of a world for an honest man to be alive in. Sir Ronald, with the prestige of his Nobel Prize—to say nothing about his Order of Lenin, and his honorary degrees —was almost impossible to get at. He would not discuss matters with anyone whose honors equaled his. And criticism from lesser people he made to seem despicable by claiming the international freedom and sanctuary of science. In an age of public men who were also ham actors, posturing before cameras and outdoing the professionals in grotesque effects, Sir Ronald had seized the part of Wisdom, like a character in the medieval church plays. But there was something wrong with this Ronald Maxwell-Spencer. David felt the wrongness though he could not define it. If at this moment he were called on to submit proof of what he felt about Sir Ronald, he would have been compelled to cite such things as the scientist's acceptance of the ridiculous germ warfare evidence in North Korea. He must have *known* it was preposterous, David thought. But assume him innocent, suppose he honestly believed those sorties had been flown to spread typhus in North Korea, even though that was in the same class of operation as bombing Newcastle with coal; suppose, all the same, that Sir Ronald honestly believed it. What then would that tell us about Sir Ronald? That he was crazy, that's all. But man, you can't say that! Shape up there, man! Sir Ronald has a Nobel Prize, and how could he have got that if he was crazy? In the quiet stacks, David shook his head, and muttered to himself. This Maxwell-Spencer could beat you either way. "New York Extremist Accuses Nobel Scientist"—he could see the headlines now. And that word Nobel, anagram for noble, preceding the all-humbling term, scientist. Another right-winger, touched in the head, attacking a great and good man, and not even sure what he was trying to accuse him of. But there was one thing sure: Sir Ronald was a great friend of Jefferson Kane's, and Jefferson kept a watchdog named Harvey September. That, at least, could be investigated further. David went to a telephone booth and looked in the Manhattan directory for Systems Analysis. There it was, at an address on Madison Avenue below Forty-second Street. He dialed the number, and soon was talking to a switchboard girl who would admit only that he had reached the number he was dialing. Systems Analysis? They did not give out that information.

"But it says in the book this is the number for that name. I want to speak to Dr. September, or leave a number if he's out. Referred by Mr. Jefferson Kane." Silence. Pause. Then a strange man's voice yelled, "Hello, who is this?" and David began to explain in a patient tone, though he felt a throb in the crater of his ulcer. He was interrupted by September's familiar Pavlovian barking. Between them they got the unknown man off the line and David said, "Doctor, I'd like to talk to you again, about those tests, and some other things you mentioned." The doctor became businesslike, and said, "Can you get here right away? Half an hour? I'll be waiting."

The building was old but without distinction; it had never been first-class. Systems Analysis was listed on the directory as 1504. One of the building's two elevators was being converted to the automatic system under a glaring naked light by large, greasy, shouting men whose tools littered the lobby and got in the way of tenants and visitors alike. The other elevator was in charge of a melancholy uniformed man who smoked a cigarette as he took David up to the fifteenth floor. There was a sign in the elevator that said, "FOR YOUR CONVENIENCE WE GO AUTO-MATIC. RELSAR CORP., OWNERS." Your convenience, David thought, is a nicer way of saying, let the customer do the work. But at least they haven't put in Muzak yet. The gloomy man stopped the car neatly and exactly; he was an old pro, and would soon be out of work. David stepped out, and saw that 1504 was two doors away from the elevators.

The reception room was empty except for a bare, cigar-ette-scarred table and a couple of chairs. A girl with a hive of hair looked out suspiciously from the information window, then repeated his name into the telephone after he gave it. She pressed a button, a lock clanked, and David opened a door marked "Entrance." He found himself in a general office with a frosted glass partition setting off six cubicles at one side. There were four or five desks in the open area, two of them occupied. At one, an elderly man was marking and filing newspaper clippings. Next to him sat a redfaced young man with a crew cut who was writing on a yellow pad. The young man looked like an athlete— possibly a homosexual of the muscle-man type. Neither paid any attention to David, who stood looking around him for a moment until Harvey September appeared at the door of the end cubicle and beckoned to him.

When David entered September's private space, he noted that the office had one wide window looking on the courtyard, and that it was equipped with maple furniture that must be second-hand. It took no expert to see that these battered pieces dated back to a time when organizations like Systems Analysis had not been thought of, and Dr. September had not been born. Now we'll see whether he makes any excuse for the looks of things, David thought.

"Sit down, Bell," September said, establishing himself behind the desk. He had the same expensive look, with the glints of gold here and there. "We've been getting a feed-back on you."

"By feedback I take it you mean report."

"And not the kind of report I'd like to have coming in on me."

"Is something wrong?" David asked.

"I'd say so."

"You can't accuse me of lighting a cigarette in the subway, because I don't smoke."

"All right, Bell," Harvey September said, "let's have it."

"I asked for the interview, and I *will* let you have it, maybe in more ways than you think."

"You're not going to get tough with me in my own back-yard," September said. "You've got too much sense for that."

"Now we're talking about getting tough," David said. "This is a little different from our first meeting, isn't it? You were telling me all about the mental tests and how you kept people away from Mr. K. Some people you kept away, others you let by. And others you dropped out of windows."

Dr. September's face seemed to have turned into some hard kind of wood. When he spoke, his voice was squeezed down in his throat almost to a whisper. "What do you think you're doing?" he asked. "Don't you know the laws of libel?"

"I doubt if they apply to you," David said. "You're not the only people in the analysis business, you know. You've been taking a look at me. I've been taking a look at you. And you look great, Dr. September. You look wonderful. No, I'll tell you what you look like—it's what a friend of mine sometimes says. You look terrific."

"What makes you get so hard with me? And who is this friend, by the way?"

"Somebody in Washington," David said.

"You're finished in Washington."

"Where did you get that, what do you call it, flashback?"

"Feedback. We got it from a big bird. The old American eagle."

"Do you believe everything you hear?"

"Almost none of it," September said. "But I believed that. You were working on a high level down there and then you were declared lousy on a psychiatric inventory. And now your friends down there wouldn't believe you if you said Sandy Koufax played on the Dodgers." A slight look of animation came into Dr. September's face along with a tone of righteous indignation in his voice. "And now you—a psychological cripple—you come to Mr. K. and say you want to mess with his business, his operations. Who do you think you are? I'll tell you who you are. You're nobody."

"You seem to be pretty sore about nobody."

"Well, I'm sore, Bell, of course I'm sore. Your whole attitude is lousy. Like you didn't give a damn, didn't have no respect. *Any* respect. That's the way it goes. Try to help people, they take advantage of you. I already explained to you, we don't allow outsiders and strangers to waste Mr. K's time. Man comes to Mr. K. with a proposition, we check him out. And mostly that's as far as it goes, screened out, good-bye, don't call us, we'll call you. And that applies to you, Bell. Nowhere is where you're going with Mr. K., because you—are—strictly—nothing."

"Then how do you explain the fact that I had lunch with Kane yesterday along with Maxwell-Spencer and his wife?"

"I hope you took a good look. It was the last you'll see of those people."

"I could almost wish you were right. As table companions, I put them down in Class Z-7. In case you're wondering, that's the bottom."

"All I'm wondering is why you're here."

"I got a little feedback on you, Doctor. It turns out you're more interesting that I thought. So I decided to have another look. I must say you don't put much into offices, do you?"

"You've been around, Bell," Dr. September said. "You know offices don't mean anything. Some of the most important men in the world got no offices at all. But, you want to see nice rooms? Look us up in Beverly Hills. Seventy-seven-Oh-Seven Wilshire. Out there we have the works, complete, everything up to date, like it's expected in L.A."

"Sounds expensive."

"We can afford it if we want it, Bell. Depends on the town, depends on what's expected. Around here, looks aren't important."

"It's nice that you think so, Doctor, because frankly, this looks like the office of a collection agency."

"Why this needle, Bell? I don't understand you. Not that you have any license. And you talk about reports. Night before last you pulled a great stunt. You threatened a man with diplomatic immunity."

"I don't recognize it."

"The State Department would like to hear that."

"I don't give a damn about the State Department," David said, getting up. "You'd better check your Washington sources, Dr. September. Maybe I wasn't run out after all."

Harvey September looked up over his glasses, and again David caught a flash of the ancient quality in his eyes, like that in the eyes of something between a lizard and a fish. "I won't take any more of your time, Doctor," David went on. "But I'm very grateful to you."

"What for?"

"For letting me know you had my apartment staked out with that guy from Lower Slobbovia."

"Did I say that?"

"You knew I told him to get out of there."

"All I know is you're looking for trouble," September said. "And it's not hard to find."

"There could be a lot of it around my apartment," David said. "But I told you that before."

David walked out through the bull-pen, noticing that the old man and the muscular young man kept their eyes down and paid no attention to him. The girl at the switchboard let him out, and after a five-minute wait, the melancholy uniformed man brought up the elevator. Walking along Madison Avenue, David felt his bloodstream gradually absorbing the adrenalin released into his system by the anger he felt toward Dr. September. It occurred to him that the doctor summed up everything David objected to in Jefferson Kane and others of their sort, and he turned this thought over in his mind until he could express exactly what it was about these people that angered him, and frightened him. It was, he decided, what must be a pathological determination to have their own way. He thought of the list of men in the history of the modern world who had been victims of this pathology, and the millions of graves they had filled . . . Marlowe's program tonight would be something of a relief, he thought.

Half an hour before broadcast time, Studio 8-H hummed with activity. The audience, standing patiently in the corridor, was not yet admitted. David looked at the space they were to occupy, some hundred and fifty tattered theater seats on an incline behind the camera locations. He thought that the shabby condition of the chairs indicated the network's fundamental contempt for its audience, both in the studio and throughout the land. David had walked past the lines of people waiting for admission, and they had filled him with horror—the rows of kindly but congealed smalltown faces, their docility as they were herded by supercilious youths in the network's livery of blue and gold. They would be as orderly and quiet, David felt sure, if they were lined up to go into a gas chamber, or to pass before scientists selecting material for human experimentation. David had given his name to the white-gloved head usher who stood at the studio door, hoping he could control his temper if the fellow proved discourteous. No such thing happened: the youth, who was almost seven feet tall, had a paper folded under the knotted gold cord on the shoulder of his tunic. He pulled out the paper, opened it, found David's name, and said, "Right through here, Mr. Bell." As David passed through

the door the usher held open, he saw the eyes in the congealed faces resting on him without curiosity, and he could
sense the words, "That's not a celebrity. That's nobody."

Don Marlowe came up to David as he stood in the
studio looking at the chairs the audience was to occupy.
Marlowe's trick of catching another's thought was working,
and he said, "Yes, I know it's not the Winthrop Ames. But
the camera doesn't show the difference when those seats
are occupied. Come over here where you can see the
action." He led David behind a black screen that carried
the trademark of a sponsor picked out in rhinestone.

"They use this for a live commercial, where the girl
comes out dressed as a can of sausages. I think you'll like
it."

"I won't have to duck the camera?"

"No, you're out of range back here," Marlowe said,
indicating two folding chairs near a portable monitor
screen and a microphone on a stand. "That mike's for the
voice-over announcer, and this screen carries what actually
goes out. But look here, cousin, where's Miss America?"

"Couldn't make it," David said. "Before you go back to
work, Don—you had something to tell me."

"We're under pressure right now," Marlowe said. "After
the show, David, okay?"

"Of course."

David watched as the three cameras, trailing cable,
were pushed into position by the dolly men. At the same
time the boom men who controlled the microphones re-
hearsed their placings under the direction of a disem-
bodied voice that came from the wall. There was a legend
that the technicians of moving pictures and television had
a collective skill, amounting to wizardry, far beyond that
of the directors and performers in their media. David had
an idea it was all of a piece, and that the studio technicians
were lucky to be so highly paid for simple jobs. But the

members of this crew did not seem to be happy, and went about their work with expressions of unutterable contempt on their faces. Marlowe was to perform in a sort of amphitheater where he sat at a desk. The guests who came to be interviewed would sit nearby in swivel chairs. A box of Kane's breakfast cereal was out of camera range behind the desk, and David knew that Marlowe worked this into a friendly chat at some point during the program. "It's the only part of the show that Jefferson looks at," Marlowe had said. "That's how he gets his jollies—at forty dollars per second." In a corner, a group of advertising men in silk suits were rehearsing the sausage girl. It was a strange scene to David: thirty or forty people hard at work pretending they had the talent and ability to put on a show that could be compared with those that people paid to see—and that they had something worth saying. All demonstrably false, and beneath notice—and yet as the door now opened and the audience shuffled in, actual tension and excitement could be felt. Ten minutes to air time: Don Marlowe had stepped out of sight. An announcer introduced him and he made his entrance; his line on the prompter read, "Good evening, all you good cousins. My name's Don Marlowe and I want you should all have a good time." But to David's astonishment, none of this could be heard, for at the sight of Marlowe, the studio audience let out a roar like that which is heard when Notre Dame goes over on a sixty-yard pass with five seconds to play. Marlowe acknowledged the yell with fists clasped over his head like a prizefighter. "Good Lord," David said to himself, and wondered if he could get out. But he was trapped now. If he came from his hiding place while Don Marlowe was warming up the audience, he knew it would be worse than trying to reach the men's room in the old days at the Club Eighteen. David thought he could stand it for half an hour, but after the program was launched he was thankful that the Marlowe program occupied only thirty minutes on the air. He made it seem like ninety minutes, and yet it would be a problem to say just what it was all about, or what the structure of the entertainment was supposed to be. At one point a guessing game was played, and a popular novelist and his wife appeared dressed as James and Dolly Madison. The rules of this game were incomprehensible, but apparently a man and wife, picked from the audience, won a pot of $2700 for knowing that Thomas Jefferson was a widower when he occupied the White House. With the connection still unclear to David, the act ended with one camera on the smiling winners, while the others rolled in for a discussion between Marlowe and the chief announcer, who seemed to be a man of vast erudition like that of an old-fashioned encyclopedia salesman. The two engaged in a consideration of oddities in the week's news, which set up jokes by Marlowe on golf, mortgages, mothers-in-law, babies, traffic, and the catastrophe of being booked to Los Angeles on an airplane that was showing a film one had already seen. In Vietnam, men were dying face down in the mud; from New York, Don Marlowe was saying to an audience of millions, "If you have any trouble meeting new people —just pick up the wrong golf ball." God save the United States, said David Bell. He could see part of the studio audience, and suddenly he looked again, back along the row of faces, to one that had stood out because it was not laughing with the rest. It was Mr. Anonymous of Third Avenue, Gramercy Park, and Lower Slobbovia. David asked himself if the man had followed him here. He thought not. Was it coincidence that the man had appeared in the studio? David could not accept that as a probability. It occurred to him then that the man could have joined the audience for some reason having nothing to do with David. The man obviously had not come there to be amused; he sat wooden-faced while the audience roared around him. From his concealed seat David continued to watch, until at last the program ended, with Marlowe and the guest star dancing a soft shoe routine and singing "Side by Side." David kept his eyes on Mr. Anonymous as a camera swung to pan across the faces in the crowd, which was delirious with joy. Now Mr. Anonymous came to life. He took out a white handkerchief and waved it, apparently in a pattern. David could see this action both in the studio and on the monitor screen, and said to himself, it looks as though my theory had something to be said for it. Let us theorize further, that the purpose of the man in coming to the studio has been to transmit a message. How would one send a message, or a signal, with absolute certainty of avoiding electronic eavesdropping? By using a public medium—a variance of Mr. Poe's principle of concealing in plain view the purloined letter. If this theory were correct, David realized, the next question was, to which one of Don Marlowe's forty million viewers was Mr. Anonymous signalling? With that question open, David decided not to mention any of it to Marlowe; and as the picture faded to black on his monitor screen, he stayed behind the commercial scenery until the audience had left the studio. Then Marlowe and Peggy Alcott came over to him.

"You can come out now, cousin," said Marlowe.

"Hello, Peggy," David said.

"David, it's nice to see you! Didn't you love it tonight?"

"Great show," David said. "I didn't know Don was a song and dance man."

"Neither did he," Peggy said.

"This flattery will get you everywhere," Don Marlowe said. He seemed to be in a state of euphoria. David surmised that broadcasters were at their happiest immediately after going off the air. There were no failures in studios.

Besides, it was possible that Marlowe was on drugs, and at this moment on the rising side of an intake, before nerves started complaining. Or, simply, he had just earned in half an hour more than the Company had ever paid David in a year. Any man would be cheerful at a time like that, with a girl like Peggy Alcott at his side. Don Marlowe now suggested they go out to a place he had discovered.

"It's called The Banjo, and it's up on Second Avenue," Marlowe said. "I guarantee you'll like it."

When the Bentley pulled up in front of The Banjo and they got out, an autograph hunter rushed at Don Marlowe with a scrambling, flopping run, like an agitated penguin. The hunter was a shaggy girl of fourteen or fifteen who said, "Vautographpleeze," shoving a book and pen into Marlowe's hands.

"I think you'll want this lady too," said Marlowe, as he signed the book. "She's the famous actress, Miss Peggy Alcott." The girl looked at Peggy and said, "Nah."

"And this is the English critic, Mr. Kenneth Tynan," Marlowe went on. The girl gave David a look of loathing and said, "Nahdowannum."

"Then get away from me, you vile little beast," Marlowe said, in the same cordial tone with which he addressed the spectators in the studio. The hunter was not going to take this. She spat at them and screamed, "Drop dead! Yah dirtyole bassard!" They heard a burst of shrieking halfway up the block, and saw a gang of autograph hunters rushing toward them.

"Inside, quick," said Don Marlowe. "These are piranhas and they'll pull you to pieces."

The Banjo was a long, low, smoky hall with red-check-covered tables and a lighted stage at one end, on which several men, each armed with the instrument that gave the place its name, were playing and singing the ballad of Casey Jones, the brave engineer. They were backed by a

piano, drum, tuba, and trombone. The customers who
filled the place were young and, to David's surprise, con-
ventionally dressed. As they stood in the lobby, the
proprietor ran over and seized Don Marlowe in a show-
business hug.

"Don, baby!" he cried. "I love this guy," he went on to
Peggy and David. "You want near the music, or back by
the bar?"

"By the bar," Marlowe said. "The waiters won't have
so far to walk."

When the proprietor recovered from his convulsions of
laughter, he said, "You just name it, Don baby, and you'll
get it." He then led the way to an alcove decorated with
antelope horns and Remington reproductions. The orders
were Scotch and soda for Peggy, a Jack Daniel on the
rocks for David and for Marlowe, a split of champagne
with a shot of brandy on the side. The band started "Red
River Valley." When the drinks came, David commented
on the conservative appearance of the patrons.

"This is a different set of people from the ones you saw
at Hudson's," Marlowe said. "Squares and proud of it."

"What's the attraction here for you, Don?"

"Just that it's cheerful."

"It is that."

Not wishing to question Marlowe in Peggy's presence,
David said nothing about the reason he had come to the
broadcast, but it became plain that whatever Don might
have had to say to David would not be communicated at
The Banjo. Every few minutes the proprietor stopped by
to re-affirm his admiration for Marlowe, who was basking
under the treatment. The man had circulated word of
Marlowe's presence among the customers, and there were
continual requests for his autograph. Some came in person,
some sent menus by waiters, and Marlowe signed gra-
ciously for all. David decided to relax and try to get some

enjoyment from the evening; he wanted to keep thoughts of his father at bay, and not think of what an addition Roxie Dean would have made to their party. With Roxie they would have had at their table two of the best-looking women in New York. From college days David had liked appearing in public with handsome women: Mary had been a beauty. His mind skidded now in Mary's direction, and he felt bleakness and a moment of panic. Then it passed, and he hung on. He looked at the waiter who had been assigned as their special attendant, and pointed at his glass. Another Jack Daniel appeared almost instantly. The band was playing "Dardanella."

"That business I spoke of," Marlowe said. "Can we let it go to the morning?"

"Of course, Don."

David swallowed part of his drink and thought, I'll go off duty now. Everyone else has. You go so far, you take a break, then you pick up the load. He realized that Peggy Alcott was looking at him.

"What are you thinking about?" she asked.

"About the greatest scene I ever saw on television," David said. "I mean the greatest comedy scene. And with all respect to Don, it wasn't on his show."

"I know your kind," Marlowe said. "You look at the opposition."

"We all looked at this, Don. It was the Kennedy inauguration."

"And had a comedy scene?"

"I'll say it did. It came while the Cardinal was praying."

"I'm beginning to remember."

"Then you'll recall that the Cardinal's prayer was exceedingly long."

"I remember that all right," Marlowe said.

"And while the Cardinal was up there, right on the front of the platform, he was completely unaware that a fire had broken out behind him. There was smoke rising straight up out of the floor, and it kept coming. The President was sitting there, absolutely disregarding it, but he could see it, and everybody else in the country could see it. And then these officials began bobbing around in the rear. Man did they look anxious. You could see it written on their faces: 'There goes my job.' And the smoke still pouring and the Cardinal still praying. And the President still rising above it, like a headmaster when something goes wrong on graduation day. But you knew he saw it, and the little guys bobbing around, they looked as though they were dying by inches. And the Cardinal prayed on. Finally they got it out, but I tell you, Preston Sturges in his greatest days never equaled that scene for pictorial comedy."

"You have a strange sense of humor," Marlowe said. "According to you, they must have had a riot of laughs in Dallas."

"Not a bit of it. Tragedy all the way. And that picture of the boy saluting will last forever."

"I think I see what David is getting at," Peggy Alcott said. "You can never be sure without the script."

"Exactly," David said. "And history doesn't write a script. We make it up as we go along."

Marlowe said, "That's known in the trade as ad libbing. If you don't mind, I'll keep my teleprompter."

"That's not the worst idea I've heard today," David said. "And now I must go." He took money from his pocket, and Marlowe said, "Are you crazy, cousin? This is on the cufferoo. Ask the owner if you don't believe it."

"I believe it." David said good night to Peggy and Marlowe, tipped the waiter, and left the place. The band was bursting into "Saints." Outside, he saw autograph hunters patrolling several places along the block, with a scout waiting for Marlowe to leave The Banjo. David's cab driver reported there were movie stars on a pub-crawl in the neighborhood, hence the deployment of autograph collectors. "There's more like what you might say action around here tonight than we had for two, three years," said the driver, a middle-aged man. "Like you may remember, a man like yahself, I don't know, Mistah. You may be a New Yawkah a man like yahself. *If* so, you remember they used to be all night clubs, night life, all parts of the city. You wannah know why? Because the people they had no fear fah themselves. Go out at night, have a good time without no fear fah yahself, fah yah wife or yah girl friend. But not any more. No, sir, not any more."

On the way downtown, the driver discussed a number of recent holdups, knifings, and rapes. "I'm pulling in now," he said as he dropped David at 15 Lexington Avenue. It was half past eleven o'clock.

David went to the apartment and found Louise Bell in the living room. "I hope you weren't waiting for me," he said.

"Oh, no," Louise said. "But your father's asleep and I thought if you came back before twelve you and I might have a nightcap."

"I'd like to," David said, and he poured a little whiskey in a glass, adding White Rock without ice. "What can I get for you?"

"What you're having would suit me nicely," Louise Bell said. David brought her the iceless drink, mixed another for himself, and sat beside her.

"Dad told me about the operation," he said. "He's worried, Ma."

"So am I," Louise Bell said. "It's a question of cancer, David."

"I think they've pretty well ruled that out," David said.

"Nonsense, my dear boy. Your father doesn't know it, but I've talked to Ted Kenyon. This must be the first thing

I ever concealed from your father in my life. Of course Ted wouldn't try to hide anything from me, and he told me to get ready for a bad time."

"If there's no hope, why does he operate?"

"There *is* hope. But only a little."

"That was what I got from Dad," David said. "He's mostly worried about you."

"Whatever it is, I'll be with him," Louise said. "That's what women are for."

"I wish I could really help. One thing—I'll stay here until after his convalescence."

"If he has one."

"I guess you're right, Ma. We'd better adjust our minds to something bad."

Louise Bell had tasted her drink and put it aside. David understood that she had taken it only so he would not be drinking alone. "I don't need this," he said, and set the glass on a table. "In spite of adjusting to what may be bad," he went on, "I'd not forget the hopeful side if I were you. Remember, he hasn't had a day of sickness in his life so far as I recall. He's in good shape for this thing."

"He's a tired man, David," said Louise Bell. "And I think right now you are, too. You mustn't try to do too much. Let's close up, shall we?"

As they walked upstairs, Louise said, "There was a message for you. Roxie Dean telephoned, about half past nine. She wanted to talk to you."

"Think of that."

"I didn't know where to reach you, so her message was, please call her at her office in the morning."

"I'll do it. Good night, Ma."

"Good night, my dear boy. Sleep well."

After a night of dreamless sleep, David went to his office and telephoned Roxie. To his pleased surprise, she wanted him to take her to lunch—they could meet at a quarter to one at the Meadowbrook, if that suited him.

"You have a date," said David. "I'll tell you about Don Marlowe's broadcast and a night club full of banjos and trombones."

His next call was to Marlowe, who sounded subdued as he said, "Ah, yes, amigo. We were going to have a little talk. Some days it doesn't even pay to breathe. But I guess we'll have to face it. Could you come up here?"

"Right away, Don."

David found Marlowe in a Japanese gown and sandals, sitting on the couch in his library and studying two poached eggs. Apparently there was something wrong with the appearance of these eggs, for Marlowe finally pushed the plate away. "No," he said. "No use."

David said, "Anything I can do?"

"Nothing," Marlowe said. "It's always like this after a show night. I can't understand why."

"Natural reaction."

"Maybe so. I don't know how I made it when I went on every night. That was rehearsals every day, amigo. Weekends excepted. Weekends, I'd get married. Well, you've read the story of my life. And now I have things to tell you."

"So you've been saying."

"Forgive the mysterioso," Marlowe said. "Things happen so fast these days, it's hard to get everybody into the schedule. Damned if I see how *you* can be so relaxed. Well, anyhow. In the first place, I want you to know I'm grateful to you for talking to Peter. He tells me you're the first grown person who ever listened to him without getting sore."

"He did make me sore but I tried not to show it."

"You succeeded and I'm very grateful. Something about that interview must have sunk in. Get this picture, David: Peter has accepted a job."

"To your surprise?"

"My complete surprise."

"What's the job?"

"Research assistant in the news department at the network. Oh, sure, I opened the door for him. And he's only
one degree above a uniformed page, but it puts him in a
necessary classification, so the Army will leave him alone.
The idea of being drafted was what had him worried."

"Maybe that had more to do with his going to work
than my listening to him."

"You don't know that kid. Anything *I* say is automatic-
ally out, he'll do exactly the opposite. And he's just no good
for the Army. They might even turn him down as a psycho.
But if they took him, he'd pull some goof and end up in
the stockade, or defect to the Cong if they ever got him to
Vietnam."

"You wouldn't mind that last too much, would you?"

"Be sensible, David. Not for my *own kid*. In spite of
going to college he's only about seven years old mentally.
Network headquarters is the ideal place for him, until that
little wife produces children."

"Even then he'd better keep the necessary occupation.
They may take men with children before they're through."

"I'll warn him about that. He'll believe it if I say you
told me." Don Marlowe pulled the robe around him. His
ankles were a sickish white. "I've got the rams this morning," he said. He pressed a button and a Japanese man
wearing a striped gray apron entered the room.

"India pale ale," Marlowe said. "And remove the re-
mains."

"Eggies no good?"

"Eggies no good. You want something, David?"

"No, thanks."

Marlowe sat muttering to himself until the Japanese
brought four bottles of ale iced in a wine bucket, along
with a heavy silver bottle opener, but no glass, on a tray.

He uncapped one bottle and handed it to Marlowe, who took a long drink.

"That's better," Marlowe said. "Yes, a little better. Now look here, David. I have a feeling about you."

"What is it?"

"I have a feeling that somewhere behind you and George Rollins, we might find Uncle Sugar."

"The federal government."

"How about it?"

"If you probe far enough *anywhere*, you're liable to run into Uncle. I can tell you this, I know people who know him pretty well."

"In other words the answer to my question is yes."

"Some questions don't get answered in words."

"I see," Don Marlowe said. "Mind your own business, and don't embarrass the man."

"I didn't say that."

"Well, I'm grateful to you, David, for your kindness to that dreadful kid, and I'd like to do something in return."

"About the Kane Foundation?"

"In that area."

"I don't suppose there's the slightest chance of Kane using any Institute people," David said.

"About the same as there is of General Sarnoff doing a belly dance on CBS."

"That's what I expected."

Marlowe threw the empty bottle into the fireplace and uncapped another. "I thought that's what you expected. Frankly, the purpose of your whole exercise has been unclear. But I've played along with you so far because you seem like a nice guy and I saw no way you could hurt my colleague and sponsor, Mr. K."

"And he is well protected by another colleague—Dr. September."

"I have heard," Marlowe said, looking away from David

and speaking carefully. "I have heard that Dr. September takes a very close look at all strangers in the parish."

"I have heard he sometimes does more than that."

"It may be. Every man to his own trade, eh, David? I'd be a little happier right now if I could be sure what *your* trade is."

"I can send you a prospectus from the Institute."

"Let's get back to your former trade," Marlowe said. "You were in Washington quite a while, I think."

"That's right."

"I wish you still were. I mean I wish you still had those connections."

"Don, this conversation is familiar to me. I've heard it all before."

"Not around here."

"Of course not here. But the general drift has been the same, so many times."

"You're ahead of me, cousin."

"I know what you're trying to say."

"Enough to say it for me?"

"What you're trying to say is that you want to report something."

"You said you know people who know Uncle Sam."

"I do," David said.

"How about taking me to somebody like that?"

"If that's what you want."

"Yes, I think it is," Don Marlowe said.

"I'll take you tonight if you can make it. Pick you up here at nine-thirty?"

"I'll be waiting."

At the office, David found George Rollins at his desk.

"Any objection to my introducing Don Marlowe to the Colonel?"

"Don wants to talk, does he?"

"It looks that way. How about it?"

"By all means."

"Who shall I tell him Colonel Andrews is?"

"Just Colonel Andrews."

"Isn't that a little offhand? I mean, secrecy about the Colonel, and so on."

"There's no secrecy about him. The opposition knows he's there. So far as Marlowe goes, just tell him the Colonel is the man to see. The end of the line." George Rollins got up, walked to the sofa, and leaned back with his hands behind his head. He went on, smiling at the ceiling as he talked. "I told you this thing was phasing along nicely. By keeping quiet on the substantive level and biding our time, we have Marlowe ready to surface the entire Kane Foundation."

"But George, we know all about it already. What's secret about a publicity-getting organization?"

"That's what I'd like to find out," Rollins said. "And as I see it, Don is the guy who is going to tell us one of these days. Maybe not in this interview, but one of these days."

"George, how did you get to know Marlowe?"

"I thought you'd be wanting to know that some time."

"I really think I need to know."

"I don't mind telling you. It was during my trouble. During part of my trouble. I was up at this place near Lenox. It's like an estate. It was an estate at one time. Now it's a good place for drunks to dry out, and for nervous people to slow down, which was what I needed. It's just like an Edwardian house-party, or so I suppose from what I've heard of Edwardian house-parties."

"The people were guests and not patients."

"That's the idea. Of course they took a certain amount of trouble to see that, uh . . . that the dogs didn't get in and bite us, you understand?"

"I understand," said David.

"And one of the guests was Don Marlowe. As you know,

he's a pleasant fellow. We used to sit on the lawn and talk and look at Berkshires. That's how we got to be friends."

"What did you tell him about yourself, George?"

"Just that I was a man who had worked too hard and needed a rest."

"Wasn't there any security up there?"

"Cleared personnel? No need of it, David. By then I was all right, just tired. Marlowe and I left the place the same day, and I've kept contact because of his Kane operation."

"I hope we get something out of him," David said.

"When do you want to take him to the Colonel?"

"Quarter to ten tonight."

"I'll set it up for you. This is good work, David. Want to lunch on the strength of it? The club? Twenty-One?"

"No thanks, I have a date," David said.

"Fine. Have fun."

At a sofa table in the Meadowbrook an hour later, David found Roxie unusually subdued for a girl who had asked a man to take her out to lunch. She seemed both preoccupied and uncomfortable, like someone looking for an opportunity to get a request for a loan into a conversation with a friend. Things did not go well. Bruno caught the feeling of it, and held solicitous hovering to a minimum. He sensed that there was no use trying to make David look good with flattering attentions: something had gone wrong. And today Charles was making no circuit of the room, but stayed at the end of the bar talking to a man David had not seen before. Roxie paid only polite attention to David's account of the Marlowe broadcast, and they had become silent by the time coffee arrived.

Then Roxie said, "David I think so much of you, and we've become such friends, that I want to tell you something that's happened in my life. I've met a man and I've fallen in love with him, and I'm going to do something about it."

"You mean get married?"

"We're going to be married next week."

David was surprised at the distress this statement caused him. He hadn't been thinking of marriage. Or had he? But now it was evident that a decent instinct had told Roxie he must be informed of what she planned to do. And what she had succeeded in doing to David, though she was not to be blamed, was to give him a feeling of sudden loneliness that went through him like a spear. David thought to himself that whatever the effort cost him, he must conceal this hurt from Roxie. His first move was to say, "You are a surprising girl. You have my good wishes, that shouldn't have to be said." In the effort to seem effortless, David's eyes took in Roxie's face as if for the first time; and he realized that what he had taken to be a subdued look was a look of quiet joy. Ann Sheridan was happy now. David asked, "Who is the man? Someone I know?"

To his intense disgust, David thereupon heard that Roxie's intended husband was a member of the Italian mission to the United Nations. When Roxie talked about him, she spoke in the stunned manner of people in love. She would leave New York when her husband was recalled to Rome, and go with him wherever diplomatic duty took them. Perhaps, David thought, he should tell Roxie that this would be no sort of life, and that her poor little boy would grow up to be a hotel child, and a foreigner. But it wouldn't do—one couldn't say such things. Roxie would have to come out of the anesthetic on her own time. Perhaps she never would. But it was odd, it was very odd, how awful he felt. Somehow he got the bill paid, Bruno standing as though at the deathbed of a valued friend. He got Roxie into a cab, her face openly joyful now that she had performed her little chore of cracking David's heart. The cab drove away. Another came at the doorman's signal.

David got in and gave the address of a bank in Brooklyn. They started out, and the driver, after a look at his passenger's face, decided not to complain about the trip across the river.

The bank was in a tall building in the middle of a business area that looked like downtown Detroit. When David paid, the driver figured his tip and was glad he had not complained when he took this fare into his cab. Sometimes things worked out all right after all.

In the bank, David went to the safety deposit vaults, presented a key, and was left with a large box in one of those fine little rooms where such boxes may be opened by the renters, and their contents examined. He sat in a solid oak chair under a good light at a solid little table, equipped with scissors, sealing wax, bank stationery, ink, and pens. However, David's box contained no financial documents. It was a cache for weapons which he had set up during a period when he sometimes outfitted refugees who planned to return to their native countries. The box contained a number of small pistols and useful things of that sort. What David was after was a sealed manilla envelope, which he put into the inner pocket of his coat. Then he locked the box and rang for the attendant.

Outside the bank, David was looking for a cab when he became aware of a man on either side of him. They were young men, well dressed, and they looked like professional football players, the sort who weigh around two hundred pounds and play defensive halfback. One of them seized David's arm and locked his wrist in the come-along grip. They walked into an alley. The passers-by who noticed the three men and what was happening averted their eyes and hurried on. In the alley, one of the men set himself to hit David, while the other got behind him and locked his arms. David knew they were going to maim him, possibly kill him. He kicked at the man in front, who jumped aside. David heard feet on the pavement, and saw Charles and another man running down the alley. The thug behind him released David's arms and ran at Charles. The restaurant owner let the hoodlum run into his left forearm, which was like an iron bar. The man fell, choking, and Charles kicked him methodically. At the same time Charles's companion bent the other man with a kick to the belly, and slapped a blackjack across the base of his skull as he went down. In five seconds it was all over.

"Out this way," Charles said, starting toward the other end of the alley.

"Hold on," David said. "I want to search them for identification."

The man with Charles said, "If you want, I'll piss on this bastard's head and bring him to."

"Not necessary," Charles said. "We know them. Out this way." They hurried out of the alley at the other end. A few people had peered in from the street at the fallen men, then continued on their way. David did not blame them. In this town you minded your business. Charles whistled down a cab and they piled in. When they had caught their breath, he introduced his companion. It developed that he was the AIPA man assigned to Charles's account. David recalled having seen him talking to Charles in the bar at lunch. The two well dressed hoodlums had also been in the bar, the AIPA man informed David. They had come in shortly after David entered, and quietly ordered soft drinks. The AIPA man had recognized them.

"They're muscle men working for Systems Analysis," the AIPA man said.

As the cab edged into the Manhattan traffic stream on the Williamsburg Bridge, Charles continued, "My doorman reported a strange hackie on the line who wouldn't take his turn. Said he was waiting for a private party. When you left, these two followed you out and got in the strange cab and looked like they were tailing you. We thought we'd better follow in another cab."

"We *knew* we'd better follow you," the AIPA man said. "If we were wrong it wouldn't matter. If we were right you'd need help pretty bad. We knew we were right when we saw their driver tailgating your cab all the way down First Avenue. You know something, Mr. Bell? Those two were college men. The Kane organization recruits for Systems Analysis right out of college. You think I'm kidding? Say there's a young fellow in college wants to go into the rackets, they got recruiters, same as Standard Oil."

Charles said, "Now do you believe me about Systems Analysis?"

"I believed you before," David said. Reaction was mounting in his nervous system, and he yawned deeply. Blood needed oxygen, he noted; adrenalin burned it up. He thanked Charles and the Appleton operative—and how do you thank people who have saved you from broken bones or worse, he thought, as he repeated conventional phrases warmed by genuine gratitude. They dropped him at 15 Lexington Avenue, and before closing the taxi door, the AIPA man leaned out and said, "You be extra careful, Mr. Bell. From now on, you pack a gun. They've got plenty more of those college graduates."

Upstairs, David found Dr. Kenyon with Louise Bell. The surgeon said, "Hello, David, glad you got in. The room I want for your father's available now so we're going to hurry things up a bit. We'll take him to the hospital right now and work on him in the morning. I have my car and I'll drive him up."

"I'll come too," David said.

"That's nice," his stepmother said. "But don't feel you have to. It's just a matter of going to bed."

"I know," David said. "Where is he now?"

"Upstairs, in the workroom."

The late afternoon sun warmed the studio with a mellow glow that showed Roger Bell looking more rested than he had when he told David of his illness. He was standing by the drawing table, looking around the room as if to print it on his memory. When he left it now, he was most probably leaving it forever. The thought was overpowering. There was no way to make light of it. Accepting it was all one could do.

"A lot of my life's in this room," said Roger Bell. David was silent for a moment, making sure he had control of his voice. When he was able to speak in an ordinary tone, he said, "Don't go up there without hope, Dad."

"I haven't abandoned hope," Roger Bell said. "You don't know what hope is till you get to be seventy. We won't give way to despair, my dear young friend. Not the right thing to do."

"Dad, that thing you asked about—the escape hatch?"

"I'm sure you have provided it."

David took out the small manilla envelope. "I'll keep it for you," he said. "If the time comes, you tell me. I'll give it to you then and stand by while you take it. Whatever happens, the bad thing won't happen. We won't let it happen. You'll have it under control."

"Thank you, David. I knew I could depend on you."

At the hospital it was decided that Louise Bell would stay until Roger went to sleep, which he was sure to do early because of a capsule Ted Kenyon planned to give him. Then David would come back and bring Louise home. Ted Kenyon recommended sleeping medicine for her also, as they would operate early in the morning.

"I'm old-fashioned about those things," she said. "If I can't sleep, I just stay awake and make the best of it."

After returning his stepmother that evening to 15 Lexington Avenue, David found that he had half an hour to kill before picking up Don Marlowe. He decided to walk part of the way, and try to arrange his thoughts at the end of as trying a day as he could remember. At the door of the apartment, he went to the hall closet and took out the taped wrench, which was in the pocket of a raincoat, and dropped it into the pocket of the light overcoat he was wearing. Then he set out, walking north on Lexington Avenue.

Organizing his thoughts as he walked along, David acknowledged to himself a feeling of loss where Roxie Dean was concerned, but as he analyzed it, he perceived that wounded pride was involved. No wonder Roxie had refused to go on an every-night basis with David. In the times of unavailability, of course, she had been with the Italian. David could see it now: he had come into contact with Roxie just at the point when a love affair turns into an engagement to marry. At such times there can be quarrels and temporary partings. There also can be reconciliations, the last one permanent, or as permanent as the marriage turns out to be. What a thing, what a thing. A bum lurched away from the wall he had been leaning on and staggered toward David. He grasped the wrench in his pocket and the wino tacked away across the sidewalk. There were many bums north of Grand Central, David knew, so there was no reason to be surprised at seeing them on midtown Lexington Avenue. He felt that the presence of these people throughout the city was not because the derelicts had spread from their traditional quarters along the Bowery, but simply because of a great increase in their numbers. It reminded David of the phonograph record that had delighted him in childhood, on which a comedian asked why the black horses ate more than the white horses, and was told it was because there were more *of* the black horses.

Old simplicities and boyhood satisfactions were utterly gone from David now. Like the city he still wanted to love, his life seemed deafened with senseless noise and choked with unnecessary soot. Why did things have to be this bad? In paying further serious attention to those two laughing academy graduates, George Rollins and Don Marlowe, was he merely acting out a farce? Jim Ewing had said as much. Yet Jim Ewing apparently knew nothing of Colonel Andrews, and David took this as good evidence that Ewing might not be quite so fully informed as he thought. After all, the Company's basic doctrine was "need to know," and there might be a great and essential fact that Jim Ewing did *not* need to know—the fact that the Company had failed, and had been replaced by another Company that would not fail. And in Washington a huge bureaucracy is left to live and grow, like a benign tumor, while the real issues are fought out elsewhere. When David thought of tumors, his mind turned to his father's illness. David was afraid to hope. If he built up hope, and then saw it taken away, it would be unendurable, like waking from the dreams about Mary. Not a bad idea of his father's, the emergency exit. Roger Bell might have to go, and David had in the small envelope something to make sure that when the time came he would go fast.

Meanwhile, as he crossed over to Park Avenue and climbed the hill by the ruined Vanderbilt Hotel, David told himself he must explore the possibility of something useful developing at last from his acquaintance with Don Marlowe. He now had fifteen minutes to get up to Marlowe's flat, and he took the subway for the rest of the trip.

Don Marlowe had rigged himself out for the visit to Colonel Andrews in a trench coat that was all flaps, straps, buttons, pockets, rings, and loops. And when he descended from the Bentley at the art store, he looked around with approval.

"This seems a little less conspicuous than the Pentagon," Marlowe said.

"I believe that's the intention," David said. He rang the bell and the young man who had admitted him before came through the shop and opened the door. In the reception room beyond the fire wall, the man said, "The Colonel is ready to see you." They entered the inner office. Colonel Andrews rose and came forward. "Good evening, Bell," he said. "And Mr. Marlowe. Sit down, gentlemen. Let's be comfortable." Don said nothing, but David observed the angriest expression he had ever seen on Marlowe's face. They continued to stand while the Colonel looked questioningly at David.

"Sit down, Mr. Marlowe," Colonel Andrews said.

"I don't think I'll need to," Marlowe said.

"Come on, Don," David said. "Save the comedy for the show."

"Let's go, David," Marlowe said.

"Did you say go?"

"Yes, I want out."

"But we just got here," David said.

"You stay if you want to. I'm leaving."

"Have you blown your wig? What's the matter with you?" David said. "You wanted to come here."

"And now I want to leave."

"Colonel, I can't understand this," David said. "I feel I owe you an apology."

"Don't worry about it," the Colonel said. He was undisturbed, back in his desk chair, a composed, solid figure. "I have known this to happen. At the last moment, Mr. Marlowe has decided to re-think his position. That's his privilege."

"Then I guess we had better go," David said. "Good night, Colonel Andrews."

"Good night, gentlemen."

Outside, standing beside the Bentley, David said, "That's not my idea of fun."

"Don't try to tell me what's funny," said Marlowe, and his voice was cold. "What do you take me for?"

"Let's not put the bad mouth on each other, old buddy," David said. "I thought you wanted to talk to somebody. So I brought you here. That man is my boss."

"Don't give me that, old buddy."

"You heard me tell you," David said.

"Then I'll tell *you* something. It's short but good: never try to fool an actor with an actor."

"I don't understand you."

Don Marlowe said, "I mean that colonel-guy in there is an *actor*. That's Kendall Andrews, an old soap opera leading man. He got that scar at the Chicago Stadium when he was hit by a puck while he was watching a hockey game between the Black Hawks and the New York Rangers. I was there."

"Are you sure of that?"

"You're damn right I'm sure. What are you trying to pull on me?"

"I'm not trying to pull anything, Don. I'm as surprised as you are. Why don't you just tell *me* whatever's bothering you? I still have friends in Washington."

"With AFTRA cards like Kendall Andrews?"

"If you really want to get something off your chest, *I* can handle it. I promise you that."

But Don Marlowe had no more to say. He got into the Bentley without inviting David to come along, and the car glided off. David stood where he was for a moment, then turned south and walked to the Westbury Hotel, and looked into the Polo Lounge. All the patrons were in couples, man and girl. He decided against exhibiting himself as a solitary figure at the bar. There was no trouble-solvent now in Jack Daniel or Chivas Regal or the Glenlivet. David had the kind of trouble that thrives on fuel of that sort, and its name was failure. He went out and walked on, alone as a man can be. What was the use, he asked himself. For he knew the humiliating truth: the Company had cast an actor in the role of bellwether for its failures—a professional who could exactly portray the figurehead they wanted to serve under. David had been discarded into a farcical situation—a charade to keep him quiet until, like the old elephants, he had the decency to die.

I I

IN THE MORNING David waked tired and aching, but to the realization that there had been no dreams. His first task was to take his stepmother to the hospital where Roger Bell was to undergo surgery at half past ten. He had breakfast with Louise in the hospital coffee shop, and looked in on Roger, who was smiling and semi-conscious with the preparatory drugs. Then David went on to the office, where he found Mrs. Martin beaming brightly.

"Mr. Rollins is here early today, Mr. Bell, and he'd like to see you."

"I'll go right in," David said.

"How'd you make out last night?" George asked when David came into his room.

"Oh, it went fine, George. One of the greatest productions the Company has ever put on."

"Give me the details."

"We've taken care of Marlowe as a source. Dried him up for good."

"Dried him up?"

"We have succeeded in convincing him that all we want to do is make him look silly."

"But what happened?"

"I took him in there and the minute he saw the Colonel he froze."

"I don't see why he should do that," George Rollins said.

"I didn't either, but when he told me the reason, I understood very well. Come to think of it, I guess I'm sore too. It turns out that our Colonel Andrews is an actor."

"Oh, is *that* all?"

"It's enough."

George Rollins swung his great chair, tipped it back, and lifted his irreplaceable Peal shoes to the desk edge. "I see nothing wrong," he said. "Of course the Colonel is an actor."

"You're not surprised?"

"I knew it all the time," Rollins said. "Certainly he's an actor. A former actor at any rate. He was also a colonel in Air Force Intelligence. What's wrong with that?"

"And you don't think he's been put in that office because he looks the part, and can pacify us elephants?"

"Pacify us what?"

"It's a phrase I heard someone use. My point is, ever since I came close to Marlowe and his big friend Jefferson Kane, I've been getting pressure from Kane's Gestapo. First I had trouble at the apartment—well, maybe that was just by chance. Then I found a bum hanging around down there, claimed he was a diplomat. I told you about him. Then a pair in Brooklyn yesterday, and they meant business I can tell you. There's something going on around Kane that he doesn't want dragged into the light of day. Maybe he's just planning to steal something. I'd still like to know what. So, Don Marlowe says he has things on his mind, he wants to talk. I say I'll take him right to the end of the line, and I show him a man who used to play soap opera out in Chicago! The result is that Marlowe doesn't trust anybody. But he just might have something important on his mind, and I think he's basically a decent man."

"I think so too, David. I expect a lot of mileage out of Don Marlowe, one way or another."

"Then let me make a suggestion."

"Go ahead," George said.

"You talk to Marlowe. He's decided I'm a fraud. But you might still be able to get somewhere with him. How about giving it a try?"

"Very well, David, I'll do it. We don't want to lose ground just when we've started blooding the troops."

Wincing inwardly at the familiar expression, which had so little meaning on George's lips, David left the room. Outside, he said to Mrs. Martin, "I'm going up to New York Hospital now. Please be sure to make a note if Mr. Marlowe calls."

"Of course, Mr. Bell."

At the hospital, David was told that his father was still in the recovery room. He spoke to Louise Bell, and then walked along the corridor with Ted Kenyon to a window that looked out over the Queensborough Bridge.

Ted Kenyon said, "David, it's turned out hopeless. That thing is all around the aorta. I felt like crying when I saw it."

"How long can he hold on?"

"We can give him a little radiation and mustard gas, but you'll have to think in terms of weeks. Very few weeks. I can't tell you how sorry I am."

"Have you told my mother?"

"Yes, as I promised."

"Is he out of the anesthetic yet?"

"I wouldn't try to talk to him till this afternoon, David."

As it turned out, Roger Bell lay quiet all that day and night. Next day he was able to talk, and in the afternoon he sent his invincibly cheerful wife downstairs to the hospital tea room so that he could speak privately to David. Mr. Bell looked bad and his voice was weak.

"It's a strange thing, David," he said, "but all these years I've been libeling a good airplane, the Caproni 450. Three Isotta-Fraschini engines, one in the back as a pusher, quite advanced for the time when you think of it."

"I'm sure you always gave the impression you really respected the aircraft," David said.

"Very unfair to Johnny Caproni if I hadn't," Roger Bell continued. "Flew at night, you know, down the valley to the Adriatic. Followed the river by starshine. Austrians tried to pick us up with searchlights from the mountains on either side and shot at us with cannon. There were six Americans in my squadron. Two killed, one wounded, one crashed in enemy territory and walked out. And two of us not a scratch. Not so bad. Nothing to complain of."

"I never heard you complain about anything."

"I did something I'm ashamed of not long ago. Asked you to provide a bit of medication. I wanted to tell you I've changed my mind. It won't be necessary. Yes, Kenyon's told me the prognosis. I won't go much farther, David. And I've decided to make it under my own power. Fact is I'm curious to see what happens."

"You're not out of the running yet, Dad."

"Not as of this minute," said Roger Bell. "Kenyon says they'll send me home in a few days, after I get a final dose of radiation. A little of that goes a long way."

"You're getting tired. Don't talk."

"I'll rest a bit now. Don't stay, David. Your mother will be right up."

"Let me wait until she comes back, unless it bothers you."

"I was thinking you might be busy, have somewhere to go. Whatever you do, you're not to worry about me."

David stayed until Louise Bell returned. She was as cheerful as though at a party, moving lightly around the room, arranging flowers and talking about nothing in particular. Yes, David thought, women are wonderful. He shook his father's hand, kissed Louise, and turned to go as the lights came on. The so-called reading lamps at hospital beds were designed, of course, only to glare in the eyes of the sick. By Ted Kenyon's order, a Tensor light had been rigged for Roger Bell's reading, and as David was leaving, Louise started opening a parcel from Scribner's bookstore. David came back from the door to glance at the titles, and said, "All history and biography, Dad. Your usual order. Why don't you go on a real binge now, and read a novel?"

Mr. Bell said, "I haven't read a work of fiction since *The Magnificent Ambersons*. And I'm one of the happiest men in New York. There may be a connection. See you tomorrow."

At 15 Lexington Avenue, David lit the living room fire, made sandwiches and tea in the kitchen, and brought a tray into the library. The room reminded him powerfully of his stepmother and his father. It was true, his father had lived in this house for forty years, and everything David saw around him in the spacious and handsome room had been there always, so far as he could remember. There must have been changes over the years, but even when David could identify them he could not have told when they took place. A picture here, a Lowestoft bowl on a table—they might have grown there, gently and slowly. It was startling to think that when his father had first lived here, he had been ten years younger than David was now. And now his father was talking of being brought home to die. David had a feeling that this would not happen. In all probability, Roger Bell had looked for the last time on his favorite coaching print, which hung over the fireplace. But whether he came home or not, Roger Bell had refused to be defeated. Or at least, he had refused to admit defeat, and had rebuked that knave death for his ill-mannered way of pushing in where he hadn't been invited.

David knew now that an overwhelming realization had come into his mind, a feeling so powerful as to mark a turning point. It was the realization that since his father was behaving in this dauntless way when confronted with ultimate terror, he himself would have to follow the example. Life was never easy. Talent and achievement made people, but neither of these was worth an instant's attention without some sort of integrity, and attaining *that* was hard. You did it on your own time, making it out of what you could find in yourself, and anything you could put together in the way of courage. And in the process of reaching integrity, you had to look at yourself from time to time, and you did not like what you saw. And when basic reality was finally revealed, you knew that you were running alone, and the fox would go to the furrier at last. The emergency exit was an imaginary thing. There was no escape. David got up, crossed the room, and tossed the small manilla envelope, with its contents, into the fire.

David thought on: Suppose he *was* cast off from the Company years before his time. He had no excuse for allowing this to break his spirit, for it had not been due to any fault of his. It had been a matter of luck. On that subject, a Mr. John Oakhurst, of Poker Flat, had said the last word: "Luck is a mighty queer thing. All you know about it for certain is that it's bound to change." Whether or not the time of change in his personal luck was near, David now decided that at the very least, he would find out what was bothering Don Marlowe. For in this situation, he said to himself, there were certain realities, in spite of all the play-acting. One reality was that persons of evil intent had taken a deadly interest in a man named David Bell. Another was that Sir Ronald Maxwell-Spencer was a most peculiar man. An odd man, a very odd man. Above all, his patron Jefferson Kane was a singular man, as powerful as he was strange. David considered Kane: here was a man with the power literally to get away with murder. And David had received a strong impression that Don Marlowe was scared.

Marlowe might have good reason to be frightened. A non-serious man involved in serious business will always come to a point, on some grim day, at which the penalty for frivolity must be paid. The powerful men of this world were humorless men, and they wanted deadpan loyalty. No jokes. No fraternizing with the enemy. If Kane resented David so much that he set Dr. September on him, then sooner or later, resentment would extend to Don Marlowe. Here a calculus of motive and pressure might come into play that could leave the network minus a star, and Peter and Jeffrey without a father. David told himself he'd be damned if he would let that poor ham be used as a tethered goat to attract the tigers; it wasn't right, that's all. He went to the hall telephone and called George Rollins' New York apartment.

"Yes, David?"

"George, about our friend the television star. Have you seen him?"

"I talked to him on the phone," Rollins said.

"Any results?"

"He's not at all happy. Seems to be afraid he's been compromised in some way by seeing the Colonel."

"All he did was walk in and walk out," said David.

"That's true, but it's made him awfully unhappy."

"When he talked to you, was he drunk?"

"It's hard to tell with Marlowe. He didn't sound drunk, more like he was scared."

"That could be important," David said.

"There's nothing in it," Rollins said. "There's no danger to this man at all. None whatsoever. I tried to tell him but he wouldn't believe me."

"How about those people in Brooklyn?"

"What people in Brooklyn?"

"The ones who wanted to take me apart."

"Maybe you just ran into a couple of wise guys, David. This town is full of people discharging aggression and hostility."

"No argument there," David said.

"Don will be all right. Just let him cool off a day or two."

"Any objection to my seeing him?"

"He might object. Better leave him alone."

"I may try to talk to him anyhow, George."

"All right, but I warn you. He can be difficult. Maybe you haven't seen that side."

"I'll be tactful."

"You're always that, David. See you tomorrow."

David took a cab to Marlowe's place, and gave his name to the polite old doorman, who telephoned upstairs, and then reported, with sorrow, that Mr. Marlowe was not at home. The Bentley, however, was parked next to the cleared space in front of the door, with the Japanese at the wheel—sure sign that its owner was soon due to emerge from the building. David walked a short distance up the block, stopped, and waited. After fifteen minutes had gone by, the elderly doorman hurried across the side-walk and opened the limousine's door. Peggy Alcott came out and got into the tonneau, and David stepped in on the other side just as the door was closed on Don Marlowe.

"Get lost, pal," Marlowe said.

"Eddie Robinson in *Little Caesar*," David said. "Not your role, amigo."

"I thought I sent down word I wasn't at home."

"Not very friendly of you, considering you *were* at home."

Peggy Alcott said, "I thought it was strange, myself. You boys are supposed to be buddies."

Marlowe said, "The mutual admiration society has disbanded."

"But you sound so unpleasant," Peggy said.

"Too bad," Marlowe said. "We regret to announce that Dr. Jekyll has sold his practice and moved to Pasadena. His patients are now being cared for by Mr. Hyde."

"I'm sorry, Don," David said. "And I'll get out now if you say so. But I see no reason for the quarrel scene."

"Because you let me down, that's the reason."

"Nothing of the sort," David said. "You two have dinner with me and we'll talk it out."

"We're on the way to eat now, at Bossanetti's."

"Cancel that, Don, and let me take you to the Meadowbrook."

"Why there?"

"The most important reason in the world. You'll be safe there."

They rolled on in silence for a moment. Then Marlowe said, "You call that a safe spot, huh?"

"Yes, and it has nothing to do with George or the man you saw last night. How about it?"

"All right, if Peggy approves."

"I'd like to go there," Peggy Alcott said.

Charles put them at a table that fitted a curved banquette in a corner of the room. Then for an instant David felt dizzy and short of breath because of two people he saw across the restaurant. They were Roxie Dean and a man who must be her fiancé. The man was extremely handsome. Hell, he looked something like Mastroianni. Roxie looked up, caught David's eye and smiled, adding a tiny wave of her hand. David smiled and bowed.

"*Who* is that beautiful girl who is ogling you?" Peggy asked.

"An old friend called Roxie Dean."

"And who's the man?"

"I believe that's her fiancé. Good-looking fellow."

"Only if you like that type," Peggy said. "I don't care for them too greatly."

"I knew you were beautiful, and I see you're intelligent as well," David said. "I now confess that I've eaten. So I'll just go on with salad or something while you two find out what Charles's chef can do."

Peggy Alcott ordered lightly, while Marlowe called for cocktails, wine, and an enormous dinner. When the food was brought, he scarcely touched it. But he had his wineglass filled to the brim, and emptied it several times. As he did so, he became a little more cheerful.

"I'm sorry I cut up rough about your getting in the car, David. The nerves are a little shot these days."

"That's all right," David said. "I'm not sensitive. But this nervous trouble. Has it just come on you?"

"Just in the last few days. Maybe I'm working too hard."

"Don't try to be the richest guy in the cemetery, Don."

A troubled look appeared on Marlowe's face. He tapped the table and said, "Knock on wood. When I was broadcasting five times a week, the wise guys used to tell me, 'No pockets in a shroud, boy.' Nice way of putting it."

David said, "Perhaps you could lighten your load by giving up the communications panel for Kane's Foundation."

Peggy Alcott said, "I've suggested the same thing."

Marlowe said, "But you have to do something to justify your existence."

"Maybe they don't need you any more," David said. "They can have page one any time they want it, now that Sir Ronald's in the country."

"Yes, it's true, Sir Ronald can have page one, Cronkite, Huntley-Brinkley, any time he likes. But I don't think that's the reason they dropped me."

"You say they *dropped* you?" David asked.

"I may as well own up to it, cousin," Marlowe said. "If I'm a press agent, I'm out of a job."

"How does one get fired from a volunteer job?" Peggy asked.

"Just the same as if they were paying you," Marlowe said. "I went to Kane to talk about that Limey being interviewed on the Great Minds series, and he said to forget it, they weren't interested. And he added that I needn't trouble myself about any of it in the future."

"That Mr. Kane," Peggy said. "A frightening old scoundrel he seemed. Something like Mr. Tulkinghorn in *Bleak House*."

"Exactly," David said. "An old guy who goes around finding out secrets. My hunch is, he has a few himself."

"He certainly didn't say thanks for anything I may have done for him," Marlowe said.

"Kane's not the type for that," David said. "Do you lose him as a sponsor, too?"

"Not till the Nielsens drop, old buddy."

"Then you're free of a job that wasn't even paid in gratitude," David said.

"That's what I tried to tell Don," Peggy said. "It was like playing a benefit. He did his best and now it's over."

"I'm glad to hear you're through with Kane," David said. "I don't think he's a man you really want to train with. But look here, you people. I've broken in on your date. Maybe I could see you later, Don? Or tomorrow?"

"Stick with me, old buddy," Marlowe said. "We only had a dinner date. I'll be alone for the evening because Peggy has a first reading of her new show."

"Off broadway," Peggy said. "And another revival, *The Second Mrs. Tanqueray*. We're doing it straight, with wonderful, authentic costumes, and the sets are by Billy Aubrey."

"Sounds like a good idea," David said.

"Wish us luck, anyhow," Peggy said. "I'll be cured of revivals if this doesn't go."

Roxie Dean and the Italian got up and left, without looking at David, and the desolate feeling came back as he watched her go. The next to leave, he supposed, would be Peggy Alcott. What had become of women who stayed where they were supposed to be? Of course, actresses weren't women. But he had to admit Peggy looked surprisingly like one. She said, "You're both as gloomy as though you'd lost your last friend. There's to be a party after the reading. Why don't you come down? New Arts Theater, Minetta Lane. Party in the Fiesole Restaurant next door. Come on, now. Both of you."

David and Marlowe agreed, and a schedule was worked out. The Bentley would take Peggy to the theater for the reading, then return to the Meadowbrook and transport the men to Marlowe's apartment. Later in the evening they would go down to Minetta Lane for the party.

"Good-bye for now, Peggy," Marlowe said, not getting up. "See you later," David said, as he stood in the gangway to allow Peggy to slip by. Passing in the narrow space she brushed against him. There's one good thing, David thought, this girl is not too damned thin. Those living skeletons in the fashion magazines make me wonder about the future of the race. But this is a woman. No, an actress. Well, never mind.

"I was slightly daunted there for a few minutes, cousin. Think nothing of it."

"I believe I understand your trouble now," David said. "And I don't blame you for being nervous."

"You think you understand."

"Yes."

"Maybe you're the guy everybody is looking for," Marlowe said. He might be a little drunk now, but his tolerance for alcohol was so great that, as George Rollins had said, it was hard to judge his condition. Thinking of that telephone call, David said, "Don, where did you meet George Rollins?"

"At an exclusive country club," Marlowe said. "Hasn't he told you? We're both alumni of dear old Shady Rest. Try it yourself some time, David. Good for what ails you."

"So I've heard."

Bruno came up and said, "Mr. Marlowe's car has returned." Like most tremendously rich people, Don Marlowe put up no fight over the check, nor did he offer any thanks to David for his untouched dinner, plus cocktails, wine, and brandy. But on the other hand, Marlowe never seemed to expect thanks when *he* provided such things. He had been in the big money so long that expensive surroundings had become natural and accepted, and he inhabited a world where every meal shared with another human being was in some way or other a business meal. And so farewell courtesy, welcome expedience. The Bentley stood at the curb.

In Marlowe's apartment all was quiet, and they went to the library.

"Younger boy's at his aunt's tonight," Marlowe explained. "That's why you hear nothing from the sound effects department. And what would you like from *this* department?" He was standing by the grog table.

"Nothing for me," David said, and Marlowe prepared a drink and sat heavily in a deep leather chair. "Solid comfort," he remarked. "Which I wish I could enjoy."

"You still haven't got it off your chest."

"Got what?"

"Whatever was bothering you."

"You don't have any way of knowing that," Marlowe said.

"But I do have a way. Common sense."

"Oh, that."

"It's all I've got, Don. I'm not clever."

"Old buddy, you're clever enough for a country boy like me."

"The point is, you still have something on your mind—whatever it was you wanted to tell somebody who worked for Uncle Sam."

"This is some kind of mind-reading act?" Marlowe asked. "If so, I can tell you it's no good."

"Listen to me. What does a man do if he wants to report something to the authorities? He calls the cops—either the New York police or the Bureau—the FBI. But not you. It was a little different, the way you wanted to play it. You were looking for people in the government, sure enough. But they had to be special people."

"How do you mean that, cousin?"

"They had to be government people who were not police. Now what makes a man back away from the police? Only one thing—the fear that they might put him in jail. And a man like you could only be jailed if he were mixed up in something that my friends call terrific. Very, very terrific. Now how about it, Don?"

Marlowe raised a pewter tankard and swallowed some of the drink. When he put the tankard down, he sat staring at the rug for a moment; then he got up, walked to the fireplace, and leaned against the mantelpiece. Above him a clown by Rouault glowed like stained glass. "Old son," he said, "you are absolutely right, and I'll give you the cold laydown. I wanted to use your channels because I did not want those Bureau types to throw me in jail."

"I'll bet you're even more afraid of Dr. September."

"God, yes," Marlowe said. He looked old, and there was no trace of merriment left in him. "And you didn't see how Kane looked at me when he said I needn't hang around any longer. To think I once took that man for a harmless, rich rube."

"So it *is* Kane."

"Yes, Kane and the Limey. David, I think these people have gone completely round the bend. And they've had their heads together since the Maxwell-Spencers got here, planning some kind of political coup."

"That's not news."

"This isn't one of their usual schemes, to get in the papers, or on the T and V. *I* helped them with those things. This one is a nightmare." Marlowe put the tankard aside, and leaned back in the solid leather chair, his hands moving on the arms as if to assure himself of that much reality.

"If you'll give me some specific facts, the nightmare can become my responsibility."

"And no longer mine? I don't think it can be that easy."

"At least I'll have a share of the responsibility."

"Will you believe what I tell you?"

"Yes."

"Maybe you will and maybe you won't. It's a real grabber."

"It must be, to turn you against those people."

"Well, man, you can only go so far. And what Kane and those Limeys are planning to do is pull off a political operation that involves the explosion of fissionable material."

"How do you mean that?"

"*Fissionable material,* I said. An atomic explosion. A big bang."

"Where?"

"At the Pathfinder Atomic Power Plant in Sioux Falls, South Dakota."

"When?"

"Three days from now, on Friday, when Sir Ronald and his lady visit the place, with honors as eminent scientists."

"They'd hardly blow themselves up, Don."

"I should have said, they will plant the nuclear trigger. After that, the big bang can come any time."

"It's not possible."

"The hell it isn't, old buddy. Sir Ronald has a little device about the size of a camera. He has it covered to resemble a cigar case. Nobody will shake him down when he visits the plant, he's too big a wheel. And you know how nasty he can be when reporters are around. So he takes this thing right in there, and it's time-set. They're to be there three hours, including lunch. During this time, Sir Ronald retires to a men's room. He hangs up his coat to wash his hands. At the same time, a Systems Analysis man comes in. He hangs up *his* coat, brushes against Sir Ronald's, palms the case and pockets it. Later on this fellow conceals the thing in the right place on the installation. And he damn sure calls in sick for the day it's set to trigger the big blast."

"He's an employee, a Systems Analysis man working at the atomic plant?" David asked.

"Certainly. Don't you think they can get one man in among thousands? I was reading the other day that even the National Security Agency had been penetrated."

"I don't say it couldn't happen."

"I'm telling you, the whole thing is laid on, as Sir Ronald says."

"Don, this does sound like a nightmare. Are you sure of it?"

"As sure as I'm talking to you."

"But how do you *know*?"

"Jim Hawkins in the apple barrel."

"You overheard."

"You catch the allusion, old cousin. I overheard."

"How?"

"It was up in Kane's suite. I had lunch with him day before yesterday. Everybody happy. Well, he took himself off after lunch and I decided to stay right where I was, and try conclusions with a bottle of Fundador the catering manager had left on the serving table. He probably meant to come back and steal it. But I got in my licks, and pretty soon—Sleepsville."

"I've seen you do that."

"Greatest relaxer in the world. I went in the main room and climbed on one of those high-backed couches, the one that faces the fireplace, remember it?"

"Yes, its back is to the room."

"You're right with me, old buddy. Back to the room. Anybody coming in wouldn't know I was there, unless they passed between the fireplace and the couch. And all my wives have admitted I have one good thing about me: I don't snore. So, I went to sleep. And so, I woke up and heard Kane and the Maxwell-Spencers talking. They were getting the bugs out of their plan and Kane was telling Sir Ronald he could depend on the Systems Analysis man at Sioux Falls. The Limey didn't think *anything* in the U.S. was any good, but Kane assured him Dr. September knew his business and he had a national set-up that amounted to a private Gestapo, and even more efficient than the Heinies ever were. The question was, did Maxwell-Spencer have his atomic trigger device ready? Oh yes. Most certainly. But how can they alert the SA cell out at Pathfinder? In your bloody country the McCarthyites have made it impossible to send a private message. This one will be private, Kane says. So private that forty million people will see it. His remark gets zero laughs from the Britishers, so Kane explains the SA people at Sioux Falls will be watching the Don Marlowe Show and an SA man in New York will give the signal when the camera pans for a crowd shot. The signal will mean, be ready to carry out the plan when Sir Ronald visits the place. So all right. You can imagine I thought I was dreaming all this. But no. I knew I couldn't be dreaming when they began checking off points in their plan like a pilot getting ready to lift a Seven-Oh-Seven. In doing this, they showed what they expected to accomplish. Oh, twenty to thirty thousand people would be killed, but that wasn't the target. The main objective would be to cause world opinion to consider that this proved the U.S. wasn't capable of handling any form of atomic energy."

"God knows what difference world opinion would make," David said.

"They thought it would make a hell of a lot of difference at the United Nations," Marlowe said. "But that wasn't all. There was Washington. There's to be absolutely nothing left of the reactor and the surrounding plant. No evidence one way or the other of what caused the big rack-up. So, suppose Washington decided this had been done by Soviet agents, even by a Soviet missile? What then? The President and his advisers would be bound to lose, whatever steps they took. Suppose it went to the limit: nuclear war, America versus the Soviets. According to these people, the war would end with the U.S. totally destroyed, but plenty still standing in Russia. This would be all to the good, for their dearest friends, the Chinese Reds, would come out in the best shape of all—unharmed, with the U.S. destroyed entirely, and Russia cut down to size. You understand, Kane and the Maxwell-Spencers would be safe in Canada during the atomic war. And whatever the final result of the caper might be, the U.S. would lose a great deal, maybe everything. That was a thought that made them very happy. Old son, don't you agree they must be clear out of their heads? I mean to say, those people must be absolutely starkers."

"And after you heard them talking, how did you get out?"

"I didn't. Not without their knowing it, I mean. The catering manager came back, looking for the Fundador bottle, the son of a bitch. Jim Hawkins had better luck in his barrel."

"The moon came up and the lookout sighted Treasure Island."

"Very convenient. But in my case, that motherin' catering manager came by the front of the couch and saw me and started harrumphing and saying, 'Mr. Marlowe, sir. Extremely sorry to have disturbed you, sir.' Then he got out of there."

"And what did you do?"

"Pretended I'd just been waked, of course. I gave the 'Wha? Whassat?' routine and got up staggering around. I was so scared, I'm sure I overplayed it. The three of them looked at me. There was something about their eyes. Jefferson says, 'How long have you been there, Marlowe?' 'Since just after lunch,' I tell him. 'I always sleep at that time. I find it's the deepest sleep I get.' 'I see,' Kane says. I can't tell whether they believe me or not about having just waked up. Lady Maxwell-Spencer says, 'The man's a fool.' I liked the sound of that. Her husband mutters something to Kane, and they all walk out. Next day I decide to go to see Kane as if nothing had happened and he fires me from my unpaid job with the Foundation. And after I saw Kane, something happened to prove I hadn't dreamed the whole thing."

"You got a call from Dr. September."

"And he asked me if I was interested in buying any stage effects for my show. I was cautious, and said it would depend on what they were. He said he had a pretty good magic effect which he'd be glad to demonstrate. He said it would make people disappear. The odd part is, he almost made me believe he was talking about making people literally vanish. But I said I didn't do a magic act.

Which of course he very well knew. Then he said he was
sorry we weren't associated any longer as colleagues of
Mr. K. I said I was sorry, too, and he talked a little longer,
all about the greatness of Mr. K. and the necessity of
seeing that he wasn't bothered, and I said I had no intention of bothering anybody. Finally he went away and I
started working to convince myself that I hadn't heard
those three in the hotel suite, that it hadn't happened at
all. David, you know it can be like that, when something
awful happens?"

"I know."

"You think at first you can make it unreal?"

"It's like that, yes."

"I did fairly well on it, with the help of John Barley-
corn, until time for my show. But then I watched the
audience, and there was that man signalling with his
handkerchief."

"Don't people do that sometimes, Don? For Aunt Minny
back in the home town?"

"Oh yes, but not the way this fellow did. And he looked
different from the usual studio fan."

"I saw him too, Don. He was an SA man. But after the
show you didn't seem disturbed. You looked happy and
relaxed. How was that?"

"I was putting it off, putting off telling you. We'd just
had a great show, I had my check in my pocket. They
pay me right there in the studio each week, did you know
that? Peggy was there, and everything familiar, so I just
decided to push it all back another 24 hours. I showed
my nerves with that autograph kid, but as soon as we
got inside and the drinks were in front of us, I began to
believe things might work out after all. Even when you
told that story of a near-disaster. So I killed the giant on
a temporary basis at least. But in the morning I knew
you can't run forever."

"You have to stop somewhere."

"Well, there you have it. What do I do now?"

"Right now, I suppose you go to that party downtown," David said.

"I think I'll give up on that. I'm too tired."

"This isn't like you," David said.

"I feel like hell. Maybe from the strain of telling you all this."

"You shouldn't be here alone."

"Then you believe me."

"Suppose I didn't? And suppose I was wrong. You'd be in danger. Let's arrange for what's known as a factor of safety."

"Not those Bureau people, David. All I have is hearsay. Remember, I've been in Shady Rest and one or two other little nooks of that sort. The Bureau might throw a net over me and there'd be publicity. And the network has a clause in the contract that would fire me like that."

"I'm thinking of worse trouble than getting fired by a network. So let's assume you need protection. Here's what you do. Call Charles at the Meadowbrook. He met you with me tonight. Tell him I said for him to get hold of his AIPA man and have your apartment covered from now on. Tell him to put a uniformed man at the package entrance downstairs and a couple of plain-clothes operatives up here. Call right now, and I'll stay till you're covered."

"The AIPA? What's that?"

"Appleton International Protective Agency."

"The Appletons."

"That's right, the people who used to be the heavies. The company gunmen. Still available when needed."

"It's like sending for a private army."

"That's what it is. We're in a Florentine period now, and private armies are a necessary thing. You know the

New York police are helpless. And the Bureau isn't for you in this case. I'll tell you one thing, the Appletons don't give a damn about SA men. So go on and make that call, or shall I make it?"

"No, I'll do it," Marlowe said, and left the room. In a few minutes he returned and said, "They're on the way."

"Good. You try to relax now. We'll work this out."

"What are you going to do?" Marlowe asked.

"I think I'll go along to that party in the Village."

"Won't you tell somebody in Washington about the Pathfinder plant?"

"There's no use trying to make anyone believe such a story over the telephone. It has to be told face to face. I'll fly to Washington early in the morning. Meanwhile, I want to be sure Peggy's all right. How many times have you taken her up to Kane's place?"

"I don't remember exactly, but quite a few."

"Then they know she's a friend of yours."

"Seems so."

"I'll have a look down at the Village punch-up."

"And put AIPA men with Peggy?"

"If it seems necessary," David said. "Maybe she'd rather get out of town."

"Not that one, with a play in rehearsal. You can take my car and driver if you like."

"No, thanks, Don. A cab will be less conspicuous."

A few minutes later David was riding down Park Avenue in a taxicab, trying to arrange his thoughts and reach some kind of firm conclusion. He had posted AIPA men at the front and service entrances of Marlowe's flat, and at the building's delivery entrance in the rear downstairs. Now he was confronted with the hard intellectual effort of identifying provable factors in a situation that might still be fantasy, even a practical joke on Marlowe's part. David had one sure element to work on: the men of Systems Analysis, Jefferson Kane's security organization, had behaved as though motivated by the arrogance of conscious power. To this he, David Bell, could testify. And Dr. September had threatened Marlowe with his talk of making people disappear. Or so Marlowe had said. But could one believe his story? Was he sane? Or had alcohol invaded the brain tissue to such an extent that he had lost touch with reality? David decided he did believe Marlowe. There were too many strange things going on all over the world for any kind of skepticism to be justified at this point. At any rate, he must *assume* that Marlowe told the truth, until the whole story could be checked out.

And if Marlowe still held on to sanity, David reflected as the cab continued on its way, what about Kane and Maxwell-Spencer? Were they sane? He mentally built the argument that they were not. Observe first a symptom of emotional obsession: their continuous, unmitigated hatred of the United States. Granted every error in the country's policies at home and abroad, still it argued mental unbalance to hold that the U.S.A. should be destroyed as the enemy of humanity. Note that Jefferson Kane was like a man busily sawing off the limb on which he was sitting; what could he possibly expect from Russians or Chinese when they no longer needed his help with their propaganda? And the Maxwell-Spencers: scientists who would accept obviously fraudulent proof of any American villainy, such as that which they had so eagerly endorsed in North Korea ten years before. Everything fell into place once you theorized that these people must be crazy. Hatred, the world's most dangerous drug, had fastened on them years before; they had become addicted, and now, insanely self-centered and self-righteous, they would meddle with the very materials they said the U.S. could not be trusted with: fissionable explosives.

As he considered all this, David's heart grew faint. In Washington, he would have to tell his tale to people who had already lost faith in his judgment. He would be talking to overworked officials, to whom his voice would be nothing but a lonely and unwelcome cry from the valley of the dying elephants.

The Fiesole Restaurant had become fashionable during a two-year run at the neighboring New Arts Theater of a brilliantly revived Elizabethan tragedy, John Ford's *'Tis Pity She's a Whore*. The proprietor had gone snobbish and installed a plush-covered rope and a maiter dee in the entrance to the dining room, something the original customers would neither forget nor forgive when the theater closed and its acting company moved to Connecticut. Tonight, however, the owner was rubbing his fat white hands with pleasure as a great crush of people overflowed the barroom and filled the stairway, pushing up to the party in the banquet room on the second floor.

David checked his hat and raincoat and joined the press on the stairs. As he slowly mounted the stairway, David thought this would be a bad time for a fire alarm. People were so close his elbows were held to his sides. Someone behind him was pushing. Unmannerly thing to do—and then David felt a sharp pain. He thought, somebody has let me have a needle in the arm. He tried to turn and see who had done it. The top of the stairs moved away and seemed to swoop off to infinite distance, smaller and smaller, while he tried to reach it on legs that would not move. Then a black curtain came down and covered all.

12

Consciousness came back a little at a time. First it was a sensation of light through a white screen. Then there was the feeling of being covered with bandages. He was lying on his back on a hard surface. That much could be determined. He felt light-headed, as one does when recovering from the anesthetic after being brought from an operating room. David thought, am I in a hospital? He could hear people talking, and the sound of feet on a hard floor. He felt that his face and head were covered with wrappings, as well as his body. He breathed deeply, raising his chest, and felt the bandages tighten. As he inhaled air, a smell came with it. Formaldehyde. He took another deep breath and caught the same chemical odor, together with another smell, faint but pervasive, and not quite definable. David moved his fingers. His hands were bandaged. He tried to hear what the people in the room were saying. All he could make out was some sort of technical conversation.

David found that he could move his legs—the bandages were not tying him down. He moved his arms, and found them stiffened at the elbows with wrappings, but not under complete restraint. Although he was wrapped from head to foot like a mummy, he was free to move. Slowly, he turned his head, the light now glaring from the right instead of straight into his eyes through the coverings.

Very slowly he moved his right hand and pawed an opening in the bandage over his eyes. Now he could see what was in the room. Believing what he saw was another matter.

The room resembled a squash court, with white walls and brilliant illumination from above. On the opposite wall the windshield, instrument board, and steering wheel of an automobile were set up, bolted between two iron beams that rose from the floor. About ten feet away from this curious arrangement, two men in white jumpsuits were working over a metal chair. The chair had a cylindrical steel shaft, like a huge piston rod, extending from its back into the wall about twenty feet behind it. The men stepped aside and David could see what their work had been. They had strapped upright in the seat a silent, bandaged, mummy-like figure.

"Let's get set," one of the men said. He was the older of the two, and had a bald head, goggles, and a trimmed red beard on his chin. The younger man nodded, and together they seized the metal chair and ran it back on railings. The piston-like steel column disappeared into the wall.

"Ready?"

"Throw it."

The younger man turned a metal wheel on the wall. There was a roar of hydraulic pressure. The chair shot across the floor, and the bandaged figure slammed against the instrument board with a cracking sound, as the head flew forward and battered the windshield.

The older man said, "Nicely broken. Take it in."

Pulling the chair back to the center of the floor, the younger man loosened the web belting that held the wrapped figure, expertly turned it over on a wheeled stretcher, and pushed it through a white door in the corner.

David sat up on the hard shelf.

Catching sight of the movement, the bald man stopped.

"What the devil's going on?" said the man. He hurried over to where David was sitting. David pawed the bandages loose over his eyes.

"How did you get in here? Who the devil are you?" the man went on, indignant as a game warden who has come upon a poacher. "In here you're supposed to be dead, man!"

"I'm not dead, as you can see," David said. "My name is David Bell. Now let me ask a question. How *did* I get here, and what are you doing?"

"We're experimenting to determine the effects of auto wrecks on the human body," the man said. "We use cadavers. We get them from the usual sources—those who will their bodies to science, and the potter's field." He indicated five long tin cases at the end of the room. Two were standing on end and open; three lay like coffins. "That is our current supply. You seem to be an educated man. How you came in, I cannot imagine. We took you out of a box half an hour ago."

"What day is this?" David asked.

"Wednesday, October twenty-five." The man looked at his wrist watch. "At four o'clock in the morning."

This meant that David had been unconscious a little less than four hours. He must have been given a standard surgical injection by someone who then hustled him out of the crowd on the stairway as a passed-out drunk. Something about this body-breaking laboratory stirred a memory. He couldn't pin it down. He said, "After you smash your cadavers, what do you do with them?"

"We send them in to the doctors."

"Are you a doctor?"

"No, a technician." The man lit a cigarette.

"And what do the doctors do?"

"Study the broken cadavers, and record their findings."

"And then?"

"The crematory."

"The doctors work at four in the morning?"

"No, but we do, to get their work ready for them."

The memory returned. David had been told that when the Mafia's overlords condemned an underling, they stuffed his body into the trunk of an automobile which was then put among those to be smashed flat by hydraulic presses and used in the foundations of concrete highways. What had happened to David was a refinement of that technique. But the SA men had not injected a killing dose. Knowing what waited at the laboratory, they would scarcely have felt they had to.

"Somebody's taken my clothes," David said. "I'd appreciate the loan of a lab suit to go home in." There were several zippered overalls hanging on the wall, and David moved toward them.

"Just a minute, fellow," said the man. "This is a restricted area. You'll have to identify yourself."

"How can I?" David said. "And what place is this, where you have restricted areas?"

"Industrial Research Foundation," the man said, following David across the concrete floor. He walked lightly, on the balls of his feet. "We're conducting this wreck damage research on a confidential basis for the auto industry. And they don't want the, uh—nature of the work to be publicized. For all I know, you could be a reporter."

"Industrial Research," David said. As he recalled from his biographical studies in the library, this was one of Kane's foundations. He had read that its building was well guarded and its achievements kept out of public view. David went on, "You people have a reputation for liking privacy. But you'd best take my word for it, I have to get out in a hurry."

At this point the young laboratory man came back. He closed the door, saw David, and croaked, "Who's that?"

"Unauthorized personnel," the bearded man said.

"I'm asking you people to lend me a lab suit and some kind of shoes," David said. "We'll look into how I got here later on. Right now it's very important that I'm not delayed."

"I don't know about that," the bearded man said. "Eddie, you go and get plant security. Hop to it."

Eddie went out in a hurry and the man came closer to David, who was standing at the wall where the lab suits hung. Nearby was a bridge table holding a half-eaten container of Chow Mein, a box of wheat germ, and an empty bottle with the label of a sugarless soft drink.

"Keep away from those suits, fellow. I'm warning you. I'm Black Belt judo."

He would be, David thought. And I'll bet he's the guy who drinks that saccharined cola and eats wheat germ. It figures. The man was within reaching distance now, and he stood poised, with his left hand raised for the judo chop.

"I wish I could convince you that I'm serious," David said. "I'll be glad to give my address, telephone number, references, anything you like, *but later*. You understand?"

"You'll go nowhere until you talk to plant security. Keep away from those suits. I'm warning you."

David thought, there's always a wise guy. His hand on the side the man could not see brushed the surface of the table, felt the carton, then the curve of glass. He grasped the bottle, wheeled and hit hard, aiming behind the ear. The man dropped like an empty sack. David ripped at the bandages, pulled his way out of them, climbed into one of the zipper suits, and then took the man's shoes. They were moccasins, a reasonable fit.

Hurrying out the same door the assistant had used, David saw the word EXIT glowing in red glass at the end of a corridor. He ran down the hall and saw a time-clock and a rack of cards beside an iron-railed staircase. This, then, was the basement entrance to the Industrial Research Foundation, where the employees checked in and out. A door near the timeclock opened and a uni-formed guard stepped through. David pulled a card and put it under the stamper.

"Hey, you. Wait a minute."

The guard came beside David and went on, "You can't go outside in laboratory clothes."

"Have a heart," David said. "I'm just going for coffee."

The guard moved close. He was old, fat, badger-like. He wore a badge, and on his cap were the letters "SA" and underneath, "Security Patrol."

"I don't know you," the guard said.

David reached to the man's belt, drew the gun, and jammed it against the beer pouch. The guard's face went gray, like a wrinkled dishrag.

"Dawn't kill me, mister."

David kept the gun, backed up the stairway, came out in an alley, and ran down to a long empty street that he identified from the corner sign as Tenth Avenue, in the Fifties. Except for a few passing trucks, there was no traffic. Two blocks away he saw a telephone booth. He ran to it, and realized he had no coins to operate the telephone. An automobile swung around the corner by the Industrial Research Foundation building and he saw that it was filled with uniformed SA men. David crouched in the telephone booth as the car went by. From where he stood to Marlowe's apartment was little more than a mile, and he could cover the distance easily on foot. But he knew the white zipper suit would mark him out for the additional SA cars that would certainly be quartering all that part of Manhattan. And they would stop all taxicabs.

Dawn was coming up the side streets. This was the one hour when there was very little traffic. Of course the streets of New York were never completely deserted, and every few seconds a Diesel rig would come along Tenth Avenue, snorting and roaring and pouring fumes from its pipe. No help there; David knew the truckies stopped for nobody. He moved from the telephone booth and looked around him. Across the street the eastern tower of a housing development rose in thirty stories of badly-laid brick, huge drafty windowpanes, and ranks of shelf-like little balconies, combining to give an overpowering impression of meanness and despair. No lights were showing, and in the courtyard the breeze of dawn was feebly stirring a mixture of old newspapers and crystallized soot. David decided to take his chances with this building and try to reach an outside line through the lobby telephone. He stepped off the curb, the traffic light snapped over, and a Diesel came pounding down, the driver leaning out to curse at him as he leaped back to safety. David thought, I'd like to put a bullet through that rig, and teach the creep some manners. But first things first. At this point, two uniformed SA men came around the side of the housing project. They carried shotguns and walkie-talkies, and ran into the street when they saw David. Again came a Diesel rig, and cut them off. Behind David was a block of empty brownstone houses with boarded-up windows. He backed toward the front stoop of the nearest house, got the brownstone stairway between him and the SA men, reached around it, and fired one shot. The uniformed men jumped flat to the sidewalk on their side of the street. David hurried into the areaway. The basement window was covered with thin boards hanging partly loose, which came away when he pulled at them. The glass had been broken out long ago, and David stepped over the low sill into what had once been the kitchen. Feeling his way into the hall, he saw a patch of gray at the other end; it was the back entrance, a door from which the glass top-half had been smashed away. He broke the jagged edges smooth with the pistol butt, climbed through, crossed the back yard, and scaled the fence. On the other side was a wooden platform that held half a dozen garbage cans. He smelled hot grease and saw that the cans were grouped at the rear of an all-night diner whose pink and blue neon sign was still burning over the doorway. He walked rapidly around the diner, pulled back the sliding door, and entered. Two shabby men were huddled over coffee at one end of the counter. David got on a stool at the other end. A sturdy man with an apron tight over his paunch came up behind the counter to serve him. This man had an air that suggested some substance, more than would be found in the average counterman.

In a low voice, David asked, "Are you the proprietor?"

"Night manager."

"Veteran?"

"First Division. Whattaya want?"

"I'm in trouble."

"With the law?"

"No."

"Husband after you?"

"No—private cops."

"And what do I do?"

"Just let me use the telephone."

The man opened a gate in the counter and motioned for David to come in. David walked behind the coffee machine and followed the man through the kitchen, where a Chinese cook was reading a paperback, to a small metal desk in the lee of an enormous icebox. Among the bills of wholesalers held in the jaws of metal clamps, and the scattered catalogues of supply houses, stood the telephone. David thought, I seem to do well with restaurant men. It must be their benevolent occupation that makes them sympathetic. He dialed Don Marlowe's apartment, and Marlowe sounded wide awake. David spoke rapidly, giving the address of the diner.

"There isn't any doubt now," David went on. "We're in business."

"What should I do?"

"Send me two of those AIPA men. Tell them to be loaded for bear. And Don—"

"Yes?"

"Have you any cash?"

"Two, maybe three thousand is all."

"Give one of the men a C-note and charge it to me, will you? I want it for a friend."

"Give him a hundred bucks? All right, cousin. Take care of yourself."

Within ten minutes an Appleton man in plain clothes entered the diner.

David said, "I need fast transport down to Gramercy Park and I'd like to keep you with me till my Washington flight. You can charge it to me. Charles is my reference."

"All right, Mr. Bell. Whatever you say."

"I don't usually go in for bodyguards, but the SA has been giving me trouble."

"We'll watch close."

"And I think you have some money for me."

"Right here, Mr. Bell."

"Thank you. I want to give it to the manager here."

David found an armored AIPA payroll delivery van waiting at the curb outside. The uniformed driver stood at the back, a Browning automatic rifle over his arm. The driver said, "Those SA people fear us more than they do the cops. If they try to stop us we'll blow them down. Get in, Mr. Bell." Peering from the window of the diner, the manager watched the armored car roll away as though not quite certain what he was seeing. He lifted a crisp new hundred-dollar bill, held it to the light, and felt it front and back. That, at least, was no phony. Well, what the hell. See all sorts in this man's town, especially on the night side.

By seven o'clock that morning, David was telephoning Ben Thornton from the Washington National Airport.

"Come on over," said Ben. "Coffee's waiting for you."

At the little house by the canal, Thornton was dressed for the day, and sitting on the living room couch with a breakfast tray before him. David said he didn't feel like eating, but he accepted a cup of coffee from the Georgian silver pot.

"It's good to see you, boy," Thornton said. "How's old George?"

"He's fine."

"Glad to hear it," Thornton said, grinning with the characteristic happy expression that made one think he really was delighted with one's presence. David saw the look, and it reminded him that he had often seen the effects of its charm. But to David, it was a warning not to forget that nothing was harder than to get Ben Thornton to look at something which he did not want to see. He started cautiously.

"Ben, I think it's safe to say that in your travels, you have come across things that could be classed as incredible?"

"God, yes."

"And you've seen bad things?"

"Yes—especially in the war. The Maquis were none too scrupulous in their use of weapons. Some of those things are best forgotten."

"I wanted to remind you of the bad strange things that can happen," David said. "I have some strange ones to report." He went on to tell what he learned about Jefferson Kane and his associates, leaving out the last eight hours. He did not feel capable of convincing Thornton that those events had taken place, but emphasized that there had been threats, and efforts to intimidate him.

"In fact, Ben," David said in conclusion, "they have tried to get rid of me altogether."

"Now let me add it up," Ben Thornton said. "Kane's friend Sir Ronald is planning to cause an atomic explosion that will embarrass us, and maybe start a war that will get us all blown to Kingdom Come. Is that what you've told me?"

"Yes," said David, but his heart was dead. The voices of people who believe and have not become hostile have a certain unmistakable resonance. When one speaks to a bore, the voice goes flat, and its tone is wooden. So also when one doubts the facts of an account presented—and so it was with Ben Thornton's voice as he talked to David.

"What would you suggest that we do?" Thornton asked.

"I think we ought to cut off access to the Pathfinder plant for Kane and the Britishers. Or if that seems too obvious, give Sir Ronald a quiet search at the gate and hush up the whole affair."

"This sounds like Bureau business, David. It wouldn't be our pigeon even if, er, that is, it's Bureau business. And I'll tell you right now, they couldn't touch it. There's a 'hold' on Kane and any foreigner who visits him."

"What do you mean, Ben?"

"Just that the Bureau has orders to leave them alone, not bother them in any way. You know, world opinion, free traffic in ideas, all that sort of thing. There'd be complaints to the UN if anyone annoyed them."

"It sounds as though you thought we were helpless."

"Well," Thornton said, as he poured a second cup of coffee, "the truth is, of course, that this Jefferson Kane is a vicious old jerk. But they're afraid of him down here, and he knows it. He's awfully hard to handle because he's always yelling about free speech. And, of course, the Maxwell-Spencers should be disposed of for sanitary reasons if for no other. But they're great celebrities at the UN and we have to leave them alone."

"Thank you very much, Ben. Thank you for listening."

"Now don't go away mad."

"Don't worry about how I feel. Not that you do, or ever did."

"What's this, David?"

"I'm going to leave before I say things I'd regret later on. But I want to tell you this: nothing is personal any more. I went beyond that some time ago. I advise you to do the same."

"That sounds like a good idea," Ben Thornton said. "Good-bye, David."

He left the house and took the brick walk beside the canal, then turned north toward Pennsylvania Avenue. Obviously, Ben Thornton did not believe that anything worth the trouble of listening to would come out of the elephant valley. David had been tempted to tell Thornton he had found out about that valley, and taxing him with the well-meant lie that he had been sent on a "terrific" project. But David had decided not to tip his hand any further with people like Ben Thornton. And it made him sick to think he could no longer trust his friends. But there was Jim Ewing. At least Jim had been decent enough to tell him the truth. Now perhaps Ewing would recognize truth in return.

David crossed Pennsylvania Avenue near the Wisconsin Avenue corner and entered a large, glaring, cut-rate drugstore. He found a vacant telephone booth and called the Tottens' number. Topsy's mother answered, her clear nice-girl voice bringing a shocking remembrance of Mary, the first that had struck him in two days. His throat closed for a moment, and he managed to gasp, "This is David."

"You sound so strange—are you all right?" asked Nonie Totten.

"Yes—just—hoarse for a moment. Something in throat. All right now. Nonie, could I stay in the garage apartment tonight?"

"Of course, David. You're entitled to it. You don't think we'd rent it out with your money in our pockets, do you?"

"No, I guess not."

"I'll run out and put on fresh sheets right now."

"Don't hurry. I'll be along."

He walked past the frivolous shops on Wisconsin Avenue, up the hill, and turned into Q Street. He realized that he intended to walk past the house where he and Mary had lived. It wasn't morbid sentimentality, and it wasn't for the luxury of self-pity. It was something that he knew he had to do, and he did it. And it was just another house. Small place, but had a lot of charm. Exactly right for young government people with a little inherited money going for them. Houses like these were never on the market long . . .

He found himself at the Tottens' house. Nonie greeted him affectionately, and mourned that Topsy had left for kindergarten most unwillingly, having heard that David was coming.

"I'll make a point of seeing her this afternoon," David said. "May I use your telephone?"

"Of course."

He got Jim Ewing, early in his office as usual.

"David, how are you, young fellow?"

"There are troubles."

"Sorry to hear it. Where are you?"

"In Washington."

"Think of that, now. Lunch today?"

"What I was about to suggest," David said. "One o'clock? F Street Club?"

"By all means. See you then."

After a showerbath, David walked through Washington late autumn sunshine to 1925 F Street, where there was a quiet and extremely agreeable club. The house had been the Curtis mansion, and the widowed owner, some years before, had accepted suggestions of friends that the spacious Edwardian rooms would make an ideal gathering place for men and women. The discreet birth of the organization followed, and now it was valued as a place where the obnoxious types so plentiful in Washington were never known to appear either as guests or on the roster of members, which had never been published and never would be. At the door David was greeted by the courteous Irish major domo, who was famed in some circles both for his tactful behavior and his extraordinary resemblance to J. Edgar Hoover. He received David in his usual suave and comforting manner, which always made one feel that whatever load of trouble one was carrying would be lightened if left for a while on this high stoop.

David went into the room behind the small drawing room on the left, and found Jim Ewing sitting on the couch opposite the bar.

"Well, David. Let me have a look at you."

"See any change?"

"None. You still look tired."

"I've lost a little sleep. You drinking?"

"Maybe one sherry," Jim Ewing said. "I don't want to roll and toss at my desk all afternoon."

They drank the sherry and went through the back hall into the dining room, careful of the step down that had been known to trip the unwary. David noticed that the food was as good as it had been the last time he had used his membership here, more than a year before. As always, the service of the deft maids was unobtrusive. It was a good place, with a home-like atmosphere. Of course very few homes had ever been so beautifully run. Still, one could imagine one's self at home, for there were no chits to sign. They simply sent you a bill. During this excellent lunch, David did not mention his reason for coming to Washington, but when they were having coffee in the large drawing room, he said, "Let's take a walk down to the monument."

As they walked along F Street, Ewing said, "Ben Thornton called me about you this morning."

"And warned you I was off my rocker."

"More or less."

They walked on in silence for several blocks, and the Monument came into view. In a clear sky the great shaft, the best piece of abstract design in America, was shining against deep blue.

"Did he tell you my story?"

"Something about Kane's Britishers setting off a cannon cracker," Jim Ewing said.

"They're going to blow an atomic reactor sky high and they don't care what happens after that."

"My friend, it's not possible."

"How do you know?"

"I made a call or two to check out. Can't be done."

"Jim, this Maxwell-Spencer got a Nobel prize in physics. You know his specialty? Something called critical mass. You know what that is in plain language? The nuclear trigger. And you know the men who arm the biggest bombs carry what they need in a briefcase. Now are you telling me Sir Ronald Maxwell-Spencer couldn't improve on that?"

"Theoretically perhaps."

"But you don't believe me."

Moving up the inclined walk to the base of the monument, they came to a vacant bench and sat down. David went on, "You don't think anybody would ever find anything out, in the elephant valley."

"David, you didn't belong there."

"You say that in the past tense. Where do I belong now?"

"Shall I answer as a friend?"

"Go on."

"I think right now you ought to be on a tramp steamer, taking a long rest in the sunshine. We've asked a hell of a lot too much from you. Not recently, but for a long time in the past. Year after year, too much. Then the thing about Mary struck with your reserves depleted. Hell, even college professors take a sabbatical . . ."

"You think the head-shrinker was right?"

"Oh God, no, David, but I do think you've got to have some rest. This report, as you call it. All hearsay. Nothing anyone could conceivably act on. No recorded voices, for example. No documentation of any kind. Not a scrap of evidence."

"Except what Don Marlowe heard."

"Hearsay, David. Don't you understand the term? And provided by a notably unstable TV announcer with a history of mental imbalance due to drink."

"Against a respectable multimillionnaire, and a winner of the Nobel Prize. All right. Let that part go for the moment. I'll tell you what happened to me this morning. Kane has a place called the Industrial Research Foundation. Now one of the things they do up there is experiment with dead bodies." David stopped. "I know that does sound fanciful."

"No, no. Go on, David. About this place where they experiment with corpses?"

There it was again, the patient tone of utter disbelief.

David said, "Never mind. Just excuse me, Jim. Time's getting short."

He got up and walked rapidly away, crossing Constitution Avenue and the baseball diamonds, coming up below the Treasury, and entering the photograph-filled lobby of the Occidental Restaurant. Here he went into a telephone booth, and called a friend at the White House.

"I want to speak to the President."

"David, the President is pretty busy this afternoon. How about telling me about it, whatever it is?"

"In your office?"

"I could see you now if you're free and want to come over."

In a few minutes David was sitting in his friend's office. This was a government friend, one of the President's advisers, whom David had worked with in the days when he had been a person of consequence at the Company. The friend was relaxed and pleasant in his sunny office. If White House pressure was inhumanly severe, this man did not seem to have heard about it. He also did not seem to have heard that David was no longer taken seriously. He leaned back in one of those great soft official chairs that was like a leather sofa upended—there was something obscene about these chairs. But David felt that his White House friend was—believing? It was possible. And when David had told his tale, the man's voice was still warm.

"Let me put in a couple of calls," said the man. He went into the next room, closing the door after him. Ten minutes went by, and the relaxed man returned and sat again in his enormous chair.

"I called the Bureau, David, and the Company. *Your former* Company, it seems. I hadn't been read in on your departure. Seems as though this thing is their baby, old man. Wrong doorstep for it here, you see what I mean? That Maxwell-Spencer is one hundred per cent poison, you know. I doubt if we'd want to ask the Boss to mess around with him. Nice of you to come in. Say hello to George Rollins for me, huh?" The relaxed man stood up and extended his hand. No use, David thought. No use here either. He shook the hand, and the relaxed man was lifting the next paper from his IN box before David was out of the room.

He picked up a taxicab in front of the White House and rode back to the Tottens' house. Fatigue weighted his legs as he walked in the front door, but he called for Topsy, who rushed at him with cries of joy. A few minutes' talk satisfied the little girl, and he sat down to rest on the couch in the Tottens' living room. His fatigue had progressed to the point where there is a feeling of emptiness behind the eyes. Next comes double vision, as David knew. He was too tired to sleep, but dragged himself to the garage apartment, now made ready for him. His nerves would not allow him to sit or lie down. He prowled in the small apartment for an hour, then he walked out and ate supper at the White Tower on Wisconsin Avenue, came back, and managed to force himself to sit in a chair throughout the night. There might be rest in keeping quiet; he knew the progress of such exhaustion, and knew that sleep might now be two or three days away. At times during the night he saw two separate cold fireplaces in the attic room. This was not only double vision, but double vision of what was not there.

At seven-thirty Thursday morning David sat in the Tottens' kitchen eating breakfast. Monty Totten said, "You look dreadful, young fellow. What have you been up to?"

"We had some night work and got behind in our sleep," David said. Now he was at a stage where mind and head were clear, and he had an idea. If the Company and the Bureau and the White House were deaf, there was one more place to try: the Department. He went on, "Monty, who was that man at State we thought so much of? Harrison? Somebody Harrison?"

"You're thinking of Walter Hamilton."

"He still there?"

"And flourishing. I see him all the time."

"Could you fix it for me to talk to him?"

"When?"

"Today. Soon as possible."

"Today? That's a lot to ask of State."

"It's important."

"Well, Walter's not the stuffy type. I'll call him from the office and see what can be done."

"Thanks, Monty. May I wait here? You'll let me know?"

"Of course, David. No trouble whatso."

At eleven o'clock Monty Totten called to say that Mr. Hamilton would see David at one o'clock at his office in New State, the Department's big building in Foggy Bottom. David was on time, and drew hope from the fact that Hamilton did not try to impress him by making him wait in the anteroom. When David entered the inner office, he thought for a moment he was looking at his White House friend again. There was the same cheerful informal manner here.

"Hello, David," said the State Department man. So we're first-naming, David said to himself. A good beginning. "How's our old friend, George Rollins?"

"He's fine."

"Glad to hear it. Now what can we do for you?"

"There's a most alarming, a most incredibly alarming situation in New York," David said.

"So I understand," said Walter Hamilton. "I called Jim Ewing when Monty said you wished to see me."

"But Walter, why call Jim?"

"This is Washington, old man. Have to keep in channels.

Surely you remember Jim is the link between your people and State?"

"Yes, of course, Walter, he's the *official* link. But why call him?"

"I thought I'd get a little advance briefing, David. While keeping in channels, you understand."

"Then you know about Kane and Maxwell-Spencer."

"I know what you're saying about them, yes. But I don't quite see where the Department comes in."

"Walter, isn't there what you call a 'hold' on these people?"

"Absolutely. Same as diplomatic immunity, only more so."

"Who says they should have this 'hold'?"

"The Department."

"Could you take it away?"

"Oh, it could be done. There'd be a certain amount of pulling and hauling. Said pulling and hauling should be preceded by someone getting up a position paper. Then to get substantive on the thing, we'd have an *ad hoc* committee laid on. You couldn't just pull one 'hold.' We'd have to review the entire procedure."

"But Walter, suppose we have to get action—and right now?"

"We can act fast when we have to, David. All that machinery can be bypassed. I don't want you to think we're tied with red tape around here. We can cut the tape any time we want to. That is, any time we feel we have to."

"And in this case?"

"David, you know I have the greatest admiration for your outfit, especially for the Director, for Henry Sedgwick, Monty, Jim Ewing, the whole crowd. Ben Thornton. Yourself. But in this case . . ."

"The answer is no?"

"I don't think, in *this* case, that the Department needs
to make any answer at all."

"Ewing and Thornton told you I was crazy."

"Oh no, David. Nothing of the sort. But they didn't ask
for any action. And the matter didn't originate over here.
So we're actually not obliged to pass on it either way."

"Then they did say I was crackers."

"Not at all. I'll tell you what they said. As they put it,
you have been operating in a vacuum. So there's nothing
pending in the file, you know? Nothing on the agenda."

It was like the nightmare in which one presents a legitimate claim, only to meet with universal refusal of attention. For a dizzying moment David felt himself trying to
wake up, as one will in a nightmare when it is realized that
so much terror and frustration must be only a dream. But
he was awake, and he could see Walter Hamilton glance
at his wrist watch. David got up and shook hands.

"All right, Walter," he said. "Thanks for seeing me."

"Don't think this Maxwell-Spencer is anything sacred,"
Hamilton said as he got up.

"No, certainly not."

"These 'holds' are technical matters, really."

"Of course."

"They involve a rather sophisticated sort of statecraft."

"Hard to explain to a layman?"

"Well, yes." They were at the door.

"Good-bye, Walter."

"Good-bye, David."

Flying back to New York on the three o'clock shuttle,
David admitted to himself that one thing had to be said
for Washington: they had raised the brush-off to the level
of a science. David had now come into a long second wind,
in which fatigue was no longer demanding, and he felt
that he saw everything with microscopic clarity and detail. Maryland was blue and tan beneath the wing; and

leaning back in the comfortable seat, David thought of the country as a whole. In his exalted state of fatigue, he had the feeling that he could see it all, not only the metropolitan area that lay just ahead to the northeast, but also the green midlands, the bronze desert, and the rocks and forests of the western coast. David thought of his life work, and his study of the organizations that are supposed to guard the country from treacherous harm—the Bureau, the Company, the Department. He had an overwhelming fear that the Bureau and the Company and the Department could only take things apart, in mighty efforts of team work and corporate operation. But putting things together again— that, one did by one's self, if it was to be done at all.

At 15 Lexington Avenue, Louise came to the door.

"He died at the hospital, two hours ago."

"Was he conscious?"

"No, David. He'd been asleep since early this morning. When he died, I was with him, and Ted, and the nurse. He gave a kind of sigh and turned his head, and Ted said, 'He's gone.'"

"Where is he now?"

"I authorized an autopsy and then Morrison's men were to take over. The undertakers. We'll have the funeral two days from now so his California relatives can get here. Is that all right with you, David?"

"Of course, Ma. Are friends here with you?"

"Yes, and the Rector has called. But I don't need anyone. I was already adjusted to the idea."

"Compared to what we'd been expecting, this is mercy," David said. "But you've got to rest. Didn't Ted give you something?"

"I don't need it yet," said Louise Bell. "Roger . . . Roger is to stay at the undertaker's, and the funeral will be from Grace Church. Do you want to go up and see him?"

"No, Ma. I'll remember him alive."

"That's the way I feel, too," said Louise Bell.

Leaving his stepmother with her friends, David went out and took a cab to Ted Kenyon's office, which was in the basement of a town house, with Kenyon, his wife, and four children living upstairs. He found the doctor ushering out the last patient of the afternoon.

"Hello, David," said Ted Kenyon. "I can't tell you how sorry I am. But from what we found in the autopsy he was lucky to go as he did."

"He was worried for fear it would get the better of him. But he planned to luck it out."

"You've seen your mother?"

"Yes. Will she be all right?"

"She'll have a reaction later. But you know what she's made of."

"I have an idea. Ted, I want to consult you about something else."

"Come in the office."

Sitting beside Ted Kenyon's desk, David arranged his thoughts and said: "I want to ask about insanity. I realize you're not a head-shrinker, but you are a doctor and I trust you."

"Thank you, David. Between you and me, I don't consider the shrinks much of an adornment to our profession. I think some of them are mongrels and jackals in the trade."

"That is severe."

"You can get them to testify either way in a trial. In the name of science, either way. And there's many a poor bastard in his grave because of a homicidal maniac that a shrink said was ready to be turned loose. Conversely, there's many a harmless old guy locked in an asylum because the relatives hired a shrink to put him in there. But what is it you want to know?"

"I want to know how you can tell if people are insane."

"The common sense answer is that people are crazy if they consistently do crazy things."

"Can the human personality be destroyed by harmful emotions?"

"Ah hah! You sound like a psychiatrist yourself, as though you could verbalize with the best of them. But give me a specific question and I'll see if I can remember what the book says. Or I'll look it up in Bleuler. Fire away."

"A hypothetical question. Consider the emotion of extreme hatred. I theorize that this emotion is destructive, and that it can be habit-forming, like a drug. If persisted in, it disintegrates the moral and ethical framework of the personality. I theorize that malign, driving emotion destroys the normal personality just as alcohol softens the brain or drug addiction destroys the nervous system. A psychopathic personality—insanity—is the result. What does the book say about that as a theory?"

"You have an interesting idea there, David," said the doctor. "But from a mundane clinical standpoint, we are more likely to see obsessive hatred as a *manifestation* of paranoia. So, as the hatred seems to mount and become more consuming, the clinical picture would be that the paranoid condition was worsening."

"But obsessive hatred *is* a manifestation—or symptom —of insanity?"

"You bet it is, David. Would you like to borrow my copy of Bleuler? That's the revealed word so far as I'm concerned."

"No, thanks. I believe you can tell me all I need to know. I have only one more question."

"Fire away."

"Can you be insane, and still walk around with no outward indications of it?"

"Yes, if you're a psychopathic personality."

"And that is?"

"We recognize psychopaths by their attitude toward other people. We never hear them say a good or sincerely kind word about anyone. That's because the psychos are unable to feel any genuine emotion of love or even liking for anyone but themselves."

"Would you call that pathological selfishness?"

"Call it that, but you'd be closer if you said the psycho's motivation is vanity. Not normal self-esteem, David. A monstrous overwhelming vanity that never subsides. The key to the psycho's personality is his eternal watchfulness that this vanity is never damaged or even threatened. And if ever the psycho is exposed for what he is, he's monstrously affronted and outraged, and he never forgives. And if he can, he destroys the person who called the turn on him. But let me go upstairs and get my copy of Bleuler, and you can read up on the whole business."

"That's not necessary, Ted. I've got what I came for."

"Well, good. Nothing like a doctor going out of his own discipline for answering questions. And by the way, David. As a friend. You look bad. Are you all right?"

"No."

"How do you feel?"

"I think I'll tell you frankly. As a friend."

"Please do."

"I feel as though I'd been dragged through hell backward and slapped in the face with a buzzard's gut."

"Take off your coat and shirt and we'll put the 'scope on you."

"Not now, Ted. Later maybe, but not now."

"How about a prescription for a tranquilizer?"

"I don't need it. Honestly, I'm used to feeling this way. I'm very short of sleep. You asked me, and I told you."

"Wait a minute, young man," said Dr. Kenyon to his former schoolmate. But it was no use, because David walked from his office, through the reception room, and out into the street.

David's next stop was at the office of the Institute for Strategic Research. At a quarter of six, Mrs. Martin had gone home, but George Rollins was happily working at a tall stack of documents on his desk.

"The wandering boy returns," George said. "What's the good word?"

"There is none," David said. Fatigue had again begun climbing along his nerves, and leaving numbness where it passed.

"Things have been phasing along pretty well in your absence, David."

"That's fine. Now look here, George. You've got to fire Mrs. Martin."

"How can you say such a thing?"

"She has been furnishing information to people outside this office."

"How do you know?"

"You were told I was coming up here before I was told."

"Well, uh—yes, David. I was told in advance."

"And shortly after I arrived, I went to see Kane's intelligence chief, the fellow called Dr. September."

"Yes, you described him to me."

"He knew about my separation from the Company."

"But you always were overt."

"George, he knew about the mental business. The reason I came on detached duty."

"The hell he did! That's a leak, all right."

"You see the one person bound to be responsible?"

"Yes I do," George Rollins said. "Confound that woman. Best secretary I ever had."

"All right," David said. "Do as you think best. That's *one* thing I won't worry about any more. Now here's another thing. I'm not sure about my usefulness here in your operation. Or rather, I'm sure that I'm not doing anything for you."

"I wish you'd let me be the judge of that."

"George, some things are hard to say. Some things are *too* hard to say. I think I'll let this business go. Pack it in. Strike the set, as Don Marlowe says. I'm speaking for myself only. If I were asked to give *you* any advice, I'd say keep right on exactly as you are. You're going fine. And it was nice to have been with you these few days."

"Won't we be seeing you in the morning?"

"I doubt it. Good night, George."

At Marlowe's apartment, the quiet Appleton Protective man outside the door recognized David and admitted him. Marlowe hurried him to the library and mixed a rye highball with so little water that it matched the mahogany of the grog table.

"Where have you been, old cousin?"

"Washington. Tenth Avenue. Minetta Lane. In reverse order."

"I don't think I want to hear anymore. By the way, I gave that man a C-note."

"I'll send you a check. Don't you want me to go halves on the Appletons?"

"No, I'll take care of it. They're a good bunch. I'm glad you put me onto those people. What a world to live in. But you said we were in business. What now?"

"Suppose I tell you all about it when it's over."

"That will be soon?"

"Very soon," David said. "Is Peggy here?"

"Not exactly. In fact, no."

"What's happened?"

"Cousin, she did not like my non-appearance at that party. You she forgave, figuring you have other duties of some kind. But me? The doghouse."

"You send the Appletons to her?"

"Yes, but I didn't let her know. She'd just tell them to go away. They're watching, and she doesn't know."

"That's fine, Don. Now you stay here until you hear from me or about me. It won't be long."

Marlowe's hands were twitching and his face was haggard.

"I'd like to get out of here. Clear out of town," he said.

"Where are you going, old buddy?"

"If the luck holds, I'm going to see Jefferson Kane."

The four of them sat there like mechanical people, waiting for the turn of a key to set them in motion. Kane, Sir Ronald, his wife, and Dr. September were seated in a row along the side of a refectory table; and to David, who sat opposite, they greatly resembled a tribunal. They were in the two-story main hall of the Kane suite. It was eight in the evening, and with only two standing lamps lit, the huge room was in darkness except around the table. David had been surprised at the ease with which he got his appointment to see Kane. It had come as easily as the maturing of his final plan, which was to have no plan, to accept the fact that a turn of luck was due, and that everything depended on whether it came in time. His tactics would be the simplest in the world: he would challenge these people directly, and so draw them to strike back and expose themselves. If Ted Kenyon was right, he knew the way to do it. And this time, he would not let anybody get near enough for a needle job.

He had gone home, after seeing Marlowe, and picked up the revolver he had taken from the SA guard. Then he had telephoned Kane's hotel, asked for the suite, and heard the canine uproar of Dr. September on the line.

"All right, Bell! Come up. Mr. K. will see you. We'll all see you."

Now they sat silently before him. And at last Jefferson Kane said, "Young man, I like your brass. I vow, I like it.

You seem to have the ginger and pep for success in the world today. But there's one thing I don't understand: *just what the hell do you think you're doing?*"

"You know the answer to that," David said.

"Let me speak to him, Jefferson," Sir Ronald said. "I want to know why he was interested in our agenda for the Kane Foundation. Why was that, Bell?"

"There's no use going through it again," David said. "You know why I was interested."

"But I don't, you see," said Sir Ronald. He took out a pipe and began to fill it from a pouch covered in the Old Wykehamist colors, the tobacco spilling on the snuff-colored suit as the pipe jumped in his nervous hands.

"Taking my interest for granted, Sir Ronald," David said, "it did have some valuable results. I had the honor of meeting you, for example. And what was even more rewarding—from an American's point of view—I discovered your plans for the Pathfinder reactor."

Dr. Harvey September shifted in his chair. "He's trying to talk like an investigator. You understand, Mr. K. and Sir Ronald, that's just his own idea. He's got no right to check on anybody. He's not even a government agent. They fired him—and it was for mental illness trouble."

"Of course, the man's mad," said Lady Maxwell-Spencer. She pronounced it, "the men's med."

"*And* a bloody fool," said Sir Ronald. A geyser of burning tobacco shot from his pipe and landed on his coat. He beat at the cloth with his hands, and then looked at David with the ancient cold look, the coelacanth watching behind rocks under the sea. David turned to Jefferson Kane.

"Will you try to understand me, Mr. Kane?" he asked. "I'm concerned with what was said in this room about a nuclear explosion. It was said in the hearing of your television man."

Dr. September said, "Don't worry about Marlowe, Mr. K. Marlowe can be handled. No feedback. No problem. This guy here is the troublemaker."

Kane said, "Bell, you have no proof that anything was said in this room at any time by anybody."

David said, "You have nothing to hide?"

"Nothing, young man."

"And your SA men aren't a private intelligence outfit? Your own Gestapo?"

"Community relations, that is all."

"They didn't threaten me, try to kill me?"

Dr. September said, "You see, Mr. K.? The man's irresponsible."

David turned to September and said, "Didn't you send for me, right after I met Kane?"

"I interviewed you, yes. I tried to tell you not to make trouble for Mr. K. But some people never learn easy. They have to learn some other way. So all right."

"That's about all we need to hear," Kane said. "Young man, for the last time, I advise you to stop making a fool of yourself. Stop being a nuisance. No? That's too almighty bad."

David's tiredness had now come to the point where he felt he was floating, and that the four figures at the table —eight figures at times—were receding to a great distance, then coming back like a closeup in a Zoomar lens. He saw the harsh hick face of Jefferson Kane, the old mean eyes with the stare of madness in them—it was all impregnable, not to be moved or altered. But he would make his final try.

David said, "I'm not the crazy one. It's you, Kane. You're out of your head and although it may be too late, you ought to be under treatment."

Jefferson Kane's mouth folded in and he clenched his big mottled hands.

David went on, "That also applies to your friends here.

They've lost their hold on reality, as I should have known from the time they went to North Korea. And your chief of intelligence is probably a borderline case. You leave me only one thing to do."

September said, "Don't talk to him no more, Mr. K. Don't lower yourself. I'll ask him. Bell, what do you think you'll do?"

"I think I'll have you committed for examination which will show at least three of you hopelessly insane."

Kane stood up, and looked at the Maxwell-Spencers. "That will be enough," he said. "Dr. September, we leave the matter in your hands."

Maxwell-Spencer nodded. The light from a standing lamp struck across his wife's glasses and made two cold moons. They stood, leaving Dr. September seated, and followed Kane out of the room. Kane walked with a rangy stride as though pursuing a plough; Sir Ronald Maxwell-Spencer had a bustling, officious walk, and the large tubular figure of the woman moved like a store-window dummy on rollers, her ground-grippers revolving like wheels beneath the long heavy cylinder of tweed.

"I'll tell you what's gonna happen to *you*," Dr. September said, dropping his pretentious accent. "You're gonna get your head shot open. Don't reach for a gun if you've got one. You were covered every minute you been here. Come in, Max."

A man holding his right arm carefully before him came from the shadowed archway. At the end of the arm was a pistol, steady as a tombstone, pointing at David's chest. The man was Mr. Anonymous, the deeplohmat.

"Stand up, Bell," said Dr. September. He ran his hands over David's clothes and took out the gun.

"All right," September said. "Now here is what we do. We go down the freight elevator. There's no man on in the evening and we run it ourselves. Automatic. Then we go over the way to a little apartment I know of. I thought you'd be trouble, and I gave the cop on the beat a double sawbuck to get lost, so don't think you'll do any good by hollering when we cross the street. Understand? Let's go."

Across the street stood one of the surviving brick houses of that neighborhood, with an all-night drugstore at street level, and three floors of flats. September opened the door by the mailboxes and held it back for David and Max to walk through.

"Up one flight," September said. "The door's open. Walk right in, but give me five minutes, Max."

Max said, "Five minutes."

"So it's good night, Bell. Good night and good-bye." Harvey September turned and walked away briskly, like a salesman heading for the Pomerania's cocktail lounge at the end of a business day.

"You heard him," Max said. "Straight upstairs."

Max turned on a bright ceiling light in the apartment on the second floor. Holding his pistol steady, he kicked the door shut behind him.

"Sit down, Bell."

David's glance around the room showed sagging velvet-covered chairs and cigarette-scarred tables. It was a typical furnished flat of the kind that went for short leases and high rentals in that neighborhood—shabby, furtive, and impersonal. He sat on a couch and Max pulled a light chair next to an end table, resting his pistol arm on its surface. With his left hand, Max drew a sheet of notepaper from his side pocket, and tossed it to David. He said, "Read that."

David looked at the paper and said, "The Bang-Jensen effect. A suicide note in my handwriting."

Max nodded, and David said, "Where did you get my writing from? Oh yes, that list of names I copied out. Looks like good work."

"It will pass," Max said. David read the note, which was addressed to Ted Kenyon. In a few conventional phrases, the letter said that David could not continue to face life, and that Dr. Kenyon would understand. The handwriting job was the best he had ever seen, and he thought, this makes the Bang-Jensen operation look like the work of amateurs. Max raised his left wrist and glanced at the watch that was strapped around it.

"Four minutes gone," he said.

David told himself that in a story, this would be where he leaped across the table and grabbed the gun—all in the instant that Max looked at his watch. Fat chance. And anyway, David was too tired to move. He would be found dead with the note nearby and the pistol in his hand. And that would be enough for the New York police. David felt no fear; complete fatigue made anything acceptable.

They heard someone in the hall and George Rollins walked in. He moved slowly, leaning on his cane. He sat down beside David and looked at the note.

"I see," George said. "Suicide job."

Max moved the pistol back and forth in a flat arc.

"I shoot you both now," he said in the whispering, husky voice that David remembered from Gramercy Park. "Make no difference to me."

George lifted his cane. There was an explosion, Max's face disappeared, and the top of his head flew across the room.

"It's a single-barreled shotgun," George said, showing David how a ring on the cane's silver band served as trigger. Taking the note, they hurried from the apartment and down the stairs, turning toward Sixth Avenue, where they stopped for the traffic light.

"How did you know I was in trouble?" David asked.

"Your friend Marlowe called me."

"Nice of him to worry."

"He wasn't worried about you, David. He was in a panic about himself. He wanted you to know he had decided to leave town for Hollywood immediately. Said he didn't know where to reach you, but you had said you were going up to Kane's place. And of Kane he wanted no part."

"But you never took the danger seriously before."

"And I hadn't talked to Mrs. Martin before. Don't I always take your suggestions, David? After you left I called her back to the office and told her I *wouldn't* have her sent to jail for revealing official secrets. That is, *if* she'd tell me about Kane's people. She told, and you were right."

The light changed and they crossed Sixth Avenue, mingling with the shuffling, nondescript crowd around the Pomerania.

David asked, "How did you spot what they were trying to do?"

"I started by watching Kane's hotel from the window of the drugstore across the street," George said. "Pretty soon Kane and the Limeys came out. They legged it for Kane's limousine, like deadbeats with the landlord after them. I noticed *you* weren't in the party, so I decided to stay awhile. A few minutes later, you came out of the alley beside the hotel and crossed the street with two characters who didn't look friendly, and went into the house above the drugstore. I came out and listened as you went into the hall. I heard one character say something about the door at the top of the stairs, and when *he* came out, leaving you and the other man up there, I thought I'd better look into it."

"All I can say is, thank God you played it that way," David said. He spotted a vacant cab and flagged it. The cab swerved in, David opened the door, and said to the driver, "Airport job."

George said, "Where do you think you're going?"

"To Washington. This note may convince them of something I couldn't get them to believe. It has to be hand-carried."

David never could recall that Washington flight. It was as though the cab on Sixth Avenue carried him all the way to Jim Ewing's house on Kalorama Road in the embassy district. There had been a dinner party, and a few guests were still in the large room that looked out on the garden, and Ewing came into the library off the entrance hall looking annoyed.

"David, your face is ghastly. What's wrong now?"

"I like that 'now'," David said. "What's wrong is that I've survived the Bang-Jensen treatment. Or maybe that's what's right." His tongue didn't seem to be forming syllables properly, he stopped trying to talk, and held out the note. Ewing took it, sat in a leather chair, snapped on the light, drew his spectacle case from his pocket, put the glasses on, and read silently. He took enough time to read the note more than once. Then he got up.

"All right, David," Jim Ewing said. As David's head fell forward and sleep rolled over him, he saw a white telephone lifted at Ewing's desk.

He waked in a sunny bedroom on the second floor of the house. Jim Ewing came in and pulled up a chair. David said, "First question. What day is it?"

"Thursday, in the afternoon," Jim said. "You've more than slept the clock around. Fifteen hours. You must have needed it."

"It's like the drunk who wakes up and calls down, what hotel is this?"

"I thought he said, what city is this?"

David smiled, and then said, "You've stopped the Pathfinder thing?"

"Dead in its tracks," Jim Ewing said. "The note convinced me. You'd never kill yourself."

"And you got action?"

"From the top, David. Just as you keeled over I was picking up the p.l. to the President's place. Yes, you might say we had action. First, the 'holds' were pulled on Kane and the Maxwell-Spencers. Yes, indeed, David. In the middle of the night."

"What results?"

"They were what you might call manifold, my boy. And most gratifying. First, the Maxwell-Spencers. That little son of a bitch *did* have a critical-mass triggering device, just as you said. And he and his lady are now on their way back to Blighty. They'll never show up in *this* country again."

"Barred?"

"Ab-so-lutely. And the Foreign Office has been given the facts. The Maxwell-Spencers are not going to pull much weight from now on, unless they move to China. Next, this fellow September. He made the Canadian border one jump ahead of the Bureau, and we will not be seeing him again. Systems Analysis is to have its license pulled and its offices closed. The few legitimate accounts it had as a front will go to agencies like Burns and Appleton. And Mr. Kane is not to have a private army anymore."

"How *about* him? He ought to be in jail, or at least under treatment."

"Well, David, we mustn't expect too much in this world. We would have a very difficult case to prove, and anyhow, you don't put people like Mr. Kane in jail and you can't commit them. It just can't be done. There's too much money there. But what's happened is nearly as good. He was called down to the White House in a hurry this morning and the President hollered at him over an hour, Texas style. They say you could hear him clear down at the Smithsonian. The only time in his life old Kane has ever had to sit still and listen to something he didn't like. And there were practical results. Oh yes, indeed. Kane won't have to go to jail, but he'll be carrying one around with him. He is to have a permanent Bureau tail, around the clock, just like a Chicago rackets boss."

"Oh, boy," David said. "That can get awfully tiresome."

"Yes, and he won't like having people on his back who don't take orders."

"He'll hate it."

"He will loathe it," Jim Ewing said, "and the beauty part is this. If he goes to Canada, he gets the same detail, from plain-clothes Mounties."

"Looks like the only answer for Jefferson is Red China."

"Yes, if the Chinese feel they don't have enough trouble already," Ewing said. "And then there's the matter of the fellow that George decapitated. Seems he was a UN type, worked for various missions, Lower Slobbovia and that sort. You can imagine. None of them wishes to acknowledge him. So, just another of the unsolved cases on the books of the New York cops. And we've kept it out of the papers. Better that way, don't you think?"

"It will be forgotten in a few days," David said.

"Then there's Kane's Industrial Research Foundation," Jim said. "That was just as you told me, in spite of my patting you on the back and saying take it easy, old man. There was one guy up there with a hell of a headache."

"I'm sorry about that," David said. "I had to knock him loose from his Black Belt."

"So you did," Jim Ewing said. "And now hear this. While I was cleaning up after Old Man Kane, a friend has been working for you."

"What friend?"

"Ben Thornton. It seems he got to thinking about that deal the Company shrink handed you. He just naturally decided there had been a lot more going on than the prayer book has a service for. So he went over Henry

Sedgwick's head, straight into the Director's office. He told him all about that fool who interviewed you, and the Director didn't take it kindly. I mean, he called in the boss of all the Company psychiatrists and yelled at him like the President giving old Kane his going-over. The boss psychiatrist lit out of the Director's office, hustled back to his own bailiwick, and passed that loud rebuke right on to your friend Dr. Greenway. Fired him on the spot, and ran him bowlegged getting out of here. I guess this Dr. Greenway is now passing through South Carolina, like a hurricane. So, David." He paused.

"Yes, so what?"

"Forget about the elephant valley and please come back. And I'll tell you something in confidence: it looks as though your old friend Henry Sedgwick might be grazing in that valley pretty soon."

"Too bad. Hard lines, eh?"

"Yes, tough. Hate to lose old Henry. How about it, David?"

"I'm still sore."

"I don't blame you in the least."

"Trusting my reputation for sanity to the Company a second time. Would you do it?"

"Now cut that out, David," Jim Ewing said. "That charade of George's has confused your thinking. Take some time off, and give us a call when you feel rested. Then we'll kill the fatted calf. And I think his name is Henry Sedgwick."

"I'll think about it."

"The maid will be up in a minute to see what you'd like for breakfast."

"Oh let me come downstairs, Jim. I can get on my pins all right."

"As you please. New toothbrush and all that in this bathroom. Shirts, shorts, and socks in my dressing room.

Take your pick. We're holding a sale. See you in a few minutes."

David sat up and swung his legs in Ewing's pajamas over the side of the bed. "Be right with you," he said.

On the following afternoon, David stood at the window of his room and looked down across Gramercy Park. An elderly gentleman in a cloak and big black hat was entering the National Arts Club, while next door a man in dungarees was polishing brass in front of The Players. The sunshine had that golden quality, both mellow and stimulating, that it seems to attain only on certain days and only in New York. As David looked down, he knew that he had come to a decision on Ewing's invitation of the previous day. He would go on with the Company, and work, and try to get better at his trade. Perhaps emotion ruled the world; at any rate, and for all its failures, David Bell was part of his native land. He would work for it as long as his life had value.

But there was no use, David thought as he stood at the window, in allowing Jack to become a dull boy. That would never do. Joy and beauty had not vanished from the world, nor would they ever, so long as men cherished women and sought their love. David picked up the Manhattan telephone book, turned pages, and found it:

ALCOTT PEGGY 115 W 11 555-2368

He lifted the receiver and began to turn the dial.